Praise for
New York Times bestselling author
Shannon Stacey

"The perfect antidote for the winter doldrums. Stacey's family drama is equal parts steamy romance and coming-of-age story."
—*RT Book Reviews* on *All He Ever Dreamed*

"Shannon Stacey is one of my favorite contemporary romance authors. Her...books are always full of fun, warm characters, great small towns and really sexy relationships."
—*USA TODAY* on *All He Ever Desired*

"A fun read with characters you latch on to and don't want to let go of."
—*USA TODAY* on *Slow Summer Kisses*

Praise for *USA TODAY* bestselling author
Jennifer Greene

"Greene's lowcountry romance is heavenly, filled with memorable characters [and] Southern charm."
—*RT Book Reviews* on *The Baby Bump*

"Distinctive characters and witty dialogue... make this one a sweet, delightful read."
—*RT Book Rev*

Praise for *USA*
B

"A charming, la
Dunlop's characters
multilayered, warm and funny."
—*RT Book Reviews* on
The Billionaire Who Stole Christmas

"Fun, fiery and utterly delightful."
—*RT Book Reviews* on *An After-Hours Affair*

SHANNON STACEY

New York Times bestselling author Shannon Stacey lives with her husband and two sons in New England, where her two favorite activities are writing stories of happily ever after and riding her four-wheeler. You can contact Shannon through her website, www.shannonstacey.com, or visit her on Twitter and Facebook. You can also email her at shannon@shannonstacey.com.

JENNIFER GREENE

USA TODAY bestselling author Jennifer Greene has sold over eighty books in the contemporary romance genre. Her first professional writing award came from RWA—a Silver Medallion in 1984—followed by over twenty national awards, including being honored in RWA's Hall of Fame. In 2009, Jennifer was given the RWA Nora Roberts Lifetime Achievement Award. Jennifer is currently raising two Australian Shepherds, is married to her own personal hero and lives in orchard country near Lake Michigan. Visit her website at www.jennifergreene.com.

BARBARA DUNLOP

USA TODAY bestselling author Barbara Dunlop has written more than thirty-five novels for Harlequin, including the acclaimed Colorado Cattle Barons series for the Harlequin Desire line. Her sexy, lighthearted stories regularly hit bestsellers lists. Barbara has twice been short-listed for Romance Writers of America's RITA® Award. Visit her website, www.barbaradunlop.com.

SHANNON STACEY

Snow Day

JENNIFER GREENE

BARBARA DUNLOP

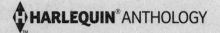

HARLEQUIN® ANTHOLOGY

ISBN-13: 978-0-373-83782-3

SNOW DAY

Copyright © 2013 by Harlequin Books S.A.

The publisher acknowledges the copyright holders of the individual works as follows:

HEART OF THE STORM
Copyright © 2013 by Shannon Stacey

SEEING RED
Copyright © 2013 by Alison Hart

LAND'S END
Copyright © 2013 by Barbara Dunlop

Recycling programs for this product may not exist in your area.

Printed in U.S.A.

CONTENTS

HEART OF THE STORM

Shannon Stacey

CHAPTER ONE

NOTHING MADE DELANEY WESTCOTT happier than four o'clock coming around on the last business day of December.

Being the deputy municipal clerk in her hometown of Tucker's Point, Maine, was usually a low-key job she enjoyed, but the stampede of people who'd realized it was the last day to register their vehicles would try the patience of a saint. And Delaney was no saint. Even after four years in the office, she had to brace herself for the panicked rush between the Christmas and New Year's holidays.

"Highway robbery if you ask me," Mrs. Keller muttered, slapping her checkbook down on the counter, just as she did every single year.

Delaney half expected the leather checkbook cover to creak and release a plume of dust and moths when the woman opened it. "How was your Christmas, Mrs. Keller?"

"I would have spent less on presents if I'd remembered you were going to rob me blind again."

Every year, Delaney thought again. "Did your grandbabies enjoy the holiday?"

Mrs. Keller's face, as worn and creased as her checkbook cover, softened. "They sure did."

"I heard Courtney had the croup again. Is she feeling better?"

"That baby takes after her mother," she said, shaking her head. "I swear my Becky spent half her childhood bent over a pan of hot water with a towel draped over her head. Now she has to do the same thing with Courtney."

By the time Delaney finished processing Mrs. Keller's registration renewal, the woman had forgotten her complaints and she even offered a "Happy New Year" on her way out. When you worked with the public in the town you'd grown up in, it didn't take very long to get everybody's numbers. Mrs. Keller had a reputation for being cantankerous, but she was a marshmallow when it came to her grandchildren.

Ten minutes later, Delaney looked up to take the paperwork from the last customer of the year and almost laughed. Mike Huckins had a rumpled and frazzled look about him that went beyond the post-holiday haze the rest of the town was in. Having a two-week-old baby would do that to a man.

"Sandy called me in a panic," Mike said. "She totally forgot we had to register the car this month."

"At least you guys have a good excuse." Delaney took the handful of crumpled papers from him and smoothed them out. "How's Noah?"

"Loud. But he's doing good."

"And Sandy?"

Mike sighed. "She's exhausted, of course. But she's doing good. You should stop in and visit for a while if you get a chance."

"I will. New moms don't get a lot of company."

"They sure don't. Brody's coming in Sunday, though, for an overnight visit."

Delaney froze, except for her fingers, which curled into fists and crumpled a paper she'd just smoothed.

"Sandy hasn't seen her brother since we all went to Vegas for our wedding," Mike continued, "so you can just imagine how excited she is."

Unlike Delaney, who hadn't seen him in the five years since his mother handed her the note he'd left, telling Delaney he loved her, but he was leaving town and wasn't coming back. So sorry.

But now he *was* coming back to Tucker's Point.

She went through the very familiar process of renewing Mike's registration while he talked about their new baby, but part of her mind couldn't let go of the fact Brody was returning to town.

Even through locking up the office and driving to the market, she couldn't stop thinking about him, which made her angry. He hadn't cared enough to tell her he was leaving town, so he wasn't worth thinking about. She'd done enough of that crying herself to sleep every night for weeks after he'd left. So he was going to his sister's overnight. Big deal. Delaney would simply put off visiting Sandy until she was sure he was gone and, since she planned to spend the weekend curled up in front of her television, there was no chance she'd run into him.

She was surprised to see how full the parking lot was, even for a Friday afternoon. Then she remembered it was New Year's Eve and figured there was a run on booze and snacks. Surprisingly, there had also been a run on bread and milk, she found as she wandered up and down the aisles a bit.

"Did the weather forecast change while I was at work?" she asked Cindy, the cashier, when it was her turn to check out.

Cindy rolled her eyes. "Not that I've heard. A little

snow, but everybody's stocking up like the ice storm of '98's on its way back through."

"That was a doozy, for sure." And now that she was a volunteer for the town emergency shelter, should it need to be open, she hoped they wouldn't have another storm like that anytime soon.

She took the scenic road home, which took her along the coast for a few miles before turning back inland to the house she'd grown up in and had rented from her parents since they made the decision to move to Florida three years before. Driving calmed her and she desperately needed that. She needed to leave thoughts of Brody in her past, where they belonged.

Pulling off into a scenic area, she pulled a granola bar out of one of her grocery bags but, after a moment's hesitation, she traded it for the candy bar she'd bought on impulse. This day definitely called for chocolate therapy.

Unfortunately, off in the distance beyond the gray winter ocean, she could make out part of the roof of the Ambroise estate, which never failed to make her think of Brody. It was a beautiful place, set out on a jutting piece of land, and she used to daydream about winning the lottery and buying it. Brody could quit fishing and they'd fill the place with kids.

It hadn't worked out that way for anybody. Sophie Ambroise had passed away and, thanks to working in the town hall, she knew the place had been rezoned from residential to commercial. Somebody would turn it into a hotel, she thought. Brody had left town and Delaney certainly hadn't won the lottery.

With her mood matching the turbulent waves below her, Delaney pulled her car back onto the road and headed for home. She was going to spend the weekend with her television, a couple of good books and the gallon of ice cream that had simply jumped into her cart.

Come Monday morning, she'd go back to work and Brody would go back to wherever he'd come from. Life would go on.

THE PLAN WAS simple. Fly into Portland on Sunday and rent a car—upgrading to an all-wheel-drive model in deference to the snow—and then drive into Tucker's Point. Once he'd done the ooh-and-ah thing over his newborn nephew, he'd spend the night and then drive right back out again Monday morning.

Brody Rollins didn't intend to spend one minute longer than he had to in his hometown. He'd left the place five years ago, and he hadn't thought anything could drag him back again. Then his only sister, Sandy, had her first child. Her need for her brother to see baby Noah had, over several phone calls, overcome his reluctance to ever step foot in Maine again.

Even though the "Welcome to Tucker's Point" sign was as familiar as the area it welcomed him to, Brody relied on the rental's GPS to guide him off Route 1 and through town. It was a blessing that Sandy's husband, Mike, worked for the town instead of fishing, so they had a small house in a residential section away from the harbor. Not the picturesque marina for the tourists, but the rough and dirty harbor the lobster boats called home. Sandy's residence wasn't necessarily in the postcard-pretty part of town, but it wasn't one of the run-down houses by the docks they'd grown up in, either.

He finally found the place—a small, tidy Cape with green shutters, set back from the road—and pulled up the driveway, parking behind the well-used navy sedan Sandy had described. After killing the engine, he climbed out and stretched his back, inhaling deeply.

At least the frigid temperature and falling snow neutralized the smell. The briny air, reeking of fish and desperation, was so pervasive he'd bought himself all new clothes when he left town because he was convinced he could still smell Tucker's Point no matter how many trips he made to the Laundromat.

At the time he'd made do with stiff, coarse jeans and thin T-shirts from the discount store. Now his jeans were almost as soft as his merino-and-cashmere-blend sweater, and the soles of his boots weren't worn through. He didn't squander his money on fancy labels, but what he did buy was good quality and made to last.

Brody was halfway up the walk when the front door opened and, despite his reluctance to return to Tucker's Point, his heart squeezed at the sight of his sister. It had been two years since he'd seen her, and being a wife and new mother had changed her. She had the soft, rounded look of a woman who'd just had a baby, and her long, brown hair was pulled into a ponytail. She was a little pale and had dark circles under eyes the same soft shade of green as his, but he guessed that came with the new, first-time-mom territory.

She hugged him fiercely. "I can't believe you're here!"

"I've missed you." He squeezed her back, then chuckled when an angry shriek echoed through the house. "I guess it's time to meet my nephew."

Sandy led him to the bassinet set up in the living room and lifted Noah out. His volume level didn't go down any but his sister passed Noah to him, anyway. Brody held the tiny bundle of ticked-off baby, looking down into his face. It was red and scrunched up, and Brody thought he was cute as hell.

"He looks just like you do when you're hungry," he said, smiling at his sister.

"Funny." She took the baby, changed him, and then curled up at one end of the couch. "Will this bother you?"

"Nope." His sister breastfeeding her son wouldn't bother him anywhere near as much as the ear-splitting decibels the miniature kid was presently producing.

He walked to the window, giving her a little privacy while she got Noah settled. "It looks like it's changing over to ice. And the wind's picking up."

"I'm still doing the *sleep when the baby sleeps* thing, so I haven't even watched the weather. Mike said he'd be working overtime, but he didn't say anything about ice."

"Neither did the radio. Some snow, but no mention of ice." Driving in snow was no big deal, but the last thing he wanted was for Tucker's Point to become an ice rink and keep him from catching his plane home tomorrow.

They caught up while she fed Noah. She told him how well working for the town was going for Mike, and asked about his business. He flipped real estate and the market was tight, but he was careful and still had enough money in the bank so he slept at night. They talked about the baby and how she and Mike were still debating on whether or not she'd return to her job keeping books for the local doctor once her maternity leave was up.

She'd just finished laying the baby back in the bassinet when a massive gust of wind hit the house, driving ice against the window panes and making her jump. "It's getting bad out there really fast."

"Hopefully this is just a fluke and it'll turn back over to snow pretty soon."

"Are you going to see Mom and Dad while you're here?" Sandy asked the question in a casual enough tone, but the way she picked at the side of her thumbnail gave away her tension.

He didn't want to. Walking into that shabby and depressing little house he'd grown up in was the last thing he wanted to do. "Did you tell them I was coming?"

"I might have mentioned it to Mom."

Of course she had. "I might stop in for a few minutes on my out tomorrow."

As tempting as it was to accidentally run late and not have time, he'd do it.

It wasn't that he didn't love his parents. He did. Talked to them all the time on the phone, and his mom had even mastered Facebook so she could keep tabs on him. And he'd seen them during the past five years. Once, when he'd been working in Connecticut, he'd talked them into driving down for a weekend at the casino on his dime. And, two years ago, when Sandy had announced her engagement to Mike, he'd talked them all into joining him in Las Vegas for what was the wedding trip of a lifetime for a couple from Tucker's Point.

He'd simply managed to avoid seeing them in their natural habitat, so to speak. Just thinking about his childhood home, with its ancient brown tweed couch and insulation-deep stench of cigarette smoke and the sea, made him feel claustrophobic.

But Brody had hurt his mom enough by taking off in the middle of the night five years before. He couldn't hurt her again by avoiding seeing her when he was only a few minutes away.

He tried not to think about the other woman he'd hurt, maybe even more than he'd hurt his mother.

Delaney Westcott had been expecting a future with him. They were nearing the point of proposal, followed by a wedding, a cheap apartment over a fishermen's bar and babies. Instead, she'd gotten a note telling her he was gone because he didn't have the guts to face her.

"You need to spend more than a few minutes with them," Sandy said in an admonishing tone that made her sound just like their mother.

"I'll visit for a while. More than a few minutes. But I can't stay too long because I have a plane to catch so I can get back to work." And out of Tucker's Point.

That was when the power went out.

CHAOS REIGNED IN the school's gymnasium. Delaney wanted to pretend it was the controlled kind of chaos, but if somebody had control, it wasn't her. All she had was the clipboard. And a growing stream of people who did *not* want to be there.

At least it was keeping her mind off the fact Brody Rollins was back in town. Mostly.

She'd gotten the phone call shortly after the storm took its unexpected turn for the worse. Homes were already losing power and there might be a lot of ice and wind yet to come, so it was time to open the town's emergency shelter at the school.

There were several other volunteers helping the displaced get settled. At this point in the storm, they'd get mostly the elderly and families with small children, which made for an interesting mix. But if the storm didn't ease up or change back to a more manageable snowfall, people would start risking the weather to get a warm bed and some food as the temperature dropped—both outside and in their houses.

She hadn't even gotten around to opening her ice cream yet. If *her* power went out and it melted, she was going to be really bummed. She'd need it after this.

When she saw Mrs. Palmer approaching her, she almost groaned aloud. "What can I do for you?"

"Where are the jigsaw puzzles? We always do puzzles."

"I'll bring them out in a little while. Right now we're trying to get the cots, blankets and food situation taken care of."

"What am I supposed to do, then?"

Delaney smiled and did *not* suggest the woman help with the cots, blankets and food situation. Nobody would thank her for that. "Maybe you could see if Penny needs any help?"

Penny was *so* going to make her pay for that later. Probably tenfold, even. But Delaney needed to get the cots set up because she had the chart from the fire department and if everything wasn't up to the safety code, they'd have to do it again. It was a lot harder once people started showing up.

At least Mike and Sandy had a generator, which meant even if Brody was there with her and the power went out, he wouldn't be showing up at the school. It was hectic enough without throwing in a lost love. Not that he'd been lost. He'd deliberately left her behind without even telling her goodbye.

Hopefully she'd get through this storm and his surprise return to Tucker's Point without telling him hello.

CHAPTER TWO

THE CHILL WAS already creeping into Sandy's small house, and Brody knew whenever the power didn't come back within a few minutes, it could be an hour or it could be *a while.* And a while with no heat was no fun.

"I can't stay here with Noah," Sandy said, as if she'd been reading his mind. "He's too little."

"You don't have a wood stove or a generator or anything?"

"We don't have a wood stove because of Mike's allergies. And we had a generator, but it died and we haven't gotten around to having it fixed yet."

"Space heaters?"

"Mike has a torpedo heater for the shed, but it's not really meant for in the house. And I don't think we have any kerosene for it, anyway."

He scrubbed his hands over his face, considering the options. If Mike hadn't been able to get the generator running, there was no sense in Brody standing around in the cold, tinkering with it. But Sandy was right. Noah was too little to weather having no heat with not even an estimated time for power restoration.

"How about Mom and Dad's?" he asked. He could drop them off, have a quick cup of coffee and then, hopefully, still get out of town and to a hotel.

"The way Dad smokes?" Sandy shook her head. "A quick visit's one thing, but Noah can't stay there."

"We might make it to a hotel, but we'd have to leave now." The motels in Tucker's Point were all closed for the off-season, so they'd have to go inland or down the coast. He'd take the chance alone, but not with his sister and a baby in the car. "It's already white-knuckle out there."

Sandy stood in front of the window, gently bouncing the blue bundle in her arms. "We can't risk that. I think we should head to the school before it gets any worse."

He agreed, but that didn't make it sit any easier. The plan was to get in, get out and not see anybody but his sister and her family and maybe his parents if he had the time. The plan didn't include sitting around an elementary school gymnasium with whatever percentage of the population of Tucker's Point showed up.

The only saving grace was that there wouldn't be too many people from his old neighborhood. The fishing families tended to be a hardier bunch and more self-sufficient, so they'd weather the storm better.

"Brody?" his sister prompted.

"Yeah. We should go." He reached out to take the baby from her. "Gather up whatever you'll need and we'll go before it gets any worse."

It wasn't a fun ride. Front-wheel, all-wheel or four-wheel drive didn't matter on ice and his fingers were strangling the steering wheel before he even reached the end of Sandy's road. With her neighborhood in darkness, it wasn't bad, but when they passed through areas that still had power, the ice refracted lights and pierced his eyeballs.

He crept along the streets and with every slip of the wheels, he grew more conscious of the precious cargo sleeping in the backseat. Sandy was quiet, probably not wanting to distract him, and they both breathed a sigh of relief when he finally reached the end of Oak Street and turned into the school lot.

"Do you want me to carry Noah?"

"You can get our bags in one trip if I take him, but I'll leave him in his seat so he'll be protected if I fall on the ice."

"Hold on to the handle if you do fall." Brody chuckled. "Otherwise he'll go on one hell of a first sledding trip."

They made it to the double doors marked as the shelter entrance without falling and Brody set their bags down to hold the door for Sandy. After picking them back up, he followed her in, blinking under the bright lighting.

"We have to sign in," Sandy said. "They need to know who's here, plus if there's a problem in my neighborhood, they'll know where I am."

He set the bags next to her feet. "I'll take care of it. Wait here."

"No, wait," he heard her say as he turned and stepped toward the woman with the clipboard.

Just as the woman with the clipboard turned toward him.

"Delaney?"

THE CHAOS AROUND Delaney faded into the background as her eyes met Brody's, and her breath caught in her throat.

The last thing she needed was to be snowed in with Brody Rollins.

He'd changed during his five years away. His clothes looked expensive and his dark hair was obviously being professionally cut now, rather than hacked at by his mother in the kitchen when it got shaggy enough so it fell over his eyes. At twenty-seven, his face had matured and he had an air of confidence he'd never had before.

But that rough and dangerous boy was still there, simmering under the thin layer of polish. As always, the girl inside who'd loved him immediately yearned for his touch, but that girl needed to behave so she didn't embarrass herself.

Holding the clipboard against her chest, as if it were some kind of cheap plastic armor, Delaney forced herself to smile. "Hi, Brody. It's been a long time."

"It has." He didn't return her smile. Instead, he looked at her so intently she felt as if she was being memorized. "You look great."

If women with windblown ponytails, crowd-wrangling crazy eyes and a fresh coffee spill down the front of her favorite Red Sox sweatshirt were his thing, more power to him. "Thanks. You do, too."

Oh, crap. The sweatshirt. Delaney clutched the clipboard tighter, as if she was trying to hide the baseball logo on the front. Maybe he wouldn't notice her sweatshirt—so much her favorite, the hem and the end of the cuffs were a little on the frayed side—had been his, once upon a time. He'd pulled it off and made her wear it one night when they took a late-night walk by the shore. It had been in her dryer, waiting to be folded, when he took off.

After crying into the sweatshirt off and on for days, she'd washed it again and thought about returning it to Brody's mom. She knew it was his favorite, after all. But she hadn't gotten the rings, the picket fence, the two-and-a-half kids or the black Lab she'd been waiting for, so she'd kept the damn sweatshirt.

"I guess I'm supposed to tell you we're here or something?"

Oh, she knew he was there. The racing pulse, tingling body and muscle-memory wondering why she wasn't in his arms let her know Brody Rollins was in the room.

An unhappy squawk from the baby seat Sandy was holding gave her an excuse to break eye contact with the man. Throwing a newborn into the mix was going to be a challenge. People would already be cranky about being displaced from their homes and trying to sleep on cots in a school gymnasium. Noah fussing to be fed every few hours, especially during the night, would grate on already raw nerves.

"Okay," she said, putting on her professional face, "let's get you checked in. And we have a very limited number of privacy screens, but I'll make sure you get one, Sandy."

The act of writing down their names and Sandy's address helped calm her nerves. They had no medical concerns to note, other than Sandy having given birth two weeks before, and she listed the medications new mom and baby had. They had to sign acknowledging they understood the rules of the shelter and would abide by them, and she was doing okay until Brody stepped close to take the pen and clipboard from her.

He smelled delicious. Slightly damp wool and leather and a hint of a very masculine cologne. Like money, she thought. He didn't smell anything like the Brody Rollins she'd known.

And it was probably deliberate. Because everything about the man seemed to trigger a memory; she remembered the amount of time he'd spend in the shower, trying to scrub the scent of fishing off his skin before taking her out on a date. He'd hated that smell—been ashamed of it—even though she'd never complained.

As soon as he'd finished signing his name and handed back her clipboard, she put as much distance between them as she could without appearing obvious. "Let's put you guys in that back corner. It's a low traffic area, so maybe Noah will be able to sleep."

After leading Brody and Sandy to the cots in the corner, Delaney slipped through the double doors they'd hung a sign on that read No Admittance Without a Volunteer and into the main hallway of the school. The doors swung closed behind her and she stepped to the right so she could lean her head against the wall.

There was not enough ice cream in the world to take the edge off this situation, even if she could get home to her freezer.

Of course, the jerk had to look amazing. Not that he could have gone too far downhill in five years, but now he was a man who'd make her look twice even if he was a stranger on the street. That kind of delicious packaging on a man she'd loved with all of her heart, though, was making her head spin.

She needed to focus. After taking a deep breath, she straightened and walked toward the closet where they'd stashed the few privacy screens they had. If they left them in the gym, a brawl would probably break out for them.

Once she'd handed it off to Sandy, Delaney would go back about her business of running the emergency shelter and do her best to ignore Brody. It wasn't what she *wanted* to do. Now that she'd come face-to-face with him, all the questions that had haunted her were rattling around in her brain, demanding answers.

Why hadn't he told her he was leaving? Why hadn't

he at least said goodbye? Had asking her to go with him ever crossed his mind, or did he deliberately leave her as well as Tucker's Point behind? And why hadn't he loved her enough to stay?

She wasn't going to give him the satisfaction of bringing it up, though. Especially in front of people she knew. It wasn't as though knowing the answers would change anything. All it would do was rip open old wounds and not change the bottom line. Brody knew where she was. If he wanted her, he would have come back for her.

Feeling steadier, Delaney carried the screen into the gym and walked it over to the corner where Brody and Sandy had gathered three cots together.

"I hope you don't mind we took an extra," Sandy said. "If Mike gets a chance to sleep, he'll probably come here."

"It's fine. If we do end up with a shortage of cots, I might have to steal it back if he's not here, but we'll cross that bridge if we come to it." She leaned the screen against the wall. "I'll let you guys figure out how you want this after you get situated."

"Thanks so much, Delaney," Sandy said.

Delaney managed not to look Brody in the face even once during the exchange. She could do this, she thought, as she brushed off her hands and started walking away. Ignoring him wouldn't be so hard.

"Hey, Delaney?" She turned and her insides quivered when his mouth lifted into that boyish grin she'd always been a sucker for. "Nice sweatshirt."

BRODY WAS DOING everything in his power not to watch Delaney as she moved around the gym, doing whatever needed to be done. Unfortunately, he wasn't a comic book hero and his powers were limited.

She'd barely changed at all in the five years he'd been gone. Her dark blond hair, judging by the length of her ponytail, was a little longer. And she'd put on a little weight, but it looked good on her.

Seeing her in his sweatshirt, though, was twisting him up in ways he hadn't thought possible. He'd looked for it the night he'd left town because it was his favorite and he didn't want to leave it behind. Then he'd remembered pulling it over Delaney's head and helping her shove her arms in the sleeves because she'd been shivering in the ocean breeze.

Brody had been tormented for weeks after he left town, imagining her wearing the sweatshirt and missing him. Eventually he figured she'd get over him and his prized Red Sox sweatshirt would go to Goodwill or be used to wax her car.

He wasn't sure what to make of the fact she was wearing it tonight. Was it just something she grabbed out of the back of her closet? Or did she still think of him when she wore it?

"Stop staring at her," Sandy hissed. "You're making it more awkward."

Forcing his attention away from Delaney, he looked down at Noah, who was starting to squirm in his car seat and make squeaky noises that were cute at the moment, but bound to get louder in a hurry. "I'm just looking around."

"If you were looking around, you'd know half the people in here are watching you watch her, hoping for good gossip."

"Nothing to gossip about."

"Everybody knows Delaney and half of them know you broke her heart. There's definitely gossip."

He rolled his eyes, mentally adding her comment to the *why Tucker's Point sucks* column. "Old news."

By the time Sandy got Noah out of his seat, the baby was at about half volume and Brody reached for the folding privacy screen Delaney had leaned against the wall. As he looked it over, trying to figure out the best way to fold it out for maximum privacy, he glanced around the gym again. He didn't figure a screaming baby was going to go over too well.

A few guys threw dirty looks their way, and Brody felt his temper rising. Maybe he'd made himself into a successful businessman and the calluses were gone, but there were some things a guy from the rough part of town didn't forget. Like how to throw a punch.

"Brody." Sandy's elbow jabbed his ribs. "Brody! Don't even start."

"I'm not doing anything."

"I know that look and I'm telling you don't even think about it."

Brody shrugged, more to ease the tension from his shoulders than in response to her words. "That guy in the green sweatshirt was a couple years behind me in school. A punk with a big mouth."

"Now he's just a dad here with two young kids who are probably already on his last nerve and he's thinking about how a newborn's going to make it so much worse."

Now that she mentioned it, Brody saw the two boys near the guy. Young and full of the frantic energy that came with being up past their bedtime, they were rough-housing and showed no signs of being tired. A newborn in their midst definitely wouldn't make the guy's life any easier.

"Can you do me a favor?" Sandy asked after he'd wrapped the screen around their cots. "I'm supposed to drink a lot of water when I'm nursing. I drank one bottle already and I couldn't fit anymore in the bags. Can you get some from the kitchen?"

At least it was something to do. Brody had a feeling if this power outage stretched on, he'd be begging for busy work. He wasn't a guy used to sitting around doing nothing. But he only got halfway across the gym before he ran into an old friend.

"Hot damn. If it ain't Brody Rollins." Donnie Cox didn't look much different than the last time Brody had seen him, downing shots after a good haul. Worn flannel shirt, faded jeans and unlaced work boots with duct tape over one toe. "Heard you were back in town."

Brody shook his hand, noting the hard, ragged calluses across Donnie's palm. It had taken almost two years for Brody's hands to smooth to the point they weren't something people—usually women—commented on. "It's good to see you again, Cox."

"Yeah, I brought the wife and mother-in-law over when the power went out, but I'm going to go back out and do some welfare checks. Hate being cooped up."

"Married, huh? Congratulations."

"I married Becks. Big surprise." Donnie and Rebecca were not only high-school sweethearts, but had been to-gether since junior high. They'd never dated anybody but each other, as far as Brody knew. "I'll be a dad in four months, too. Our first."

Brody said all the right congratulatory words, but mentally he was acknowledging that guys he went to school with being married and having kids made him feel a little as if he was missing out on something. Sure, he'd been working hard and putting money in the bank, but he'd be thirty soon. It wouldn't be long before he started looking for a wife and planning a family.

As the thought took hold in his mind, his gaze was drawn to Delaney. If he hadn't left town, they'd be married now. Probably have at least two kids. And he'd work his ass off every day just to keep a roof over their heads and food on the table while Delaney scrounged for coupons and did laundry that would always smell like a fishing boat.

He couldn't regret not letting them turn into his parents. But he regretted not having her. He regretted that a lot.

"It was good to see you, man," Donnie said. "I need to get back."

He shook Donnie's hand, and then continued toward the kitchen. Delaney seemed to be the only volunteer there and he didn't know where they kept the water, so he headed toward her. When she saw him coming, her expression grew guarded and he hated that.

"What can I do for you?"

So formal and cold. She'd been his best friend once and her voice had always made him feel good, whether she was talking about her day or whispering sweet invitations in his ear. "Sandy's out of water and she's supposed to drink a lot when she's nursing Noah. She said you'd have some."

"We lock the kitchen at night, but water we keep in the coolers under the main table so people can help themselves. Feel free to grab some."

When she started to turn away, he said her name to make her stop. He didn't know what to say to her, but he couldn't stand getting the cold shoulder. Not from her.

"Was there something else?"

"I'm sorry." It seemed like a good place—the only place—to start. "I'm sorry I didn't say goodbye."

She folded her arms across her chest and lifted her shoulders a little in a very familiar defensive reaction. When she was afraid a conversation might make her cry, Delaney's body language closed up, as if she were wrapping herself in a protective blanket. He wasn't surprised he remembered that. There wasn't much he'd forgotten.

"Thank you for the apology, Brody. I did get your note, though. That was thoughtful of you."

Ouch. So it was angry tears, not sad tears, she was afraid she might shed in front of him. "Let's go somewhere and talk."

"No, thanks."

"Come on, Delaney. I want to talk to you. If you just give me a little consideration, I'll—"

"I'll give you the same consideration you gave me. How about that?"

"I did what was best for you. For both of us."

"That's weak, Brody. Really weak."

Maybe it was, but it was all he had. "Delaney, seriously, can we talk?"

"No, Brody, we can't. I have to dim the lights and start spreading the word it's quiet time so maybe these kids will get some sleep."

"After that, maybe we can slip out in the hall and talk?"

"There's nothing to say. Now, if you'll excuse me, I have work to do."

She left him standing there alone, feeling as if there were a whole lot of things he wanted to say to her, but the words were all stuck in his throat. No matter how straight she tried to play it, there was still pain in her eyes. He'd known her too long and too well to miss it.

The least he could do while he was stuck here was try to make that pain go away.

CHAPTER THREE

BRODY WASN'T SURE what time it was when he opened his eyes. The gym was quiet, except for the creak of cots as people tried to find comfortable positions in their sleep and an unfortunate amount of snoring. Glancing up at the row of small windows at the top of the walls, he could see it was still dark. And if he listened closely, he could hear icy precipitation still being slapped against the glass by the wind.

Now that he was awake, he had to take a leak, so he rolled out of the cot as quietly as he could and stepped out from behind the privacy screen in his socks. The polished floor was slippery, but he was afraid if he tried to get his shoes out from under his cot, he'd jostle Noah's car seat. Since it felt as if it had only been about ten minutes since the last time the boy cried, nobody wanted that.

Movement near the set of exterior doors serving as the shelter entrance caught his eye. A woman, who thankfully wasn't Delaney, was talking in quiet tones to a man. Across the gym, in the dim lights they had to leave on 24/7 for safety reasons, he saw it was Sandy's husband, so he made his way over.

When the volunteer turned to point in the direction of their cots, Brody lifted his hand and waved as he approached. "Hey, Mike."

They shook hands. "Glad you made it into town, Brody. Sorry you can't get back out, though."

He was, too. "Spending some quality time with the loudest baby in the history of man."

Mike grinned. "Kid's got a set of pipes."

"They letting you crash for a while?"

"Yeah, there's nothing we can do with this ice and, barring anybody trying to get here, everybody's off the roads. We'll sleep for a few hours, then start checking on people. Thanks for getting Sandy and Noah here, by the way."

"It was no problem."

"I could have driven them here, but I wouldn't be able to stay because it's all hands on deck. I appreciate you being here to help with the baby."

"Nowhere else I'd rather be," he lied. "We got three cots, and we're behind that screen over there."

Once Mike had gone to join his family, Brody made his way to the men's room. The lights were brighter in there and, when he stepped back into the gym, he had to stop for a moment to let his vision adjust.

He found himself looking around the huge room, looking for Delaney, but all the sleeping, blanket-covered lumps looked the same. He guessed she was probably over near the entrance, so she'd wake up if somebody went in or out, but he wasn't sure.

Stupid to be looking for her, anyway, he told himself as he made his way back to his cot. She wanted nothing to do with him, and he couldn't blame her. But as he tucked his arms under his head and stared at the gym ceiling, he couldn't stop the slideshow of the loving, laughing Delaney he'd left behind from playing through his mind.

Light was streaming through the windows the next

time he opened his eyes, and he realized it was Mike grabbing his outerwear and boots that had awoken him. "Heading back out already? Was there breakfast?"

"Little girl's missing. Mother went into her room this morning and she wasn't in her bed."

"Oh, shit." Brody swung his feet to the floor and scrubbed his hands over his face. "She's not hiding anywhere in the house?"

"They searched it so thoroughly I wouldn't be surprised if they have to rehang the Sheetrock. She's not there."

Brody stood and picked up his bag, careful not to jostle Noah's car seat or Sandy's cot. "I can be ready to go in ten minutes, if you can wait."

"Dressed like that, I'll spend more time taking care of you than looking for April."

The little girl's name was April. Brody's gaze fell on his sleeping nephew and his breath caught in his throat. Somebody's child was out there in this storm and her name was April. "I'm not stupid. I've got winter gear, including boots, in the trunk of my rental."

"Can use the extra eyes and ears, then."

By the time Brody washed up and changed his clothes in the men's room—which wasn't ideal, but was all he had—the activity level in the gym had ratcheted up a notch. There were more men pulling on cold-weather gear and a group of women scrambling to brew coffee and put out doughnuts.

Delaney was one of them, and she scowled when she saw him. "You're not going out there, are you?"

"I'm going to go out with Mike. I can be an extra set of eyes."

"You're not dressed to be out in this kind of weather."

He took the disposable cup of coffee she handed him

and noticed she'd put one sugar and a splash of milk in it, just the way he liked it. "I've got a good coat and some boots in the rental. I'll be fine."

"Brody, nobody expects you to go."

"So you all think I'll just sit here drinking coffee while a little girl's lost out there in this storm? Thanks a lot."

She held his gaze for a long moment, her jaw set in a grim line. Then she shook her head. "Fine. Be careful and don't do anything stupid."

Not much in the way of a vote of confidence. Brody downed a couple of doughnuts and another cup of coffee before heading outside to get his stuff out of the rental. The wind stole his breath and the sheets of freezing rain made walking a challenge, but he made it to the car and back without killing himself.

By the time he was ready, a guy named Baker who was—according to Mike—a volunteer with the fire department, had handed out location assignments.

"Okay, people," the guy said. "Most of you know April, but for the few that don't, just watch for a nine-year-old girl who isn't safe at home where she belongs. She's wearing a purple coat, a white hat with a purple pom-pom and pink boots. Let's bring her home."

As they filed out of the gym, Brody looked back at Delaney. He caught her watching him, and he raised a hand to say goodbye. She turned away.

BREAKFAST WAS NOTHING short of a nightmare. Being a short-order cook for a large group of cranky people who hadn't gotten a good night's sleep was even less fun than registering vehicles for a mob of people who'd forgotten it was the last day of December.

One of the reasons they used the elementary school

for the town shelter, rather than the high school, was the fact the kitchen was attached to what they called the gym, but was actually a multi-purpose room that doubled as the cafeteria. With space, a kitchen and restrooms in a central location, it was the perfect space.

What was not perfect was people passing through the line and settling for doughnuts, pastries and cold cereal when there was a fully stocked school kitchen behind them. Some of the women wanted to fire up the stoves and turn the place into the neighborhood diner. Delaney was going to lose her voice explaining over and over why that wasn't possible.

Lunch would be primarily do-it-yourself sandwiches, but she wasn't looking forward to supper.

As soon as she could escape the serving line, she brewed more coffee and then grabbed a box of trash bags. There were at least half a dozen garbage barrels in the gym and it seemed as if every time she turned around, they were full again.

It also annoyed Delaney to no end how much she worried about Brody. No matter what she was doing or what minor crisis she was handling, in the back of her mind she was constantly aware of just how long he'd been gone. And it had only been about three hours. Though she didn't forget he'd been born and raised in Tucker's Point, she worried five years in warmer climates had made him soft.

"I'm sorry, Delaney."

She hadn't even noticed Sandy standing next to her, gently bouncing the baby on her shoulder.

"I wouldn't have come," Sandy continued, "but the house was cooling off way too fast and Noah's too little to weather it out."

Delaney jerked a full bag out of the garbage can and

shoved down on the contents so she could tie it off. "Of course you had to come, Sandy. Don't even worry about it. If he gets too fussy, we'll take turns walking him and…well, people are going to have deal, that's all."

"Thanks, but I was talking about Brody. I'm sorry for bringing Brody here."

Delaney sighed and looked at the sleeping baby. Noah looked a lot like Sandy, who looked a lot like Brody. Her heart twisted as she wondered if her and Brody's babies would have looked like little Noah.

"It's been five years," Delaney said in a quiet voice. "And it was inevitable I'd run into him eventually. I'm fine. Really."

"I wish I could have given you a heads-up, at least."

Delaney laughed. "Then I might have stayed home and made s'mores over emergency candles and who would be here to take out the garbage?"

"Would you really have avoided him?"

"I wouldn't have gone out of my way to see him." Delaney sighed. "Fine, it's a little hard."

"At least you didn't bean him with your clipboard."

"I thought about it. You know, he'd been acting weird for a couple of weeks before he left." She gave a derisive snort. "I thought he was working up the nerve to ask me to marry him."

"Oh, Delaney." Sandy looked as if she was going to cry, so Delaney focused her attention on putting a fresh bag in the can. "We thought he was going to propose, too."

"Guess he fooled us all."

"I don't think he meant to. Not that it helps any, but I think he was scared and confused."

She wasn't really in the mood to hear Brody defended, but Sandy *was* his sister, after all. Delaney knew she was only trying to help. "It was a long time ago. I'm over it."

That was a lie, but Sandy was too busy shifting Noah's weight to her other shoulder to see it on her face. Delaney hadn't spent the last five years—okay, four and a half years, maybe—pining away for Brody Rollins, but she hadn't found a man to replace him yet.

She'd dated. She'd even had a couple of relationships that might have grown serious enough to head to the altar and give her the family she wanted if her stupid, stubborn heart had been able to give up on the man who'd broken it.

But, even though she'd met some really nice guys who would have made good husbands, she hadn't met one yet who made her feel the way Brody had. And, judging by her reaction to being around him, maybe still did.

THE ONLY THING worse than driving back into Tucker's Point was riding shotgun around Tucker's Point during an ice storm. The big plow truck with the massive sand-and-salt hopper on the back went okay, but it was still white-knuckle tense in the cab, especially with a little girl lost.

Brody kept his focus on the passing scenery, eyes peeled for a flash of purple or white or pink, but he saw nothing but the town he'd grown up in. They'd been at it for hours, going around the outskirts since people were searching the main downtown area on foot.

"This is a waste of time," Mike said, not for the first time. "She's not going to be walking down the side of the road. She's hiding somewhere. Taking shelter."

"You never know what a kid will do. She could be trying to walk home right now."

"Not giving up. Just think it's a waste of time. Now we've not only got a lost kid, but a whole lot of people who should be safe inside are out looking for her." He handed his Thermos to Brody, signaling he was ready for another hit of coffee.

He poured Mike half a cup, strong and black, then screwed the lid back on. His brother-in-law was going to start getting jittery soon if he didn't lay off the caffeine. "Hopefully somebody will find her soon."

"Yeah. If it was Noah out there..." Mike swallowed some coffee, then shook his head. "I'd want every able-bodied person in the whole state of Maine out looking for him."

Brody had to agree. He'd only known Noah less than a day and he'd already take on a pack of dragons with nothing but a butter knife for the kid.

"If this gets any worse, we're going to have to head back," Mike said in a grim voice. Ice was sheeting over the windshield so fast the defroster and wipers could barely keep up, and the kids could play pond hockey on the streets. "They'll keep looking. Red'll be out on Betsy—that John Deere of his—and they'll keep searching on foot. Some of the guys have ATVs with chains on the tires. They'll go out."

Brody could hear the reluctance to give up in Mike's voice, but he had to agree. Conditions were moving past treacherous and straight into deadly. "It's like you said. She's probably hiding somewhere under cover, anyway. It's the door-to-door searches that'll turn her up and we don't want to pull people off that to come rescue us."

He looked out the window, still looking for a flash of purple, while Mike radioed in for an update and to voice his concerns.

Cased in glittering ice, his hometown looked beautiful and peaceful, like something out of a snow globe. And he had to admire the way the town pulled together. He'd been listening to the chatter on Mike's radio and this was a community that knew how to stand together and help their neighbors.

Maybe it was only as a grown man he could appreciate qualities like that. Growing up and in the few years after he graduated from high school, he'd felt nothing but resentment. Now he'd seen a little more of the world. Played cards in places like Atlantic City and Las Vegas and Miami. Flipped houses in almost every kind of suburban neighborhood, working his way up to some commercial stuff. It was easier to appreciate the bonds a town like Tucker's Point fostered and why people might stay instead of getting out at the first opportunity, like he had.

"We're heading back in," Mike said, breaking into his thoughts. "We'll take a different route back to cover the ground, but they're pulling the road crews in."

Brody would be lying if he said he wasn't relieved, but that didn't make it any easier to abandon the search. And with Mike, Sandy and Noah together as a family, Brody was going to be left to his own devices, and there was nowhere to hide in the gym. Either for him or for Delaney.

They were almost back to the school when Mike changed the subject from his job, which Brody now knew more about than he'd ever wanted to, to the past. "We might have run with different crowds, but I remember you used to date Delaney. Sandy said you were still together when you moved away."

There was no question, but his brother-in-law seemed to be waiting for some kind of response. "Yeah."

"Must be weird, seeing her again."

Now that the sucker punch of seeing her face had been absorbed, Brody was starting to like the idea of seeing Delaney again.

They definitely had unfinished business between them.

CHAPTER FOUR

BECAUSE, DESPITE HERSELF, she'd been watching for his return, Delaney knew the first thing Brody did when he walked through the gym door was scan the room until he found her. Their eyes met and she held his gaze until Mike said something to him, drawing his attention.

She was in trouble. Now matter how often she reminded herself of how badly he'd hurt her, the magnetism that had first drawn her to Brody and the chemistry that pulled them together were still as strong as they'd ever been. He was a rip tide that would suck her in and pull her under, but some reckless part of her wanted to throw caution to the wind and dive in headfirst.

But several members of the road crew, besides Mike, were arriving, so she went into the kitchen to brew a fresh urn of coffee. Most of them would crash for a while, but she wanted to have it ready, just in case.

"Miss Delaney?" The small voice startled her, and she turned to see Mariah Turner standing in the doorway. "Did those men find April?"

"Not yet, honey." Mariah and the little girl who was lost would be classmates, she realized. And no matter how discreet adults tried to be in their conversations, she'd obviously overheard somebody talking about April. "There are still people out there looking, though. They'll find her, honey."

"Did she run away?"

"I don't know." Delaney gave her a comforting smile. "Did she say anything about running away? Was she unhappy at school?"

"Nope. But if she didn't run away, did somebody take her?"

Delaney didn't know what to say. There was no training for this during the town's emergency response drills. "I don't know what happened to April, Mariah. But we're going to think positive thoughts and when the searchers find her, we'll be able to ask her ourselves, okay?"

"Okay. Can me and my sister have some oyster crackers?"

That she could deal with. She reached into a big box the restaurant had donated and took out two packets of oyster crackers. They were good snacks for antsy young people. Tasty, crunchy and—most importantly—not loaded with sugar.

"Thanks, Miss Delaney!" Mariah skipped out, almost colliding with Brody.

"Whoa!" He did a side step to keep from tripping over the child, then smiled after her. "The world was a less complicated place when a package of oyster crackers made everything better."

"I'd give anything to have half her energy right now."

"I was hoping for some artificial, caffeine-fueled energy."

"Then you've come to the right place." The conversation was so...*normal,* Delaney could hardly believe she was having it with Brody. "The fresh stuff's still brewing, but there's some left in that pot that's not too old."

"It could be motor oil and, with a little cream and sugar, I'd drink it right now."

"Bad out there?"

"Pretty bad. I think I'm going to be here awhile."

Was that a warning? "Sandy will be happy to hear it. She's missed you."

"I can help with Noah, too."

"And John and Camille must have been happy to see you."

"I, uh…haven't been to see them." She gave him a look designed to make him feel like something scraped off the bottom of a shoe, but he only shrugged. "I was going to stop by on my way out of town tomorrow, but the power went out."

"Sandy talked to them while you guys were out. Not for long because Noah woke up in a really bad mood, but she said they're doing okay."

"They're hardy. And stubborn." He took a sip of the coffee and, when he closed his eyes to savor it, she looked away. "I really am sorry about the way I left town, Delaney."

She forced herself to shrug, as though it was all so far in the past it didn't hurt a bit. "It's been five years."

"Which means you're five years overdue for an apology. I should have called you after I left."

"You know what would have been better? If you'd called *before* you left."

His mouth twisted and she saw the guilt on his face. "I knew if I told you I was leaving, you'd be hurt and I'd see it on your face. I was afraid you'd cry and I wouldn't be able to walk away from you."

"Oh, clearly it's all my fault, then. Shame on me for loving you, I guess."

"I knew if I stayed, eventually I'd hate you."

She blinked, feeling his words like a slap across the face.

Brody shoved his hands through his hair. "I hated fishing. I hated my parents for not wanting a better life. I hated this town. If I stayed for you, in time I would have hated you, too."

"I thought we were happy and that it would be enough."

"You were happy because, at the end of the day, you went home to your parents. No matter how much time we spent together, it wasn't the same as being married and on our own. It wouldn't have been a few years as my wife before you were exhausted from doing laundry that smelled like low tide no matter how many times you washed it and trying to pay bills and feed kids on short pay. And I would have been a bitter, chain-smoking drunk, just like my old man."

If that was truly his vision of their future, it was no wonder he'd run. "The fact you couldn't tell me that just proves it wasn't meant to be. You saw me as a burden, not a partner."

"Delaney, I—" He was interrupted by the angry shriek of a newborn echoing through the gym. "Damn. Mike's exhausted. I'm going to go see if I can walk the baby and let him and Sandy get some rest."

She nodded, simultaneously relieved this conversation could end and disappointed he was walking away from her. It was probably for the best. He couldn't unbreak her heart and, even if he could, nothing had changed.

Tucker's Point was her home and it was a place he didn't even want to visit, never mind return to for good. They could be civil—maybe even friendly—but there was no point in looking into the past. Brody Rollins wasn't part of her future.

THERE WAS NOTHING like trying to keep a fussy infant soothed and quiet in a gym full of people to kill a guy's new and fragile urge to start a family.

His arms ached, he had a tweak in the small of his

back, his shoulder felt damp and his feet hurt. And, when he'd managed to sneak a peek at his watch mid-jostle, it had only been a half hour.

Parenthood was not for sissies.

He had nobody to ask for help, either. Not long after Mike and Sandy lay down, he'd seen Delaney slip behind a screen to the cot she and another volunteer were taking turns using. With those three people all napping, Brody was essentially alone in a room full of people.

He'd walked away from this community and he knew, from the looks he'd been getting, they hadn't forgotten he'd snuck out in the dark, leaving them, his family and Delaney behind.

"Why don't you let me help you with him?"

A woman who looked vaguely familiar stood next to him. While it was a relief to know he wasn't alone, after all, he wasn't too sure about handing Sandy's baby over to just anybody who asked.

"I'm Dani Harbour." He must have looked blank, because she arched one eyebrow at him. "I was a year behind you in school."

"Delaney's friend."

"Yeah, Delaney's friend." The *you jerk* was implied by her tone. "Let me walk Noah for a little bit. You look beat."

She knew the baby's name. And it's not as if she could go anywhere. "Are you sure you don't mind?"

"In this town, we help our friends and neighbors." She paused. "Sandy and Mike are both."

Just so he knew he wasn't either. "I appreciate it."

He handed Noah to Dani and then pressed his hands to the small of his back, twisting to work the kinks out. Relaxing was an entirely different thing, however, and he found himself hovering as the storm's refugees took turns passing the baby. While he appreciated the way the community stuck together, that was his nephew they were playing hot potato with.

He breathed a sigh of relief when Sandy emerged from behind the screen almost an hour and a half later. Noah was obviously winding himself up for a good bawl and even the comfort of snuggling against Rebecca Cox's really ample breasts wasn't doing it for the little guy anymore. He wanted to eat.

Sandy looked well-rested, though, which was good. With her husband safe and her baby being looked after, she'd managed a power nap she desperately needed. She smiled when she spotted them and made her way over.

"Time for the little monster to eat," she said, taking Noah from Becks. "Thanks for babysitting. I feel so much better now."

"You needed the rest," Brody said. "I wish you could have slept longer."

As he said it, he caught Delaney slipping out of her sleeping area through the corner of his eye. She should have slept longer, he thought. Wearing herself out taking care of things did nobody any good.

She disappeared in the direction of the bathrooms and, when he saw her again, she was fresh-faced and looked ready to tackle whatever the next thing on her list was.

Well, she wasn't going to tackle it alone. Brody wasn't used to sitting around and he was more than capable of helping in any way he could. He made his way over to the check-in table, where she was drinking orange juice and reading something on her clipboard.

"What can I do to help?"

She jumped, almost dropping her plastic cup of juice. "Brody! Don't sneak up on people."

"All I did was walk. What are you reading?"

"I'm trying to find anything at all I can to justify putting off the next thing on my list."

If Delaney was avoiding it, it couldn't be a pleasant task. "What is it? I can help."

She sighed, dropping the clipboard on the table. "It's time to go around and clean and disinfect. With so many people in one place, it's important to stay on top of the germs so I have to wipe everything down with bleach water."

"Point me towards a bucket, oh fearless leader."

She laughed, shaking her head. "I don't really see you in rubber gloves with that sweater and those shoes."

"What about them?"

"I know quality when I see it, Brody. It's obvious you haven't had to do manual labor in a while."

That wounded him for reasons he couldn't quite put his finger on. "I'm not afraid of hard work. I might have crews to do the heavy lifting now, but don't forget I'm from here—from the docks. I know hard work."

Her eyes met his and she tilted her head, as though he were a puzzle she was trying to solve. "Gee, Brody. That almost sounded like hometown pride there for a second."

"I'm just saying I can do whatever you need done. That's all." Pride wasn't an emotion he connected to his childhood.

"I'm not going to turn down the help. Let's go get the stuff."

He followed her through the double doors in the hallway, trying to keep his eyes above her waist and not on the gentle sway of her hips as she walked. Especially since they were being watched. They were *always* being watched in the gym as people kept watch for any scrap of gossip.

The supply closet was next to the gym, and he waited while she found the right key on the ring he assumed the school supplied to the emergency management volunteers. The small room must have been on the same circuit with the gym because, when she flipped the switch, the overhead light flickered and turned on. He followed her in and wrinkled his nose at the chemical smell.

"I saw that," she told him, amusement in her voice. "I can probably find you other work, like holding Mrs. Cameron's ball of yarn while she knits, if this is too much for you."

The amusement in her eyes and the light teasing in her voice dragged him back to five years ago, when Delaney had been his only joy. The hours he'd spent with her had been the bright spots in a dismal life, and his body reacted to their achingly familiar chemistry with a rush of desire.

Her eyes widened when he stepped toward her, needing to touch her again. "Brody…"

"Delaney." There were shelving units behind her and she couldn't retreat. "Have I mentioned how much I've missed you?"

He watched her face, looking for anger or rejection or anything negative, but all he saw was the hot blush across her neck and cheeks, and her eyes focused on his mouth.

"I've missed you, too," she whispered.

It had been inevitable from the second he stepped through the doors and saw her for the first time, he realized. Five years hadn't cooled what sizzled between them. Under the ashes of his abandonment, the embers burned and now the fire flared again. This was the only woman he'd ever loved and there was no way he could stop himself from touching her.

BRODY WAS GOING to kiss her. Delaney knew the man more intimately than she'd ever known any other, and his intention was made plain in the hot and hungry look in his eyes and the way he moved toward her.

She should shove him away. There were plenty of other things he could do that didn't require being near her. Kissing him was a dead-end road and she should bang a U-turn before she ended up stuck in that lonely place she'd ended up before.

But she was going to let him kiss her because she had no resistance against him. She never had. And she wanted the kiss, too.

With his hands braced against the shelves on either side of her head, Brody lowered his forehead until it came to rest gently against hers. His eyes closed and she knew he was fighting the same internal battle she was.

A kiss would be a very bad idea.

"Kissing you is a bad idea," he whispered.

At least they were on the same page.

"But I want to," he continued. Definitely on the same page. "It's all I can think about. And I don't have to wonder what it'll be like. I *know* kissing you is like pulling a royal flush in a high-stakes game. It's a total rush and nothing will ever beat it."

Warmth curled through Delaney and she felt the soft breath of his sigh over her face. She placed her hands on his chest and felt his body stiffen under her touch. She could push him away. She *should* push him away.

Instead, she ran her palms over the soft wool of his sweater and up to his shoulders. A slight nudge, pulling him in, was all it took. His mouth covered hers and the sweetness of it tugged at her heart.

His lips were gentle and she shivered when his tongue danced over her bottom lip. He was savoring her, and she reveled in the sensations that swept through her. No matter what her mind said, her body and her heart knew this kiss. Nobody had ever made her feel the way he could with a simple touch of his lips.

Delaney's fingertips bit into Brody's shoulders as he deepened the kiss, but she still didn't pull away.

She knew she should. Letting herself get too close to Brody Rollins would bring her nothing but a second helping of heartache, and yet there was something about his kiss that felt so right. His tongue danced over hers and she leaned into him as his hand slid up her back. Her body remembered this—the feel of his touch—and wanted more.

It was the sound of the door handle jiggling that finally gave her the strength to break away.

Good lord, a quarter of the town was just a few feet away and here she was, making out with Brody in the custodian's closet like a teenager.

"Delaney?" It was Alice, one of the other volunteers, and Delaney slipped out from between Brody and the shelves as the door opened.

"I'm in here. What do you need?"

Alice's gaze bounced between Delaney and Brody a few times, and Delaney was dismayed when she saw understanding dawn in the other woman's eyes. This would be a nice bit of gossip for everybody to chew on for a while. "Sorry. We're running low on paper towels."

She grabbed a few rolls, balancing them in her arms, and then gave Delaney a quick smile on her way out. "I'll just…go. Take your time."

Delaney wondered if she'd meant that to sound as suggestive as it came out. "Just grabbing some bleach, rags and buckets. We'll be right out."

When the door swung shut behind Alice, Delaney had to stifle a groan. Even if she hurried, half the people in the gym would know she'd been kissing Brody Rollins in the supply room before she got out there. The news would trickle through to the other half whether she was in the gym or not.

"I probably shouldn't have done that," Brody said quietly.

"I didn't exactly put up a fight."

"No, but now everybody will be talking and…I'm sorry."

She grabbed two buckets and put a cleaning rag and a plastic gallon of bleach in each one. They'd fill them with hot water from the kitchen. "At least it's only a matter of time before you get to leave. Again. So you won't have to hear it."

"Delaney, come on."

"At least this time you have to sign yourself out so, as long as I'm manning the clipboard, I'll know you're going this time."

He put his hand on her shoulder, making her stand still. "I don't know how many times I can apologize for not telling you in person I was leaving."

"Screw the note, Brody. Has it occurred to you I'm having a little trouble with the fact you didn't ask me to go *with* you?"

He didn't know how to make her understand. "If I'd asked you to go, you would have wanted to think about it and make plans and…I don't know. Sort through all your stuff and come up with a whole pile of stuff you wanted to take."

"Like any normal person would."

"If I'd had to wait for you, I would have lost my courage. I drove out of here in a beat-up car with a duffel bag of clothes and two hundred bucks in my pocket because right then, at that moment, I was more afraid of staying than leaving."

"Fine. Just don't lie to me—or to yourself—and say that right then, at that moment, I factored into your decision at all."

He blew out a breath, then took one of the buckets from her. "You sure know how to take the blush off a good kiss."

That was the point. "I have work to do."

She left the supply room and hurried into the gym before he could say anything else.

They worked in silence, washing down almost every touchable surface in the gymnasium with the diluted bleach mixture. He took some good-natured ribbing from some of the guys about his bright yellow rubber gloves, but Delaney tried to ignore the rich sound of his laughter. She tried to ignore the way he stopped to talk to people now and then, rebuilding old bonds he'd severed so unexpectedly.

But no matter how much she tried to focus on the past and wrap herself in a security blanket of old hurts, her gaze was drawn to him time after time. More often than not, he'd catch her looking and his expression would be pensive, as if he were trying to gauge her mood. And she was keenly aware that most of the people in the gym with them were watching them watch each other.

Probably making little *tsk* sounds under their breath. Poor Delaney. That Rollins boy broke her heart once and now she's going to let him do it again. Foolish girl.

That thought finally ignited the anger and resentment

his kiss had cooled and she held on to it throughout the rest of the day. Even when he helped her clean up after they'd served supper to the crowd, she managed to be polite and appreciative, but decidedly detached.

But when they dimmed the lights and everybody around her started drifting into restless sleep, Delaney lay awake, staring at the ceiling because every time she closed her eyes, she relived that kiss again.

And ached for another.

CHAPTER FIVE

TUESDAY MORNING CAME early, thanks to the kids who couldn't sleep in when away from their homes. Or maybe kids never slept in. Brody didn't have a clue, but he knew *these* kids were up and at 'em like a horde of two-legged, overeager roosters.

Brody sat on the floor, his back up against the wall. He felt trapped and restless and, from all reports, the freak storm wasn't abating any. He'd already powered up his phone to deal with some email, including responding to the message from his office manager, who thought her boss being stuck in a school gym was the funniest thing that had ever happened.

He'd helped serve breakfast, with nary a word from Delaney. Then he'd suffered through watching her lead the kids in a fun but energy-burning morning exercise. It had been torture, watching her bounce and shimmy, but it would be worth the physical suffering if the kids napped later.

Brody was nodding off himself, his head against the hard gym wall, when Sandy nudged him with her foot. He took Noah and, after nestling him in one arm, used his free hand to help guide his sister into a sitting position.

"I turned my phone on for a few minutes and I had a voice mail from Mike."

Her voice had a serious undertone that immediately

concerned him. "He's okay, right? Did he go off the road?"

"No, he's fine. But I had asked him to stop by and check on my parents—*our* parents, I mean—and their power went out Sunday night shortly after ours did. Ma had the burners on the stove lit, trying to stay warm."

"They've been without heat for two nights?"

"Yeah, but you know how Dad is. He can't smoke in here, so he didn't want to come."

Brody shook his head, not surprised by their stubbornness, no matter how stupid it was to use your gas cookstove for heat. "I hope Mike gave them a stern lecture."

"He did. He also made them pack a bag and they're on their way here. I just missed his call, so they should be here any minute."

Great. His parents were just what this involuntary group reunion was missing. Though seeing them here was better than having to step foot in the house he'd grown up in. "I'm surprised he got them to leave. They can be pretty stubborn."

"He said he told them I was having a hard time here because he couldn't be with me and Noah." She paused to smile. "And he told Ma you were stuck here and couldn't get away."

"Smart guy." He paused, debating on how best to phrase his next question. "Did he tell her anything else?"

"You mean that you got caught making out in the janitor's closet with Delaney Westcott?"

His sister wasn't known for being subtle. "We were not *making out*."

"Not what I heard."

"We weren't." He cleared his throat. "I kissed her, though. Just a kiss."

"Just a kiss because that's all there was to it, or just a kiss because Alice walked in on you before it was more than just a kiss?"

"Leave it alone, San."

"I've known you my whole life, so I know you can be an idiot sometimes. I didn't know you had a mean streak, though."

That pissed him off, but he forced himself to stay relaxed. He'd figured out pretty quickly babies were sensitive to the emotions of the people holding them. "What the hell is that supposed to mean? I didn't force the kiss on her. Trust me."

"You're playing with her emotions and that makes you a jerk."

"Is that just your opinion or did the fine people of Tucker's Point discuss it and come to a consensus?"

"Except for a few incurable romantics who think you came back to sweep Delaney off her feet and carry her into the sunset, it's pretty much a consensus."

"Great." He shouldn't care what a bunch of people he hadn't seen in years and wouldn't see again in the near future thought of him, but it stung a little. Why did going out in the world and making something of himself make him a bad guy? And he wasn't the first guy to break things off with a girl, either.

Brody wouldn't have thought it possible, but he was so relieved to see his parents enter the gym he wanted to let out a cheer. The conversation with Sandy was over. He didn't like having his relationship with Delaney poked at and prodded. He didn't know what was going on himself, so he couldn't very well explain it to anybody else.

After Sandy stood up, she took Noah, freeing him to stand. His butt hurt from sitting on the hard floor, but there were only so many places to sit and the women and older men had dibs by right. The floor was actually more comfortable than trying to sit on one of the cots, but it didn't make getting up any easier.

His mom met him halfway across the gym and Brody hugged her so tightly, he lifted her right off the floor. "It's good to see you, Ma."

"Let me look at you." She took a step back and cupped his face in her hands to get a good look. "I swear, you get more handsome every time I see you."

"With a mother as beautiful as you, it's inevitable."

She laughed and swatted his arm. "Go say hello to your father."

He hugged his dad, though the embrace was brief and he left the old man's feet on the floor. "Looking good, Pop."

"You, too, son. Glad you were here to take care of your sister and little Noah."

"Sandy would have been fine, but I'm glad I was here, too. And, trust me, if I'd known you had no heat, I would have gone after you and Mom, too."

John Rollins scoffed. "We were fine."

"That's why mom was warming herself over a stove burner?"

"Now you sound like your brother-in-law. I swear, you two nag like a bunch of women."

"Hey," his wife and daughter said at the same time.

Brody laughed and took their bags. "I guess we should get you two some cots. Squeeze them over by ours."

"Delaney said she'd get them," his mother said, and he saw the speculative gleam in her eye.

Damn. A growing audience to whatever—if anything—was going on between him and Delaney wasn't helping matters any. "That's good. Once you warm up, you're probably going to sleep for hours."

As if on cue, his mom yawned. "I gotta smooch on my grandson for a little while first."

Another entry in the *why babies were good* column. They were excellent distractions when you needed to change the subject. "He'll be glad to have another familiar body to cuddle with. He's been passed around a lot."

"I hope he doesn't get sick." She took Noah from Sandy, fussing over him as he waved a tiny fist at her.

"Brody's been doing his best to keep that from happening," Sandy said, her voice light with amusement. "You should see him in his rubber gloves, scrubbing things down with bleach water. It's really cute."

His dad gave him a skeptical look. "Rubber gloves?"

"There's not a lot of call for splitting wood, changing motor oil or other manly endeavors, Pop. I help where I can."

"Women love a man who's not afraid to do a little housework," his mother added, giving him a knowing look.

Please God, Brody thought, *let the storm stop soon.*

DELANEY WASN'T IN too bad a mood for a woman trapped in a school gymnasium. Maybe it was sleep deprivation, but nothing—not even painful memories of kisses or intense looks from the woman whom she'd always thought would be her mother-in-law someday—could dim the satisfaction of a job being done well. Even with the added stress of Brody and his family in the group, she'd received several compliments on how smoothly the shelter was running.

She even smiled at Brody as he approached her, fighting the urge to turn and run. Or at least hide behind something so everybody wasn't watching for her reaction to him. "What's up?"

He gave her the smile she knew was meant to charm her into doing his bidding. "Any chance we can go poking around the classrooms for a jar of buttons or something?"

"Why would there be jars of buttons in the classrooms?"

"I don't know." He shrugged. "Or... Oh, paperclips! Some boxes of paperclips would do."

"The classrooms are locked."

"You have the keys. At least you did when we got the bleach."

Busted. "We're not stealing office supplies from the school, Brody."

"Borrowing. We'd be borrowing office supplies for the *children*."

She sighed and rubbed the back of her neck, realizing he wasn't going to leave her be until he got whatever he was after. "Why do the children need boxes of paperclips?"

"Because we have no poker chips."

"Why do the children need poker chips? Just who is *we*?"

"The older kids. Some adults, too. Pop and I are going to teach them how to play poker. Everybody's bored and my parents are starting to bicker. Most of them know how to play already, though, so we'll have tournaments once the ones who don't grasp the basics."

He looked excited about it, so she refrained from laughing at him. "Don't you think Go Fish would be more appropriate? Maybe Rummy? And we have about five hundred jigsaw puzzles."

"Mrs. Palmer has laid claim to most of the puzzles and she gets really nasty if you don't do all the outside pieces first."

"It's easier that way."

"She slapped Mr. Bergen's hand. He's gotta be almost seventy. A kid could have nightmares for life."

This time she did laugh, until he laughed with her and the warm sound tied her stomach in knots. "You're trying to distract me from your plan to corrupt our kids by teaching them to gamble."

His green eyes sparkled with amusement, so she focused on his mouth. That was a mistake. "As corruption goes, it's fairly mild."

"But why poker?"

"Because I'm good at it."

Delaney sighed. She knew he was good at it. During downtime on the boats, the guys played poker and they learned young. He'd tried to teach her how to play a few times but she was so bad at it, even the incentive of winning her clothing piece by piece couldn't overcome his impatience with her.

"Do you know how I made my money?" he asked, his tone serious now.

"When Sandy and Mike were buying their house, she said you answered a lot of questions for her because you flip real estate."

"But I bought my very first flip property with money I won on the poker circuit. That's how I got out of here and how I got my start."

She hadn't known that, but it concerned her even more than the possibility of gambling for paperclips raising some judgmental eyebrows. "Brody, don't fill these kids' heads with big dreams of gambling their way out of here."

"What's wrong with big dreams?" He crossed his arms over his chest.

"Nothing. But a lot of these kids will grow up and fish or work for little more than minimum wage and be just fine. The ones who dream big will either fight for their dreams or they won't. Just because you got lucky doesn't mean there are shortcuts."

"Delaney, I'm not going to lure the adolescent population of Tucker's Point away with me like some kind of poker-playing Pied Piper. It's just something fun to do for the in-between crowd and the older folks who don't want to play—and I quote, 'baby games'—or risk getting their hands slapped by Mrs. Palmer."

"I'll make a deal with you. I'll help you scrounge up fake poker chips, but you have to get permission from parents for the younger kids."

"Deal."

"One of the first grade teachers is a good friend of mine. We'll forage in her classroom."

She knew even as she led Brody through the doors into the main hallway that tongues would start wagging the second they closed behind them, but it couldn't be helped. Sending another volunteer to accompany him wasn't really an option because she wasn't totally comfortable rummaging around the classrooms and she was personally responsible for the big ring of keys. Only the fact Patti Worth was a personal friend made it okay.

The squeak of their shoes on the waxed floor was the only sound as she led him down a maze of hallways to the door marked by a sign reading Miss Worth in colorful, hand-drawn letters. Delaney felt slightly naughty as she unlocked it and slipped inside, but she wasn't sure if it was being in the classroom, or being alone with Brody.

And they were very, very alone.

"It's so quiet here," Brody said, kicking the door closed behind him. "Makes me want to grab a pillow and blanket and hide under the desk until the storm's over."

"I wish we could use the rooms, especially for Sandy and Noah, but there are rules and most of them boil down to insurance and liability."

"You wouldn't even sneak down here for a power nap?"

She gave him a stern look, and then glanced around the room to find the most likely hiding spot for boxes of paper clips. "It's against the rules."

"You always were a good girl."

The way he said the words—the warm timbre of his voice—had flashbacks rolling through her mind. Stolen kisses. His hand sliding up under her sweater for the first time. Making love in a borrowed boat under an endless sky. "Not always."

"No. Not always." He was closer and, when she turned, she found himself close enough to touch.

This time he kissed her swiftly, with no time for deliberations. His mouth was demanding and she surrendered to him, tired of fighting her feelings. The kiss went on and on, until her knees were weak and it seemed as though his hands on her back were all that were keeping her from falling.

When he broke it off, he kept his face close to hers, his arms wrapped around her. She liked being in his arms. She felt safe there, and treasured. The world had always seemed right when she was in Brody's arms.

His breath was warm against her cheek and she

closed her eyes, inhaling the scent of him. Reality seemed to shift between the present and their past. His subtle, expensive aroma and the feel of fine wool were strange, but the feel of his body against hers and the way he touched her was so familiar her heart ached.

When his hand cupped the side of her face, she turned into it, savoring the feeling of his thumb brushing her cheekbone.

"Your skin is so soft," he said in a quiet voice. "Every time I touched you, I hated my hands. They were rough and callused and you deserved to be touched by somebody whose hands didn't scratch like sandpaper against your skin."

"I loved your hands. Strong and capable. You worked hard and you loved hard. That's what your hands meant to me."

"I want to make love to you again, Delaney."

Words clogged in her throat. Reasons why they shouldn't. Confessions of just how badly she wanted that, too. But none of them came out.

"I don't have any protection," he said after a long moment of silence.

"And this is my friend's first-grade classroom. I can't have sex on her floor."

"Or her desk?"

"Oh, God no." She laughed, burying her face in his sweater. "I'd never be able to look her in the face again."

"So we have to stop." He paused, as if waiting for her to argue, but she was silent. "I don't want to."

"I don't want to, either." She took a deep breath. "But we have to."

"Then we need to stop touching now."

Very reluctantly, she backed away from him. Her face felt hot and flushed, and he looked a little hot and bothered himself. "Let's find some paperclips and get you back to your poker buddies before they come looking for us."

Brody held her hand for the walk back to the gym, and Delaney couldn't help but feel things had changed between them. The hurt that had flared up when she saw him again had faded away and they were falling back into their old passionate but comfortable relationship.

She needed to remember that relationship she'd been so comfortable in had ended in pain and tears, though. Five years ago, Brody had kissed her and held her hand, and then he'd taken off in the night. No matter how good it felt to have him back, Delaney couldn't forget he was only there because he couldn't leave.

He released her hand before going through the doors into the gym, but not before giving her a quick kiss. Then he looked into her eyes for a few seconds. "I'd ask if you want to play with us, but now I remember just how bad your poker face is."

She wanted to ask him what he saw in her eyes, but before she could work up the courage, he'd opened the door, brandishing the boxes of paper clips as though he'd been foraging for food and returned with a bounty.

Delaney watched as a group of kids swarmed him, their excitement obvious. But then she noticed Camille watching her watch her son and turned away. She was going to have to work on that poker face.

"HARD TO BELIEVE you made a living out of playing poker, son."

Brody snorted, but it was hard to deny the fact his pile of paper clips was significantly smaller than the old man's. "Maybe it's strategy. Sucker you in and make you feel safe so you start betting large."

"Or maybe you're spending too much time watching that girl and not enough time watching your cards."

If Delaney had been in the casinos and back rooms, fussing over people and checking things off her clipboard, Brody would probably have about two dollars to his name and be living in his car. If he still had one. She was one hell of a powerful distraction.

"What girl?" one of the kids asked. Jason, he thought his name was. He was the son of the guy who'd been a mouthy punk in school but was now, as Sandy had said, just a dad stuck in a room with his two boys waiting for the storm to end.

"No girl. My dad thinks he's funny." But he couldn't keep himself from glancing in Delaney's direction.

She caught him looking and smiled. He smiled back. The awkwardness between them had eased up and she wasn't dodging his gaze anymore. He liked that. A lot.

"Much more of this and I'll take everything you own," Donnie Cox said, laying down his cards and sweeping the pile of paper clips into his own growing pile.

"Dammit." Brody tried to force his attention back to the game.

"That's a bad word," Jason said. *Really* loudly.

"Sorry," Brody said in the general direction of all the heads that swiveled to glare at him.

Most of the younger kids had grown bored with all the thinking that went into playing poker and were, probably much to Delaney's delight, off playing Go Fish along with some game that seemed to consist of the kids slapping each other's hands every time a jack turned up in the pile.

Once Jason moved on, probably lured away by the idea of slapping his brother, the guys played a few more hands before they lost interest. Brody shuffled the cards, strangely comforted by the familiar feel and motion in his hands, but he didn't deal again.

"Becks is after me to pump you for information, you know," Donnie said. "Took you guys quite a while to find paper clips considering every room in this building is, you know, a *school room.*"

"Delaney wasn't comfortable taking them from just anybody's classroom. One of the first grade teachers is a friend of hers, so we had to walk all the way to her room. And back."

"Not judging. I wouldn't mind a little alone time with my wife right about now."

Brody wanted to point out he and Delaney hadn't had *that* kind of alone time, but he figured it would go in one ear and out the other. People seemed to have made up their minds they were a couple again and nothing he said was going to keep the speculation down. It would only make them more determined to be right.

Maybe they were. He really wasn't sure what was going on with them, but whatever it was felt right to him. It felt natural to kiss her and hold her hand in the hallway. What hadn't felt natural was ending things in the classroom before it got any more physical. He'd wanted her badly—hell, he still did—but he hadn't packed condoms for his less-than-two-days trip back to his hometown.

He glanced up again and caught Delaney looking at him. She was pretending to listen to the women around her talking, but the steamy look in her eyes almost made him flub his shuffle and blow cards everywhere.

"You two have to stop making eye contact," his dad said, "or your mother's going to get all kinds of ideas in her head."

Brody jerked his attention back to the cards and dealt them out, without even asking if his dad and Donnie wanted in. He needed the distraction because he was starting to get ideas of his own in his head.

And those ideas were going to get him into nothing but trouble.

CHAPTER SIX

THINGS WERE QUIET in the gym on Wednesday morning. Nobody was sleeping soundly and it was starting to take a toll on people. And the sense of adventure was wearing off for the kids. They wanted their video games and favorite foods and their freedom. Everybody was doing their best to stay upbeat, if only for the children, but spirits were flagging.

Even if it came with an air of depression, Delaney was thankful for the quiet. She'd seen so much of Brody from a distance. He played with the kids and talked with the adults. Helped out wherever he could. Nobody would ever guess he'd been dragged back into the community against his will.

But she liked sitting on the floor with him in a quiet corner, on small cushions he'd made by folding up their blankets. They were side by side, and he had a sleeping Noah cradled in his left arm and the fingers of his right hand were laced through hers.

She'd be lying if she said it didn't tug at her heart, the way they were sitting there like a little fake family. He was so good with Noah—and with the other kids—and she'd done a lot of thinking about what a good dad he'd be. Way too much thinking, actually. Images of him as a dad were getting all tangled up with her increasingly ticking biological clock and leading her down an imaginary path to heartbreak.

He'd been telling her about his early days on the poker circuit, when he was scrimping and saving every dollar he could make at odd jobs to pay his way into tournaments. It didn't sound as glamorous as she'd first imagined, and she wondered how she would have fared if he'd taken her with him. Probably not very well. She wasn't much of a risk-taker and never had been.

"I thought about you a lot in those days," Brody said. "Correction—I still *think* about you a lot. I've missed you."

"Not enough to pick up a phone and give me a call?" It was hard for her to reconcile all the times he'd told her he missed her and thought about her with the fact he'd never reached out to her.

"Sandy's never forgiven me for the way I left, so she never mentions you on the phone and I was too proud to ask, but whenever I thought about you, I wanted to imagine you married, with some cute kids. A dog and a picket fence and a minivan." There was a hint of sadness and maybe regret in his voice.

"Haven't gotten there yet. Seems a little odd, though, if you missed me so much, that you'd imagine me living happily ever after with somebody else."

"I needed you to be happy in my head, Delaney. If you were happy and had a good life, it made missing you worth it."

She leaned her head against the wall and drew her knees up, wrapping her arms around them. "You felt less guilty, you mean."

"That, too. But mostly I'd picture you living a life I couldn't give you and know I made the right decision."

"It wasn't."

"I think you're right."

"Tell me about your life now," she said, because she

was tired of rehashing the past. Maybe it was a little like rubbing salt in old wounds, but she wanted to picture him in *his* world.

"I work a lot. Actually, that's pretty much all I do. If I'm not on a site dealing with a remodel, I'm meeting with real estate agents or financial backers. When I'm home, I'm usually on the computer, researching foreclosure lists and property values and a whole lot of boring stuff."

"So what you do now is as risky as poker. You're just gambling with properties instead of on cards."

He chuckled, then bounced his arm gently up and down when Noah squirmed. "Maybe, but luck gets less of a say. I have good instincts, but I also do my research. Flipping real estate might be a gamble, but I stack the deck in my favor."

"Where do you live?" It felt ridiculous, having to ask that question, but at least it was a reminder he'd made a life for himself somewhere else, and it didn't include her.

"I have a condo in Connecticut, but I travel a lot. I don't have an office to speak of, even though Marjorie picked the title office manager for herself. She runs things for me, but out of her house."

He lived in Connecticut. Only a couple of states away. She couldn't quite wrap her mind around that. She wanted to ask him what his condo looked like, maybe so she could picture him in it, but she didn't want to sound weird.

"Sandy doesn't tell me much about your life," she said. "I think she's afraid to say something that might hurt me, so I know almost nothing about the last five years of your life."

"Just work, like I said."

What about women? Of course he'd dated. He was young and attractive and he'd never wanted for female attention, even when she'd been on his arm. But had he been in love since Delaney? She didn't think a marriage and divorce would have stayed quiet with his family still in Tucker's Point, but what about other serious relationships?

He squeezed her hand. "If you're thinking what I think you're thinking, the answer is no."

"What do you think I'm thinking?"

"I haven't loved anybody else since I left you."

Delaney had to blink back the tears that suddenly blurred her vision. "I tried to replace you. It didn't work."

"Good. That would make us sitting here together a lot more awkward."

She laughed softly and turned her head to see Noah looking at her with his solemn baby eyes. "He looks like you."

"He definitely has a lot of Rollins in him. Mike and Sandy should probably start bracing themselves for his teen years."

At the sound of his uncle's voice, Noah shifted his intense gaze to him. He seemed fascinated by Brody's face, not that Delaney could blame him. Brody was looking a little scruffy, like the other men at the school, but it only added a little edge to his good looks.

Watching man and infant gaze into each other's eyes was too much for Delaney, and she looked away. She couldn't push back the resentment. Brody had taken her dreams for a family with him when he ran, and that was a hard thing to forgive.

"He's such a cute little bugger," Brody said in a painfully soft voice.

"How long do you think it'll be before he starts wailing?" she asked, looking around to see if Sandy was in sight.

Of course she was. And she must have been feeling the need to nurse because all Delaney had to do was look at her and the new mom was moving toward them. Once she'd taken Noah and gone back toward their cots, Brody slipped his arm around Delaney's shoulders and pulled her close.

When he kissed the top of her head, she sighed and tried to relax in his arms. There was no sense in holding on to past hurts. Life hadn't turned out the way she'd thought it would, but she could embrace this moment for the short time it would last.

BRODY HELPED PREPARE the evening meal and serve it, so Delaney refused to let him help clean up after.

"I like spending time with you," he argued. "Even if it's dish duty."

She laughed. "That's really sweet, but there's a rotation and some people have been getting lazy because you're doing their share."

He caught her pointed look toward Alice. "Fine. I'll go hang with Pop for a while. The more entertained we keep him, the fewer times he goes out in the cold for a smoke."

He found his old man stretched out on a cot, reading a hunting magazine. As far as Brody knew, his dad had never hunted a day in his life, so he assumed the magazine was borrowed from one of the other guys.

"Learning anything?"

"Yeah." His dad closed the magazine and sat up on the cot. "Learning you can buy pretty much anything in camo."

Brody sat on the cot next to his dad's, breathing a sigh of relief. He'd been on his feet a long time, and he couldn't imagine how Delaney felt. "I think I saw a camo teddy bear at Sandy's before the power went out."

His dad nodded, then fell silent for a few minutes. Brody got the impression he had something on his mind, but talking emotions didn't come naturally to John Rollins. Usually it was Brody's mom who conveyed their feelings back and forth. "You know your father loves you, Brody" and the like.

"You seem happy, son. You've done well for yourself."

"Thanks, Pop. It's a lot of work, but I'm pretty happy with where I am in life."

"Wish you hadn't broken your mother's heart doing it, though."

Brody bowed his head, focusing all his attention on a fuzz on the cuff of his sweater just so he had a place to look. "I don't know how to explain why I left the way I did without sounding like I'm putting you down."

"Son, you think I don't know my work is hard and pretty thankless? Nobody knows more than me that my house ain't grand and my wife doesn't have a diamond ring and my truck don't run half the time. But you and your sister never wanted for a meal, dammit."

"I wanted more. There was always food on the table and I appreciate that, but I wanted more for myself and if I talked about doing something else, you'd just shake your head and walk away. Fishing was good enough for you so, by God, it was good enough for me."

His dad was quiet until Brody finally looked up. The old man's voice was as sad as his eyes when he did speak. "I didn't know *how* to want more for you, Brody. I'm a fisherman, just like my father and my grandfather and two generations before him. Hell, your mom's mother was a fisherman's wife and so on before her. We don't *know* any life but this."

Brody had to swallow past the lump in his throat. "Maybe it's because Delaney came from a family that didn't fish, but every time I'd try to picture our future, I saw her looking tired and older than her age, with worry lines from years of juggling bills."

"And you saw yourself being me."

He didn't know what to say to his dad. The words were true, but admitting it out loud seemed like a cruel blow for a man who'd done his best. He hadn't been running away from his parents. He was running *to* the man he wanted to be.

"I went through the same thing," his dad said. "I was maybe a little younger than you were when you left. Looked around and realized I was going to spend my whole life fishing like my old man and I'd end up just like him. The only difference between you and me at that age is that you had the guts to leave."

It had never occurred to Brody that his father might have felt that way. And maybe his father before him. "I love you and Mom. I hope you know that."

"We do. And even though we hated losing you, we're both proud of what you've made of yourself."

Brody had to clear his throat twice before he could speak. "Thanks, Pop."

"Your big screw-up, though, was not taking your girl with you."

Yeah, he knew that now. But at the time… "I had two hundred bucks in my pocket and no plans. No safety net. No family. No nothing."

"Once you started making some money for yourself, why didn't you call her?"

Brody couldn't meet his dad's piercing gaze, so he focused on the sweater fuzz again. "I didn't have the guts to tell anybody I was leaving. I didn't say goodbye to her. I guess I didn't have the guts to call her, either. I thought about it. A lot, actually. But I didn't think I could take her hanging up on me."

"Kind of gutless for a young man who left everything he'd known to go off into the world with only two hundred bucks in his pocket."

"Being cold and hungry wouldn't kill me, but Delaney turning a cold shoulder to me might have."

"And now you made the girl fall for you all over again and we all know you won't stay. Guess that makes you a… What's that word the young people use nowadays? Douche bag?"

Brody almost choked. "Pop! What?"

"Pretty sure that's the word I'm looking for." He gave Brody a sly look. "Unless you're planning to stick it out this time."

He wasn't sure yet what he was going to do, and he couldn't come up with the words to explain that since his brain was busy trying to wrap itself around the fact his old man had called him a douche bag.

"Sure is a pretty lady," his dad continued, his eyes fixed on Delaney across the room. "Your mom told me this morning you guys would make pretty grandbabies."

Babies. Brody watched Delaney lean down to speak to one of the kids and his gut tightened. It was too easy to picture her with a smaller version of herself and maybe a little Brody. She'd be a great mom.

What wasn't easy to picture was the home they'd live in. Not his condo. It not only wasn't kid-friendly, but he couldn't imagine Delaney away from Tucker's Point. This wasn't simply the town she lived in or the people she knew. This was her home and they were like family to her. Even an idiot could see that after the days they'd all spent cooped up together.

But he couldn't picture himself in Tucker's Point, either. Sure, he'd bonded with people again. There were old friends, like Donnie Cox. His parents and his sister and Mike. And there was Noah. The kid had weaseled his way under his uncle's skin and visits to the kid would be frequent. He'd make sure the boy could Skype before he could even talk.

But nothing changed the fact Tucker's Point was a place he'd left behind for a reason and he'd never intended to look back.

WEDNESDAY MORNING MIGHT have been quiet and slow, but Wednesday evening was anything but. Delaney and Alice had barely gotten the dinner mess cleaned up when they got a call over the radio. One of the market's generators was failing and they were shutting down the freezers in an effort to keep the other one going.

One of the road crews was coming in for a much-needed break and they were bringing an impromptu ice cream party with them. Jenny, who ran the market, had even donated some toppings and whipped cream, and the kids were practically losing their minds over the build-your-own-sundae buffet they'd set up.

Sure, it was a lot of sugar, but most of the parents were so relieved to have a fun distraction they weren't even thinking about bedtime yet.

"Maybe an adult should be in charge of the jimmies," Brody muttered to Delaney.

"That's no fun." Spending hours sweeping up chocolate sprinkles wasn't going to be fun, either, but at least it was something to do.

"Only in Maine do we have an ice cream party in the middle of an ice storm."

She laughed, then gave Jason a subtle shake of her head to signal enough with the whipped cream. His leaning tower was going to end up on the floor if he wasn't careful. "I wonder what the rules are on using the pots and pans sink as a bathtub. There aren't enough paper towels in Tucker's Point to get these kids unsticky now."

"If it has a sprayer attachment, I say we line them up and hose them down."

There was a lot of laughter, more than a few spills and chocolate stains abounded, but everybody had a great time. They really needed it, Delaney thought. The adults were worried about their homes. They had jobs they weren't getting paid to do and bills they'd have to pay. There were trees down and Delaney had heard a lot of worry about property damage voiced. And the kids just wanted to go home.

Tonight, though, spirits were high. Delaney even helped herself to a second serving of the strawberry ice cream. They'd be throwing away what was left, anyway, as the cartons were already starting to melt through. And she'd burn off the excess calories cleaning up the mess.

The fun went on for well over an hour before the little tummy aches began and the adults did a little groaning themselves. The mostly empty cartons of ice cream and all the paper bowls and plastic spoons were disposed of and all that remained was dealing with the sticky mess left behind.

"I think we're going to break out the bleach water for this," Delaney said, eyeing the gobs of melted ice cream covering the tables.

"Does that mean a trip to the supply closet?" Brody whispered in her ear.

"Are you offering to help clean up?"

"I'll wash anything you tell me to if it gets me two minutes alone with you."

They made the most of those two minutes, too. Their kisses were fervent and sweet like strawberry ice cream. They were both breathing hard when she finally took him by the shoulders and pushed him away. "The longer we're in here, the harder it gets to scrub the ice cream off the tables."

"I don't care."

She cared. Not about the ice cream, but about the fact they didn't have a condom and she was *this* close to doing something really stupid and irresponsible. "Your two minutes is up."

"One more."

"Just a quick one."

But Brody apparently didn't do quick kisses. His mouth was firm and demanding and he kissed her until every care and worry she'd ever had slipped away. All that mattered was this moment—his lips on hers and their breaths mingling—and she didn't want it to ever end.

It was a no doubt scandalous ten minutes before they entered the gym with the buckets, and thankfully Brody had stopped her in the hall to straighten her sweatshirt. They hadn't done anything irresponsible, but he'd stretched just one quick kiss into a full-fledged make-out session that had her feeling both exhilarated and frustrated at the same time.

It was tempting to ask Mike to give them a ride to her house. His truck would make it, and she didn't even care if she had heat or not. Brody would keep her warm.

But she couldn't ask the father of a newborn to risk life and limb so she could have sex. That would be wrong. Instead, she channeled that unspent energy into scrubbing all the evidence of their ice-cream party away.

They'd had to shove some of the cots out of the way and put up some extra tables to hold the frozen bounty, and Brody enlisted the help of Donnie Cox to put them away as Delaney cleaned them. With Alice running the dry mop around the floor, catching stray jimmies, the cleaning up wasn't as bad as Delaney had anticipated.

"Rumor has it the storm's supposed to let up tonight," Donnie said after they put the last table away and straightened out the cots for the people who were using them. "Bet you'll be glad to get out of here."

Brody snorted. "You got that right."

His words hit Delaney square in the heart, almost taking her breath away. He hadn't even hesitated. He was so eager to leave Tucker's Point he hadn't had to think twice about his answer.

Delaney was a big girl. She knew he was leaving town. The man had a business to run and no doubt things were piling up and putting him behind schedule while he was stuck in the shelter. But, for once, she wanted to be first in his mind when he thought about leaving and she wanted the thought of leaving her to give him pause. For a few seconds, at least.

The two helpings of ice cream she'd enjoyed turned over in her stomach, but Brody didn't seem to notice the joy had leeched out of her evening. Donnie was showing him something in a magazine and they weren't paying any attention to her.

Unable to think about anything but how eager Brody seemed to be to see Tucker's Point—and her—in his rearview mirror, she peeled off the rubber gloves and dropped them next to the bucket.

She needed some air or she was going to have an emotional breakdown. That couldn't happen. Maybe she wasn't any stronger now than she'd been five years ago, but she would pretend she was if it killed her.

CHAPTER SEVEN

BRODY SPENT ABOUT ten minutes looking for Delaney before Alice finally told him she thought she'd gone outside.

"Why would she go outside?"

Alice shrugged. "I don't know. But she had her coat and her boots on."

It was on the tip of his tongue to demand to know why the volunteers didn't take better care of each other, but Delaney was a grown woman. If she wanted to go outside, it wasn't anybody's business but hers.

And his. Whatever she was doing, she shouldn't be doing it alone.

It took him another few minutes to change into his boots and put his coat on, so he knew she'd been out there at least fifteen minutes. He didn't like that idea, and he prayed it had nothing to do with him shoving his foot in his mouth earlier.

After Delaney disappeared without a word to him, it took Brody a little while to figure out what he'd done wrong. When he'd agreed with Donnie he couldn't wait to get the hell out of there, he'd meant the gymnasium. He was really tired of being in an oversize jail cell with these people, whether some were family or not.

There was no doubt in his mind Delaney assumed he meant Tucker's Point. And, yes, he'd be leaving town. He had responsibilities. But he intended to leave in a very different way than he had the first time. Unfortunately, he hadn't told *her* that, and she'd jumped to the wrong conclusion.

After telling his old man he was going outside to find Delaney, he also let the volunteer manning the clipboard know and stepped outside into the storm. Rumor or not, it didn't seem to be abating quite yet, though there was less ice and more snow. That was a good sign.

The driving wind was so cold he was almost afraid to blink in case his eyelids froze closed. After pulling the collar of the coat a little higher around his neck, Brody looked around. He didn't see Delaney, but there were tracks leading around the corner of the building, so he followed them. The dusting of snow over ice made for treacherous footing and several times he had to brace his hand against the cold brick to keep from slipping.

Once he'd reached the corner, he saw the bright red of her coat. She was standing in a semi-enclosed area off what looked like a delivery dock, and she shook her head when she saw him coming. It didn't stop him.

Stepping under the overhang with her was a relief not only because he hadn't fallen, but the walls blocked most of the wind and ice. It wasn't exactly warm, though, even without the wind chill, so he shoved his hands back his pockets.

"What are you doing out here? It's freezing."

She shrugged, even though she was shivering a little. "I needed some fresh air."

"Kind of hard to tell if it's fresh when it freezes your sinuses solid every time you inhale."

"Wimp."

Snorting, he moved closer to her. Maybe it was a subconscious attempt to share body heat or maybe he just wanted to be near her, but he was disappointed when she took a step back. "You should go inside. It's too cold to be out here."

"Why couldn't you leave me alone, Brody?"

Her words—and the sound of unshed tears in her voice—sliced through him. "We've been trapped in a gym together. There's only—"

"You could have ignored me. You could stayed in the corner with your sister and the baby. Talked to your parents and your old friends. You could have left me alone."

"No. I couldn't." Tears shimmered in her eyes and he cursed himself for being a selfish ass. "Once I saw you again, I couldn't stop myself from being near you."

"I still have the note you left the first time, so don't bother wasting the two minutes to write another when you leave."

He wanted to reject her words—to claim they were unfair—but he deserved her anger. She had no reason to trust he wouldn't leave her like that again. "When I told Donnie I couldn't wait to get out, I meant the gym. I don't think I'm alone in wanting to get the hell out of there at the first opportunity."

"But you're going to leave Tucker's Point, too."

"You know I have to. I have a business."

She took a deep breath and the way it shuddered when she exhaled broke his heart. "I know that. I do. I've been telling myself that over and over."

"That doesn't mean I have to leave you behind again." He was winging it, just letting what he felt come out with almost no filter. "Come with me."

Her eyes met his, filled with surprise. "I can't just leave."

"Why not? I've done it. It's easier than you think."

Now that he'd said it, he felt as if it was the right thing. He could sell his condo and they could buy a nice house somewhere. He'd do his research and find a town with a top school system. They'd have kids and buy a black Lab and live the American dream.

"It was easy for you because you didn't want to be here, Brody. This is my *home*. I love this town. I love the people here. And the ocean. I love watching the fishing boats come in and the tourists walking through town. I take pride in how much they enjoy being here."

"Why the hell are you talking about tourists?" Brody had always hated the tourists. They turned their nose up at the smells and the grubbiness that came with the industry that built the quaint little town they'd chosen to spend their vacation in. "I'm talking about you and me, Delaney. I don't give a damn about watching yuppies buy their kids ice cream and Tucker's Point T-shirts."

"I grew up in my house. This is where I'm from. It's not as simple as packing a bag and getting in your car."

"Of course not." He blew out a harsh breath and ran a hand through his hair. "I didn't mean you had to run away with me the second the roads were open. But we could work toward you coming to Connecticut."

"You're from here, too. Your family's here. Why can't you come home?"

Because the idea of living in Tucker's Point again filled him with dread. Because, on some level, wouldn't it mean he'd failed? He'd worked so hard to shake his hometown. "This isn't my home anymore."

Brody saw he'd made a horrible mistake when Delaney's face fell, frustration giving way to resignation.

Her eyes were sad when she looked at him. "Someday you'll meet a woman who means more to you than where you live. It wasn't me five years ago and I guess it still isn't me."

"No, Delaney, it's not—"

She shoved by him, nearly knocking him over. "It's over, Brody. Just…please leave me alone until you can run away again."

He called after her, but she didn't look back. Maybe it was for the best. He wasn't sure he could say what she wanted to hear, anyway. Going around and around would only make it hurt more.

Ducking his head against the wind, he made his way back to the gym. He didn't see Delaney when he walked in and he forced himself not to seek her out. She'd made it pretty clear she had nothing else to say to him.

Even in the confines of the school gym, she'd managed to leave him just as surely as he'd left her the first time. He'd thought leaving her had hurt. It hurt so much more being on the other end.

DELANEY KNEW FROM the second she opened her eyes on Thursday morning that Brody would leave today.

There was a stillness surrounding the school and the sun already shone brightly through the high, narrow windows. Mother Nature was over her hissy fit and, as what passed for normal New England weather, it was going to be a gorgeous winter day.

While it might take the power crews a while to restore electricity to everybody's homes, the road crews were probably already out. With the streets treated and their parents around to help Sandy with Noah, Brody could probably be on the road by noon.

The pain was already a slow throbbing in her heart, and Delaney wondered—not for the first time—if she'd made the right decision when she told him she wouldn't leave town with him. She loved him. She'd never *stopped* loving him.

But Tucker's Point was her home. She'd always felt

like the community was almost family and that feeling had only deepened since she'd started working at the town hall. It was a brutal choice. The man she loved versus everything and everybody else she loved.

With a weary sigh, she pushed back her blanket and, after grabbing her bag, went into the bathroom to clean up. If the power crews came through, it could be a busy day as people left. Delaney and at least one other volunteer would stay until the last person could go home, and then they'd have to put everything away and restore the shelter back to school-gym status.

She'd just finished brushing her teeth when the door swung open and Sandy walked in. She looked surprised to see her, so at least Delaney knew she hadn't been ambushed by Brody's sister. "Good morning."

"Morning," Sandy said, setting her bag on the counter. "I don't know about good. Not filling the kids with ice cream right before bedtime should be written into the emergency management guidebook for future reference."

Delaney laughed. "I didn't think some of those kids would ever settle down. But at least they slept in a little this morning."

"So…want to tell me what happened?"

"Too much ice cream."

Sandy rolled her eyes and dug in her bag for a washcloth. "Don't be a smart-ass. What happened with you and Brody?"

"He asked me to go to Connecticut. I said no. I asked him to come home to Tucker's Point. He said no. That's what happened."

She managed to beat back the urge to sob and said the words matter-of-factly. That wasn't how she felt, though. Inside she was a hot mess and she just wanted to go home and have a good, long cry.

"You guys belong together. You always have."

"I wish you were right, Sandy. But I guess not."

"Can't you compromise? Find some other small town to live in. Closer to Tucker's Point than Connecticut, but without Brody feeling like he's back where he started."

"It's not that easy."

Delaney meant what she'd said to Brody outside. *Someday you'll meet a woman who means more to you than where you live.* She desperately wished she was that woman, but he'd made it very clear she wasn't.

"It could be that easy," Sandy said. "But you're both being stubborn."

Said the woman who fell in love at first sight with a man who adored her, and who got the wedding, the baby and cute house without shedding a single tear of heartbreak.

"I have to get started on breakfast," Delaney said, grasping any excuse to escape the conversation.

Alice already had a head start on the coffee, so Delaney broke out the supplies she'd need to scramble dozens of eggs and make several loaves of bread worth of toast. Parents already knew they could help themselves to the cold cereal for any kids who turned up their noses at eggs.

She heard Brody's voice before she saw him, talking to somebody in line, and she cursed the spatula for shaking in her hand as she scrambled the third batch. Glancing up quickly, she saw he was still several people down the line, talking with his parents. Groaning mentally, she tried to focus on the pan in front of her.

Of course, Camille either didn't know what had

transpired between Delaney and Brody, or didn't care. She was determined to make conversation.

"I don't know how you do this, day after day. Taking care of everything, I mean. But I'm so glad you do it. And you can bet I'll be letting everybody at the town hall know that, too."

"Thanks, Camille. I appreciate that. Alice just buttered some more toast, so grab it while it's hot."

But the older woman reached out and put her hand over Delaney's. "We're so lucky to have you, honey."

"Well…I'm not going anywhere."

Camille moved on to get her toast, but Delaney could tell by the look on Brody's face he hadn't missed her comment. His jaw was tight and his eyes were about as flat as she'd ever seen them. "How lucky for Tucker's Point."

"Hey, you heard your mom. They feel *lucky* to have me." As opposed to a certain man who didn't seem to think she was worth moving back to Maine for.

He followed his mom and John stepped up for eggs. Fortunately he did nothing but give her a sad look and shake his head, which was easy enough to ignore.

Finally, everybody had eaten—including the volunteers—and Delaney could hide in the back of the kitchen, where the sinks were. Brody's closed expression haunted her and she wasn't halfway through the dishes when she sank to the floor, soapy hands and all, and broke into tears.

ALL IT TOOK was a road crew stopping in for coffee and telling them the roads were passable for excitement to buzz through the gym. Between the salt they'd dropped throughout the storm and the sun shining today, the ice had melted off the main roads fairly quickly. Some of the back roads were still treacherous and nobody wanted the citizens of Tucker's Point going out needlessly, but there was light at the end of the tunnel.

Unlike the others, Brody knew the light was a train. A big, black, smoke-belching steam engine of heartbreak chugging steadily toward him and no matter how he braced for impact, that sucker was going to hurt.

He'd hoped to get a chance to talk to Delaney privately, but she'd suddenly become the most sociable person in existence. She was never alone. Alice or one of the other volunteers made the trips to the supply closet, and Delaney flitted from person to person, never giving him the opportunity to pull her away without making a scene.

When she'd come out of the kitchen earlier, he could tell she'd been crying. The thought of her tears twisted him up inside and he knew he couldn't leave things like this between them. But she wasn't making it easy for him.

Sandy, who was lounging on the cot next to him with a sleeping Noah on her chest, reached her foot over and kicked his leg. "Hey. Earth to Brody."

"Just lost in thought. You need something?"

"Nope. We're good."

Mike had gotten called out just as he was wolfing down the last of his eggs, and Brody suspected it would be a while before he got another break. With roads to salt and downed trees and who knew what else out there, he'd be racking up some overtime.

"The roads are open now," Sandy said. "You should go."

Brody shook his head. "I'm not leaving you and Noah here. You're stuck with me until you can go home."

"Mom and Dad are here, and Mike will be in and

out for breaks. You've already missed so much work, and you really don't have to stay."

"I'm staying."

Sandy sighed. "You hanging around here isn't going to change her mind. It's just going to drag out the pain of you leaving again."

So her concern wasn't for him. It was for Delaney. "I never pretended I wanted to be here. Or that I'd be staying."

"You're going to be as stubborn as she is, and it's not going to get either of you anything but a cold, lonely bed at night."

"So you see that she's being stubborn?"

"Yes. But maybe you missed the part where I said *you* are as stubborn as she is."

"I don't want to talk about this."

She glared at him over her baby's head. "Of course you don't. You don't talk about what's going on in your life. You just leave a note and disappear."

Brody groaned and scrubbed his hands over his face. They'd hashed out Sandy's feelings about his running away several times in the first few months after he'd left Tucker's Point, but she didn't pull punches when she was mad at him.

"I don't mind talking if I think it'll do any good."

Sandy's cell phone rang and she fished around under her hip for it. Having forgotten her charger, she'd only been turning it on a few times a day, but once she found somebody with the same type, she'd started leaving it on.

Brody tuned out the conversation which, by the sounds of it, was with her husband and kept his eyes on Noah so he wouldn't be tempted to look around for Delaney again. He might be having his heart ripped out of his chest but, dammit, he had some pride, too. No mooning over a woman who wouldn't move to Connecticut for him.

Okay, that wasn't totally fair, he told himself. There was a difference. Brody lived in a condo that meant nothing to him in a town he had no emotional ties to. It wasn't that simple for a woman who not only loved her hometown, but somehow felt as if her identity was wrapped up in it.

Sandy ended her call and dropped the phone next to her. "Mike said he went by the house and the power's back on. He checked the pilot lights, too, so I can go home now. And so can Mom and Dad. He went by there, too."

Those were the magic words offering him parole from Tucker's Point. He could take his family home, then point his rental south to the airport.

"It might take a while for the houses to get back up to temperature," he heard himself saying. "And all the pipes need to be checked."

"He said the pipes all looked okay, and he checked the faucets. The water lines didn't freeze."

His mind raced, trying to cover any and all reasons they couldn't go home yet. Which didn't make sense, seeing as how that was all he'd wanted since he drove past the welcome sign on his way in. "The roads are probably still pretty bad."

"Mike wouldn't have said you could take me home if he didn't think it was safe. He'd do it himself, but they want to get all the side roads done so everybody else can go home, too."

So this was it, then. He was free to go. All he had to do was help his family get their things together, drop them off at home and he could head to the airport. Or maybe he'd drive back to Connecticut just to clear his head. He was already so behind on work, it wouldn't make that much of a difference.

But he also had to say goodbye to Delaney. He had to look her in the face and do it like a man this time. And, as much as leaving her the note had hurt, he knew this would be so much worse.

CHAPTER EIGHT

DELANEY KNEW IT was coming. She'd seen Sandy on the phone and a few minutes later she'd started packing up her belongings, as had her parents. And Brody. Their power had been restored and they were leaving.

With each trip he made out to his rental carrying bags, her stomach knotted up a little more. She had no idea if he'd try to talk to her. She'd managed to avoid being alone with him since the disaster outside, and he might just walk out the door and not come back.

But after his last trip out to his car, he scanned the room until he spotted her. He moved with swiftness and purpose, and she knew there was no dodging him this time. When he reached her, he simply gestured toward the doors that led to the hallway. She went, but only because she was afraid she might cry and she didn't want to do that in front of an audience.

"I'm taking my family home," he told her once they were alone. "And then I'm leaving."

Even though she'd expected them, the words sounded wrong to her ears. "At least you're saying goodbye this time."

"I don't want to."

"You made your choice, Brody. Again. Go back to your life and don't worry about me."

He shook his head. "We can figure this out."

She wished she could believe that. "We want different things in life. No amount of figuring will make that work out."

"I'm going to call you."

And wasn't *that* a promise sure to make her sit and mope by the phone for days? Even weeks? "Please don't. It'll just make it harder to get over you. Again."

She looked into his gorgeous green eyes, wishing words would magically come out of his mouth that would make everything okay.

"What's between us is real, Delaney."

"But it's not enough, is it?"

"That's not fair. The choice you're asking me to make is not fair."

"There's no answer that's fair to both of us." Her bottom lip started to tremble as tears formed in her eyes. "Please don't make this harder. Just go. Please."

He went and, even though she'd told him to, every step he took away from her felt like a dagger to her heart. Maybe notes *were* better, because she hadn't had to see the look on his face as he walked away.

Brody had looked as devastated as she felt, and Delaney knew it would be a long time before she could think of him without reliving this moment. If ever.

When the door swung closed behind him, she wrapped her arms around her stomach and sank slowly to the floor. He was gone and there was a good chance, after this, she'd never see him again.

Except when she closed her eyes.

BRODY DROVE SANDY and Noah home first. She was exhausted, and she was so excited to sleep in her own bed she didn't want to wait the extra time to drop their parents off.

"I can stay with you," their mom offered. "Help with Noah so you can catch up on your sleep."

"I love you, Mom, but I honestly want to curl up in bed with him and be alone. There have been so many people hovering and holding him and, while I really appreciate it, we need some alone time."

"I understand, honey. But once you've had alone time, you call me if you get tired or overwhelmed and Mike still isn't home."

She promised she'd call if she needed help and then wrapped her arms around Brody. "I'm going to miss you. And so is Noah."

"I'll be around more often," he promised. "And I'll check Facebook every day so make sure you keep it updated."

"Brody, are you sure you—"

"Don't." He kissed the top of her head and gave her an extra big squeeze. "I'll call you soon, okay?"

The ride to his parents' house was slower. The roads were narrow and trickier to navigate, and there was a lot of debris littering the way. But it wasn't the drive that made his shoulders tense and his fingers tighten on the steering wheel. As the houses got a little more run-down and became more multifamily units than single family, his tension ratcheted up.

When he pulled into the driveway of the small Cape he'd grown up in, with its faded and splintered shingle siding and an ancient roof, he hesitated before taking off his seat belt. Part of him wanted to sit in the car and tell them he'd call them later, but he couldn't do it. These were his parents.

After grabbing their bags, he walked slowly up the familiar walk with its uneven pavers and followed his parents through the front door. Cigarette smoke, old meals, the pine-scented cleaning stuff his mom used and a lingering trace of the fishing boats, though his father had retired. The scents of his childhood.

The sight of the battered kitchen table and the ancient brown couch and recliner beyond it made him twitch.

"You're going to have some coffee and food before you go," his mother said, and her tone brooked no argument so he took off his coat and draped it over a kitchen chair. "Help your father check the basement and the pipes while I cook up some tomato soup and grilled cheese sandwiches."

It was Brody's comfort food, and he wondered if she remembered that—if she'd chosen those foods deliberately. Because she was a mom, he assumed she had and it warmed his bruised heart some. Here was a woman who loved him unconditionally.

Because he was helping his old man check the heating system and the basement, Brody got to visit every room in the house. His old twin bed was still in his bedroom, though the rest of it had been taken over by what looked like crafts. He saw some knitting stuff and a sewing machine and a lot of magazines that touted counted cross-stitch patterns inside. He wasn't sure if his mom actually did any of those crafts, but she'd sure collected a lot of it.

The pipes seemed fine and there was no water in the basement, so they made their way back to the kitchen just as his mother was cutting the grilled cheese sandwiches. Brody sat in the seat that had always been his and breathed in the aroma of his mom's tomato soup. Nobody made it like she did.

Maybe it was the soup or the perfectly grilled sandwiches, but Brody found himself relaxing as they all shared a meal. The Rollins family wasn't in the habit of talking much while they ate, and he found the silence familiar and as comforting as the food.

"I'm going to go unpack our bags and maybe start some laundry real quick." His mother pushed back from the table and stood. "I'll only be a few minutes."

Brody leaned back in his chair and rubbed his stomach. "That really hit the spot, Mom. Thank you."

She leaned down and kissed his forehead. "I like having you home, even if it's only for a little while."

"I'll come around more often," he promised, and he was surprised by the fact he meant it. It would be awkward, of course, avoiding Delaney, but the idea of coming back now and then didn't make him do a mental recoil as it had in the past.

So what if the furniture was rough and he'd have to pay extra to get the cigarette smoke smell out of his clothes. This was his family and he loved them. The house was just…the setting. Nothing more or less.

"This place doesn't define who I am."

"Doesn't define me either, and thank God for that," his father said, and Brody winced. He hadn't meant to say that out loud. "This town doesn't define me. This house doesn't define me. Having a wife I love stick by me for thirty years defines me. So does having a son and a daughter who make me proud. And now I have a grandson I'll teach how to fish and tie a decent knot someday. The people I love and the people who love me make up the man I am."

It was the most he'd ever heard the old man say about love and family, and Brody felt his throat closing up. This place he'd always thought made him somehow *less* had actually made him into the man he was. It was a house full of love and hard work and loyalty, even if the furniture was ugly.

Brody didn't want to be defined by a slick condo in Connecticut and expensive sweaters. He wanted to have a wife who'd love him for thirty years and more, through good times and bad. He wanted kids who'd grow up and make him proud, even if they occasionally broke his heart along the way. He wanted to be the man Delaney had always believed he was.

"I have to go, Pop."

"The highway's going to have some black ice, so you take your time and get home in one piece."

"I'm not going on the highway." Brody stood and grabbed his coat off the back of the chair. "Tell Ma I'm not leaving town yet—I hope—and that I'll call her later."

"Hey, Brody." He stopped with his hand on the doorknob and turned back to his dad. "Your pride means nothing when it comes to loving a woman. Leave it all on the field, son."

DELANEY HAD GIVEN herself a few minutes to cry, but then she'd splashed icy water over her face and told herself to suck it up. She could keep it together until she got home and then she'd cry herself into a state of dehydration.

The power crews were working fast so they could head to harder-hit towns to give assistance, so almost two-thirds of the storm's refugees had gone home already. The others were anxious to go, calling the power company or people in their neighborhoods so often the people on the other end of the lines were probably going crazy.

When the main door opened, Delaney looked over, expecting it to be a working crew looking for a caffeine fix or somebody come to taxi a family home.

It was Brody.

The wild look in his eyes as he zeroed in on her made her shiver, even as she told herself there had to be a perfectly logical explanation for his being there. Maybe Sandy had forgotten something, or one of his parents.

Of course, it had to be her that was out front, instead of Alice, who was cleaning the bathrooms.

"Did you forget something?" she asked when he was close enough.

"Yeah." Her heart sank. Sometimes logic sucked. "I forgot to tell you I love you."

Even though she'd known he did, hearing the words come out of his mouth made her heart do a funny leap in her chest. "I love you, too. I always have. But—"

"Don't say but. Not yet. Not until I'm done." He shoved a hand through his hair and blew out a long breath. "I ran away from turning into a man I didn't want to be. But that guy who loved you... No, that guy who was loved *by* you? I want to be him again."

"You've never stopped being the guy I love."

"I want to be the guy you marry. I want to be the father of your children."

Delaney could hardly breathe. "What changed, Brody? I don't understand."

"I changed. I stood in my parents' house and I felt... I don't know how to explain it. The house isn't the home. My mom and dad are. I want you and me to be a home, Delaney. I'll live in Tucker's Point if it means you'll be living here with me. Hell, I'll live in my parents' house again if you want me to."

She could feel the tears streaming unchecked down her cheeks, but she didn't have the strength in her arms to wipe them away. "I don't want to live in your parents' house."

"Oh, good. I mean, I would, but I was hoping you would say that." His usually cocky smile was a little shaky and it gave her a thrill to know he was as shaken up inside as she was.

"You could live with me."

"I'd like that. You know I have to go back to Connecticut. I have projects in various stages I can't walk away from. But I'll come home to you on the weekends and work toward transitioning my business to the coast of Maine. Maybe the Portland area. I can make it work if you'll be patient." He paused and reached for her hand. When his fingers closed over hers, she felt like everything was right in the world again. "Will you marry me, Delaney?"

"Yes," she whispered. Then she threw her arms around his neck and yelled it out. "Yes!"

As the remaining audience broke out in applause, Brody held her tight and pressed his face against her neck. "I promise you, for the rest of my life, you'll be the candle in my window."

"Welcome home, Brody."

* * * * *

To
SOLON
A Hero In Training

SEEING RED

Jennifer Greene

CHAPTER ONE

WHEN THE FIRST fat snowflake plopped on the windshield of Whitney Brennan's rental car, she saw red.

It was already past midnight. She was already past exhausted. And she had another two hours of driving before she could possibly reach Tucker's Point.

She wanted to be in Tucker's Point like she wanted warts.

She needed to take a week off work to make this trip like she wanted more warts.

But there was a principle involved.

Her mom and sister undoubtedly believed they'd badgered her into this trip. Both were outstanding badgerers, and Whitney had grown up as the "good girl" in the family, the one who tiptoed, the one who always caved.

This time, the family crisis was about some mysterious locked box that Mom had read about in one of Gram's journals. It referred to something Gram "treasured," and that was enough to ignite both Jane's and her mother's emotional fires. They couldn't stand not knowing what was in the box. It wouldn't wait until spring. Jane couldn't go now because she was too pregnant, and Mom pulled the nerves-with-winter-driving card. Whitney had said "yes" before they even had to try the Heavy Guilt tricks.

She'd wanted to go back. Maybe not in crazy winter conditions, and certainly not to capitulate to unreasonable demands from her family. But for herself. Ten years ago, she'd been a crazy-in-love 18-year-old with a broken heart. Man, had she changed.

She'd made a great life for herself, had a terrific job in Philadelphia, was no longer that anxious-to-please sucker she used to be. She wasn't afraid of anything anymore.

Occasionally, though, becoming fearless wasn't exactly a great character recommendation.

The weather was deteriorating fast. Damn fast. In the past hour, the first big, fat, beautiful snowflakes had turned the dark forest into a fairyland of white, but then the temperature rose—up one degree, then up five.

Her driving problems changed from annoying to downright ominous. The snow turned sharp, a furious mix of snow and rain, then pumped up the volume. The sleet pecked at the car like sharp needles. She switched the windshield wipers on higher, watched the blades pick up a skim of ice with every swipe.

She hadn't seen another car in miles—didn't expect to. Normal people would never travel to Tucker's Point on January 2. She'd easily found flights out of Philadelphia, but not to Portland or Bangor or Waterville or anywhere else near Tucker's Point. The airlines to these locations had been grounded. They all seemed to think there was a serious winter storm coming.

As far as Whitney was concerned, that was like saying that cows mooed.

This was Maine. Tucker's Point was a coastal town. So of *course* there was a storm coming.

She'd expected the snow, just not the ice. Not so *much* ice. She had to slow to a crawl, which meant it was past three in the morning before she finally crossed Pine Street, then Maple, then Oak…and finally hit the seaside road. By then the wind had picked up a scream, making traffic lights sway and tossing branches and debris in the air. The windshield wipers could barely keep up with the torrential blast of icy snow, and Route 1 was a skating rink.

She couldn't see the houses. Couldn't do anything but white-knuckle drive through this, but everything was familiar. Closest to town were the hotshot homes—upscale beauties, brick, several stories, sturdy as rock, with traditional white shutters locked because of the storm. Then came the curve of the harbor—a silver piece of glass to drive on—and after that the more modest homes and cottages.

She was a quarter mile from her grandparents' place when she heard a crack. A magnificent old maple tree suddenly came crashing down from the west side of the road. She had to jam on the brakes to avoid being hit, and that sent the car into a scissor-sharp skid. She bumped into something—a bush, a curb, something completely concealed in white ice. The car stopped. Didn't want to start again. She gave it a minute—a long, *long* minute—and finally the engine turned over.

Right around then, she realized her hands were shaking. This trip was supposed to be a cathartic journey. So much for catharsis. So she'd been dumped in high school. So she'd lost the only guy she'd ever loved. Big deal. Right now all she wanted from life was to survive the next half hour.

It took all of that time to sludge the last half mile to her grandparents' place. By the time she skidded into the dark drive, she was dead tired. Her eyes were gritty, her spirit wilted. The old bungalow was hardly welcoming—no one had been here in months, so there were no lights, no amenities, no heat. Still, just being here helped erase the miserable drive. Everything hadn't been terrible in Tucker's Point. Her gram and grandfather were so, so loved; her memories of the house were packed with smiles and laughter. Whitney might not have fit in with her nearest blood kin, but her grandparents had snuggled her close to their hearts.

She sighed and glanced at the backseat. Exhausted or not, she still had to bring in supplies. She was a Mainer. She'd come prepared for a storm, even if this was turning into an unexpectedly ugly blizzard. Cell service was unlikely in these conditions, but she had everything she needed to get by—food, water, a propane heater, warm clothes.

She wasn't afraid to be alone. Unlike ten years ago, she no longer needed anyone. Alone was safer, and she could take care of herself.

She opened the car door and had to gasp for breath; she was immediately attacked by the deluge of sharp ice-rain. The next time she needed a little cathartic trip, she decided, she'd open a bottle of cabernet, put on some old movies and stay home. Darn it, the chances of her even running into Red in this kind of blizzard seemed beyond remote.

And that was the last clear thought she had. It took the rest of her energy to get all the supplies in the house, after which she planned a complete and total crash.

AT FIVE IN the morning, when every sane soul was sound asleep, Henry Redmond—alias Red—stood in front of his third-story window, mesmerized by the view below. A storm like this was magnificent. The Atlantic was furious, pounding wave on wave at the shore, spitting and frothing as if she were rabid.

The ice storm started from the north a few hours

ago—after most people in Tucker's Point had likely gone to bed, early on a Sunday, thinking about work the next morning.

There'd be no work today, Red knew. His best guess was a three-day blizzard. Kids would be over the moon to have Christmas vacation extended by another few days. Parents would be pulling their hair out. Most would have stocked up on emergency food supplies, because they were Mainers, which meant they'd be prepared for a storm at this time of year—but Red was still starting to feel antsy.

She was hardly the worst storm he'd ever seen, not by a long shot. But the wind was a screamer, driving with whip force, and he'd watched three inches of ice accumulate in the past hour. The ice could do a whole lot of damage if it didn't slow up soon.

A saw-buzz noise made him dig a hand into his pocket, reaching for his pager.

"You sure answered that quick." The sheriff's bark of a laugh was familiar. "Thought I'd ask if you minded waking Betsy up."

"Hey. I always take care of my best girl. Did a good rubdown on her an hour ago. She was purring when I left her." He earned another laugh from the sheriff, but then he quit messing around. "I figured you'd be calling up the auxiliary team."

"Yup. You know the drill. Just starting to call, but Roger, Will and Baker will be on track shortly. Delaney'll set up an emergency shelter at the school. I assume you've got your generator going so you can plug in communication devices."

"I'll be darned. After all this time, you think I don't know the drill in an emergency?"

"I know, I know. Waste of breath. Come daybreak, I

need you to take the usual stretch off Route one, after the cutoff at Pine Street. About two dozen folks to the north there, appreciate your checking on them. Then there's a big maple down on Route one. Nothing to do about it now—I can't imagine anyone is on the roads— but hoping you can do something about the tree once the storm lets up. At least clear an emergency lane if you can."

"Betsy lives for problems like that. What else?"

The sheriff sighed. "There could be a kid missing."

Red straightened. "You mean there's a kid out in this weather? *Now?*"

"I'm not certain yet. It could be a misunderstanding. Right now I'm just passing on the story—and the worry. You know the Shuster place, two houses down from the Brennans?"

Red clawed an itch at the back of his neck. Not that the Brennan name was a sore spot, but he wasn't likely to forget the Brennan family in his time. Here he was. Twenty-eight and still single. Because of the one girl he had both loved and jilted—and even after all these years, he still hadn't forgotten her. "Yeah, I know the Brennan place."

"Well, the child's name is April Shuster. She's nine. Her parents are in the middle of a big, messy divorce. Mother just called me a few minutes ago."

"She didn't realize her kid was gone until this hour?"

"It wasn't like that. The mother thought April was with her dad. The dad thought April was with the mom. The dad had the visitation time, but brought her home early because of the storm forecast. The mom was out getting supplies for the storm, came home, never thought to look for April—"

"Less backstory, Sheriff."

"Well, I know. But the backstory's the point of how the parents mislost her."

"Mislost?"

"Ayuh, I can't think of another way to put it. It's too soon to be sure if she's misplaced or lost for real. The mom got home, put the car in the garage, put the groceries away. Power went out, and she went to bed. Woke up in the middle of the night, heard the storm, wandered around to look out windows, see what it looked like. Went into April's bedroom, saw the bed had been slept in and clothes were all over the place, but the girl was missing. She called the dad's landline, but lines were down by then. She called his cell, but lost the connection—except for hearing that April was supposed to be with her."

Red cut to the chase. "You want me out there searching now?"

"I'd like to send the whole town out searching for her, but that just wouldn't make sense. Even if she did go outside, got lost, she'd have holed up somewhere by now. And I know you and Betsy are an unbeatable team, but there's no visibility, no way you could really do a search. I'm going to try to get through to the father's place, talk to him, see what more I can find out. Then I'll let you know what's what. Not to worry."

Right. As if he could sleep after that. He clattered down to the second floor, pulled on gear—a tech-serious base layer, socks with warmers, flannel. Hit the stairs to the first floor, checked to make sure his hand warmer had fresh lighter fluid, stashed two of them inside his work gloves, grabbed his parka and hat, pulled on serious boots.

A Thermos of hot coffee, and he was ready. First-aid supplies were already stashed in the garage, including

bottled water, blankets and food packs. He unplugged
Betsy and gave his John Deere an affectionate pat on
the rump. "I know, honey, you've been waiting for action all day. Believe me, now you're going to get it."

He climbed into the cab, started up the heater, turned
her on. As expected, once on the road, conditions were
beyond awful. It was biting cold, tear-freezing cold. The
ice storm was what his granddaddy would have called
a humdinger of a storm. Ice came down in a treacherous downpour. The beams from Betsy's lights were his
entire field of vision.

He made his way to Route 1, mentally planning his
journey—to take the coast road to Pine, then double
back. The houses to the north were under his charge, for
the obvious reason that he lived the farthest out. Unlike
those in town who volunteered for the auxiliary emergency team, he could get through anything with Betsy.

Near Pine, the houses were fancy, boarded up,
wealthy owners off to wherever they wintered every
year. The harbor was centered at the core of town, with
a white beach for summer swimmers and dock space for
any size boat under the sun. After that, the road rose,
curved like a pregnant belly, a cliff edge over rocks and
stony shoals. Homes were more spread out—and a lot
cheaper—but built sturdy, made to weather storms and
capricious seas.

No lights were on in any of the houses. Red didn't
expect to find any places with power. He'd check in
later in the morning, see if anyone was in trouble, but
for now he aimed for the Shuster place. No sign of life
there, either. He edged two more houses down—a quarter mile distance—and abruptly put Betsy in neutral.

A rush of memories shot through his mind at the look
of the Brennan place. Whitney's grandfather had died

early last summer. The shake-shingled bungalow had been vacant since then, but for years, Jack Brennan and his wife had taken in Whitney, Jane and their mother.

Staring at the Brennans' brought back the best year of Red's life. Back in high school, he'd been a hotshot athlete, star quarterback in football then the best hoop shooter in the state. Girls had flocked. He had the world by the tail, got an athletic scholarship to the University of Maine, even attended that first year. But one wrong ball game, and he'd cracked a knee bad, broken the right ankle in three places. He was benched permanently from competitive sports, which meant his athletic scholarship went down the tubes. That abruptly, he was suddenly careerless, aimless and more lost than a pup in the woods.

His senior year of high school, though, he'd owned the world. It struck him now as funny, because there was only one thing he ever wanted. Naturally, it was a girl.

Snow White. That's what they'd called Whitney Brennan. She'd picked up the tag in her junior year. She was a delicate cameo, blonde, blue-eyed, made soft and serious both. Red couldn't count the number of guys drooling after her. She wasn't prissy. Nothing like that. She was just a hard-core good-girl, and the prettiest girl in school—hell, probably the prettiest in the whole country. But when none of the guys could coax her into more than a peck of a kiss after a date, she'd naturally picked up the no-touch-princess reputation. The Snow White reputation.

At least until she went out with him.

He wished he could shake it off. The memories. The images that flooded his head. It was the middle of a storm, for God's sake...but that was exactly why he couldn't help but notice the car parked in the Brennan driveway. The sedan was coated in snow and ice, but he was pretty sure he could make out rental plates. A thief? A stranded motorist? For damn sure he hadn't seen anyone in the house in months now.

He chugged in behind the car, yanked on gloves. Didn't turn off Betsy—didn't figure he'd be here that long—and opened the door of the cab. A beast of a wind slapped his face, pushing against him as he tried to walk forward. The front porch showed recent footsteps, but it was impossible to guess what size because snow and ice had already filled in the spaces.

He rapped his knuckles on the door, once, twice. Waited. When there was no response, he pushed the door latch. The door wasn't locked—another thing that didn't make a lick of sense.

"Anyone here? Hello?"

The startled shriek that answered him made his heart pound.

The shriek was distinctly soprano.

A soprano he hadn't heard in a long, long time.... But he'd know her voice anywhere.

CHAPTER TWO

WHITNEY HEARD THE KNOCK on the door—although heaven knew how. She'd been trying to sleep for a good half hour. She was so exhausted she figured she'd drop like a stone, but instead the relentless, screaming wind and the ice pelting the windows made it impossible to relax, much less sleep.

The second rap made her scowl.

This was no time to lose her mind. There was no one there. How could there be? It was past five in the morning; the roads were unnavigable, and it seemed mighty unlikely someone would be stopping over for tea.

She'd crashed as fast as she could, leaving food supplies in the car, only bringing things into the living room that she absolutely needed—the propane heater, an eight-hour candle for the mantel and bedding. Lots of bedding. She'd started with a down comforter on the old couch, followed by a sleeping bag, and once she'd zipped herself in, she'd pulled another down comforter on top. She was loath to leave the nest.

With the third rap on the door, she firmly reminded herself that serial killers didn't knock. Neither would robbers or vandals. Crooks probably wouldn't have the ambition to be out in this storm. So she needed to quit imagining things and go to sleep… A plan that worked for another couple seconds…until a large black shadow suddenly loomed over her.

A scream hurtled out of her lungs, almost loud enough to shatter glass.

"Yikes. Stop. I'm sorry. I'm part of the emergency auxiliary team—I'm not here to scare you. I saw the unfamiliar car in the drive, thought someone might be stranded in this storm—"

"Red?" The scream died the instant she heard his voice. The instant she *recognized* his voice. She tried to scramble into a sitting position, but she got tangled up in the heap of covers. For a brief, bleak millisecond, she tried to convince herself that this was only a nightmare. She'd be *thrilled* if this were a nightmare.

The looming shadow hunkered down. "I must be losing my mind. You can't be Whitney Brennan."

She heard a switch, then a thunk when he turned on a heavy-duty flashlight and set it on the carpet. The beam lanced at the ceiling, adding enough light for her to really see him. He wore foul-weather gear, enough to make him look big as a bear, but it wasn't his shoulders and height that grabbed her attention.

It was him. The brush of dark hair, thick and rumpled, framing that square face, the sharp bones, the sexy gray-blue eyes, the mouth softer than butter. A few creases here and there, but being ten years older hadn't diminished his good looks. If anything, he looked more dangerous, more compelling, more…sexy. In high school, he'd been every girl's heartthrob. He'd been crazy handsome, but his appeal was more than that. His slow smile made any girl melt. That sudden fire in his eyes could ignite any girl's hormones.

Heaven knew, she'd fallen. More than fallen. He was the first boy she'd ever slept with, the only man who'd ever stolen her heart…. At least until he'd jilted her out of the complete blue, thrown her over as if she'd never mattered to him.

But she was long over that.

"Whitney—" he repeated.

"I don't know who Whitney is, but my name's Jane Smith."

A grin stole over his face. The same grin she'd melted for when she'd been a stupid, naive teenager. "Good try, but I heard you scream. I'd know your scream anywhere. What on earth are you doing back here, and in this weather?"

He sounded so friendly, so glad to see her. How mean was that?

She finally managed to get the sleeping bag unzipped. Covers were still tangled everywhere, but she could sit up, feel a little more on equal ground—never mind that her hair hadn't seen a brush in hours, and the circles under her eyes had to be bigger than boats. Still, this was the cathartic thing she'd hoped would happen on this trip. A chance to see him again. A chance to show him that she was strong and happy and doing great. So if he wanted to be friendly, she could cheerily out-chat him any day of the week.

And she started by answering his question—or at least the short version of why she was here. When Gramps died last May, her mom and sister couldn't face doing anything with all the belongings and land. Translation: she wasn't willing to do it for them. So they voted to close up the house, wait a full year before making any decisions about the place. In the meantime, though, her mom and Jane still had things of her grandmother's, including a box full of journals. Several referenced a locked box in the attic, filled with "treasures of the heart."

"That was the end of any peace at Christmas. For both of them, it was like a hive they couldn't itch. They had to know what was in that box. Jane and Mom are in Boston now—Jane's seven months pregnant, so there was no way she could travel at this time of year. And Mom played the nerves card—"

"I remember your mom and her nerves. Particularly when she wanted you to do something."

Whitney wasn't about to go down that road. "Anyway, these days I'm living and working in Philadelphia. I took the week off for Christmas, but it was really no hardship for me to take a little extra time. The box wasn't really a motivation. I mean, I'll find it, send it back to my mom. But really, it just kind of hit me…how long since I'd been here, how many good memories I had of both Gram and my grandfather."

"Then this storm blew up out of nowhere."

She shook her head. "I heard the forecast. I just took it with a grain of salt. You know how much wild weather we get around here in the winter. Even when it's bad, it's mostly an issue of being prepared. My flight was cancelled—that was a nuisance. But I just rented a car and stocked it up—candles, flashlights, the heater, food, a first-aid kit…."

She started to relax. He'd always been easy to talk to, and as crazy as the circumstances were, now seemed no different that way. At one point, he popped to his feet and headed outside to his mammoth front-end loader. He shot back inside with a Thermos of coffee and a bag of Oreos. "Breakfast," he said with one of his infamous grins.

Just like she remembered, he couldn't sit still, bounced to his feet like the athlete he'd once been. He put a hand on the windowsills, under the fireplace, near the doors. "No draft anywhere. Your grandfather sure built the place sturdy. So what's in the box your mom and sister want?"

"No idea. I figure I'll look for it when there's more daylight."

"Well, if you find it's something heavy, don't tackle it on your own. Through the blizzard, I'll be covering Route one, from the middle of town north up to Land's End. I'll be by here again this afternoon, at least twice tomorrow."

"I'm not a kid anymore, Red. I can take care of myself." She didn't realize that she'd come across defensively until his eyebrows rose and he responded in a gentler tone.

"Well, of course you can. But you're still no bigger than a sprite, and if there's one thing I'm good for, it's brawn. No reason to risk carrying something heavy if you've got free labor."

He clearly wanted to coax a smile from her, so she gave him one, but on the inside, she was kicking herself. Being in the dark house alone with him was stirring emotions she'd locked away, feelings she never thought she'd experience again. After all this time, she should be over him. She'd wanted to come home to prove how totally over him she was.

There was just that one tiny, ticklish problem she hadn't considered.

The stupid embers were right there, hot enough to burst into flame, just as volatile as they'd been years ago.

Thank God she was grown up enough to cover the awkward moment. "So you're on the auxiliary emergency team?" she asked cheerily.

"Yup. Have been for a bunch of winters—ever since

I bought Betsy. Or, should I say, since Betsy put me in hock to the bank for the rest of my life."

"Betsy?"

"The John Deere out there, the front-end loader with the back blade." He chuckled with her, then added, "Roads have turned bad, as you must have experienced. Less snow than ice. And there isn't much I can see at this hour, but there was a report about a child missing, a little girl. Name's April Shuster—"

"I used to know the Shusters. They lived a few doors down."

"Mrs. Shuster and April still do, but I gather there's a divorce in the works, and somewhere between the dad and the mom, they misplaced their nine-year-old—or she ran away. She's everyone's priority. But more mine, because she's on my route."

"I totally understand."

"So if you see her, or, for that matter, if you need any help, hang a towel or something with color outside. I'll be looking for signs like that, in case people need a hand." He sighed, popped to his feet again. "And even if it's still dark, I want to get back on the road. The storm's too bad to go anywhere on foot yet, but I just want to make a patrol run, see if there could be any sign of her."

She climbed out of her cocoon to see him to the door—and immediately realized that was a mistake. His gaze slid over her, slow as a summer-sipping bourbon. She knew perfectly well what she looked like— she was wearing the faded jeans and ancient sweater she'd driven in, stuff she should have stashed in a rag bag. But the way he looked at her kindled a hot flush of warmth. The house was freezing, for Pete's sake.

But not where he was.

And then the devil brought on one of those wicked grins of his.

"Hey," he said, in a voice suddenly more tender than melted butter. "Don't tell me you're married."

"Okay. I won't tell you I'm married."

"Quit teasing. Show me the left hand."

Her ring finger was naked. Which she didn't show him. She wasn't about to show him anything naked.

He wasn't looking at her hands, anyway. "I'm glad as hell to see you again," he said quietly, honestly. "You look great, Whitney."

She remembered that hitch in her heartbeat. It worried her then, and worried her now. "Easy to look good when it's this dark."

"I can see enough." He cocked his head. "And I remember even more."

Talk about a louse. Just like that, he turned heel and headed out, leaving her flushed and cranky. If that wasn't a flirt, she didn't know what was. He acted as if he still had feelings for her, wouldn't mind striking that ten-year-old match.

Hands on her hips, she watched from the window as he climbed into the tractor cab. Lights flashed like giant eyes when he backed the monster out of the drive. Finally, he disappeared from sight, back into the storm.

He'd left plenty of storm behind him. She shoved a hand through her hair, exasperated with herself.

It was amazing—and annoying—how seeing him invoked all the tediously old insecurities. Growing up, she'd adored her dad, did everything but stand on her head to please him, brought him all As and honors, even in grade school. But her dad had been a fisherman, a hearty Mainer who valued the more athletic Jane. He loved both his daughters, Whitney never doubted that.

But she always knew that she didn't measure up, that she couldn't be the kind of daughter he wanted.

When her dad died, drowned in a wild storm in the Atlantic, their shortened family moved in with her grandparents. Whitney had had a hard time shaking her grief, spent a long time aching that she'd never made her dad proud. There had to be something wrong with her, that she was so hard to love.

She knew *now* that she'd brought that insecurity into her relationship with Red. When he dumped her, he broke her heart. But she wasn't surprised. Deep down, she'd never believed he would stay. She'd known from the get-go that she wouldn't be enough.

Swiftly Whitney squeezed her eyes closed. Man, it was painful to revisit those old emotions, that old history. But maybe it was for the best. She never wanted to go down those roads again.

THE INSIDE OF Betsy's cab was like a cocoon. No one there but him and his thoughts, and Red couldn't get her off his mind. Whitney was the same in so many ways. She had the same silky fine, sunny-blond hair. The same crystal-blue eyes. She was fine-boned, everywhere from her slender hands to her cheeks.

Describing her wasn't a simple thing. She never had the looks a guy would notice in a crowd, but once you really saw her, you wondered how any other woman could possibly be as pretty. Or not pretty. *Gorgeous* wasn't the right word, either. Whitney was more… lovely. Lovely, in that pure female way, like the scent of vanilla and camellias.

That's what she'd worn to their senior prom. Camellias. Otherwise he wouldn't have a clue about that flower or its fragrance. He hadn't smelled it before or since that prom night, but it was still a scent that had lingered in his head all these years.

Prom night was the night he'd broken up with her.

Betsy let out a serious screech, forcing his mind back on track—for the dozenth time in the past six hours. He was starting to run on fumes. He'd checked his whole stretch along the coast. Didn't mind the cold, the snow, the ice—never had—but that raw, relentless wind was starting to get on his nerves.

Whitney was stretching on his nerves, too, but he had to scrub up some discipline, deal with what needed dealing with first.

In an emergency—any emergency—the sheriff claimed a single channel. It worked similar to a police radio, in that the whole emergency team was tuned to communicate that way. The messages were frequent, and filled everyone in on wherever there was trouble.

The little girl, April Shuster, was still missing, her parents beyond frantic. Roger, one of the EMTs, reported a young mom had gone into labor. It wouldn't be a major blizzard if a baby didn't show up earlier than expected. Roger called in an update every twenty minutes. The mama was hanging in there, doing fine. The dad had keeled over at his wife's first scream, knocked his head and now had a lump the size of a golf ball.

Red himself had reported in about the Tuckers—the grandkids of the original Tuckers of Tucker's Point. The pair were well over 90, not about to be bothered by a plain old blizzard. They had a fireplace set up to cook on, and served him lunch—steak and potatoes. Matthew Tucker believed a little hair of the dog was helpful in weather this bad. Red had never known if Mrs. Tucker realized her husband of 60 years was a tippler, but he wasn't about to tattle.

The deputy municipal clerk, Delaney Westcott, was part of the team setting up an emergency shelter at the school. She reported whoever came through the doors, so no one would waste time searching for a "missing" person who was no longer missing. Others radioed back to her with the usual questions—did she know where Grayson Whitson was because he wasn't answering his door, or Martha Beam, who'd broken a leg days before the storm and no one knew if she'd gone to visit kin or could get around on her own.

Will—retired coast guard—wanted Red to move the downed maple tree on Route 1, said he could get in to clear a path, but didn't have the right equipment to push away the monster. Red said he'd get to it on his next pass, but was doing the people check thing first.

Baker was part of the volunteer fire department. He had the nightmare job. Fires seemed to spring up every darned time there was a power outage, especially in a winter storm like this. People used fireplaces that hadn't been cleaned in years, or they used a kerosene lantern that should have been thrown out a century before... or they dropped candles. Baker was already tired and reaching the barking stage.

"Red. Need crack-open meals at 401 Pine. Had a fire in the kitchen. Won't be able to use any of their food stuffs for the duration of the storm. Three people. One dad, two kids. Need water, dry milk, as well as the usual."

"Got it," Red promised him. It was like that. At first, fun. Everyone geared up for a good storm. Maine didn't raise any sissies. But hour after hour added up, and he did what he always did wrong—gulp down too much coffee, which he loved, but which his stomach wanted only in moderation.

He'd never been good at the moderation thing. Which made him think of Snow White again. For damn sure, he'd never done anything halfway with her. When he'd fallen, it had been like a brick. When he loved, he loved whole hog.

The radio lit up, static adding to the sheriff's crabby voice. "Red. Phone your mother. You'd think she'd know better than to call during a storm, for cripes sake. Especially when she's from here. But your mother, she's beside herself. Three calls in the last hour, interrupting the lines—"

Red winced. He knew his mother's strident voice well. One of her favorite sayings growing up was "You're just like your father!" He used to hide in the basement with his dad, watching the tube, popping corn, when she was on a real tear. But that wasn't the sheriff's problem. "I will. Sorry, Sheriff."

"Make sure you've got the weather report on. We're just getting into this. It's going to get a lot worse before it gets better."

"Still. Not as bad as the storm in 2002."

"Ayuh. Just say it in a whisper. We don't want to encourage her to get any worse."

Nor'easters were male. Capricious, evil storms were always female. Red never knew why.

He couldn't take a break until he'd made one more stop. The Shuster house was less than a quarter mile from Whitney's. As he pulled into the driveway, he could see two lanterns in the front windows, and a woman pacing in the background.

He climbed down from Betsy, headed for the door—

which Mrs. Shuster hurled open before he was close enough to knock. He'd seen her around town, the way you did in a small community. She had brown hair, brown eyes, maybe 40 or so? Jean, he thought her first name was.

Her shoulders sank when she saw his face. "I know you couldn't have found her yet, because the sheriff would have called."

"Everybody's searching. We'll find her." He stepped inside, closed the door, but stayed right on the doormat. He was dripping snow. He started to talk, but never had a chance.

"It's all his fault. April's only *nine*. When he left us, April just couldn't understand it. She doesn't want us to get divorced. I tried to make sure she never heard ugly things, no fights, no arguments, and I thought she should have regular time with her father. That's where I thought she was! With her father! How was I supposed to know he'd dropped her off early? He said it was because of the storm, but that's exactly why I was out getting groceries, because of the storm. I had no way to know he'd dropped her here—"

Red could feel his throat tightening up, as if he'd worn a tie and it was starting to strangle him. He just had a bad feeling the story was going to be long and complicated, with a lot of details that were none of his business.

"We all got a report of what she was wearing, but I wondered if you'd tell me in more detail. Or if you had a picture. And if you could give me something— mittens, a sweater. When the storm lightens up, we'll add dogs to the search."

"I could have been home *ages* before. Once I got

groceries, I dropped some off at my neighbor's. We had a glass of wine, talked for a while. I had no reason in the universe to think she was home alone! I'd never have left her alone!"

"I know you wouldn't," Red said, although truthfully he didn't much know her from Adam.

She stalked to a closet, pulled out mittens and a scarf, but never stopped talking. "She should have been with him—her father! The thing was, I got home well before nine thirty, but I couldn't have known she was here, that she'd gone to bed. We always go to bed early on Sunday night because school's on Monday."

"I know, ma'am. I live here. These mittens and scarf'll help us all—"

She interrupted again. "Her boots are pink with white fur around the top. She got a purple down jacket with a white belt for Christmas. There's no way she'd be wearing anything but that, she loves it. She has a white hat with purple pom-poms. But her mittens are here." She motioned to the mittens she'd just given him. Tears filled her eyes. "She doesn't have her mittens. She left them here when her father picked her up. And it's freezing out there!"

Tears started spilling like a faucet set on gush. Frantic, terrified tears. Hell, he hated it when a woman cried like that. "We're going to find her," he promised.

He checked that she had food and ample fuel for the lanterns, discovered she'd started up a small generator, so checked she had enough propane for that, too.

"It's so cold out there. Too cold—"

"Yup, it is. But she wouldn't still be walking. Once it got bad, she'd have holed up somewhere. Maybe a neighbor or another mother who had no way to call

you once the power went down. No one kidnaps a kid
in a blizzard, so there's no reason to worry about something like that. She probably had the good sense to seek
shelter. Soon as we can do a complete house-to-house
search, we'll probably find her safe and sound."

"You think?"

"I *really* think."

"I didn't even know she was missing until I walked
into her room. I just wanted to look out her east window, see the storm from that direction, and that's when
I saw her bed had been slept in, that the suitcase she
took to her father's was on the floor. So she'd gone to
sleep and then gotten up. I don't understand what she
was thinking, why she would have left in the night
like that."

"I don't understand it, either, Mrs. Shuster, but we're
going to find her."

"Promise. I need you to promise."

He promised a bunch of things before he was able
to get out of there. He'd have been comfortable giving
her a hug, but he didn't feel he really knew her that
well. It was just a tough visit, that was all. No way
around it. She was petrified. What mom wouldn't be,
in her shoes?

Now that he'd collected a few of April's belongings
to take back to the sheriff's, he was free for a few hours.
Good thing. Betsy's cab had heat, air, Sirius, wireless
phone and computer connections—everything a guy
could need to spend long hours with her. But negotiat-
ing the storm with her was still exhausting.

Being with Mrs. Shuster only underlined where he
was going next. Back to Whitney's. Whatever had bro-

ken up the Shuster marriage had clearly torn up three lives. Divorces were like that.

Breakups were like that.

All these years, it bit in his craw that he'd never told Whitney why he'd broken up with her—and seeing her sharply reminded him of everything he'd thrown away. He wasn't sure if he'd been right or wrong ten years ago.

But now, if fate had been kind enough to throw Whitney in his path again, for damn sure he didn't want to blow it.

CHAPTER THREE

WHITNEY FEARED HER watch must be broken. She shook
it, turned a flashlight on it, but the time refused to
change. Her watch seemed to think it was 3:30 in the
afternoon.

Could she really have slept all day?

She swung her legs over the side of the couch. From
a crack in the curtains, she could see the storm reigning
like an angry queen—the sky was still a dark, gloomy
charcoal, the wind screaming and rattling anything it
could beat up. Inside, the view was more comforting.

Her grandmother had decorated the place before
Whitney was born, so nothing was remotely new. Tables were early American maple, couches and chairs
done up in a faded colonial print. Gram had called the
couch a chesterfield. When Whitney was a little girl,
she'd thought the look was corny, but now it felt as comfortable as old slippers.

She stood up, wishing desperately for three things.
Coffee. A bathroom. And food.

Coffee wasn't going to happen. The bathroom issues weren't going to be easy, but she'd brought the
right supplies. It wasn't as if she'd never been stranded
in a storm before.

Once she'd cleaned up, she pulled on fresh clothes—
silk long johns, old black cords, a blue alpaca sweater,
big wool socks. She dug in her bag for a brush, but a

glance at her purse mirror revealed what she already knew. It was a bad hair day. Actually, it was a bad hair life. The pale blond color was okay, and she had lots of it, but it was all fine as silk, straight, no way to beg, borrow, steal or threaten it into something fancy. On the other hand, it sure didn't matter here.

She scrounged in her duffels for food supplies. Nothing special. Trail mix that she'd embellished with extra raisins and M&M's. Bread, peanut butter, guava and grape jelly. Dry cereal. Water bottles, pop bottles. Tediously repetitive, but little silverware was required, and after all, she'd only planned on being gone twenty-four hours. As she closed the door to the manic storm with a boot, that twenty-four hours seemed a little optimistic.

It didn't look as if she were getting out of here any time soon.

Once she'd packed in some food, she decided she might as well head up to the attic. Maybe she'd find the "sacred" box and maybe she wouldn't—but at least the chore would keep her mind off Red.

BY THE TIME Red could head for Whitney's, the temperature had dropped, which was both good news and bad news. Snow was hurling down instead of icy sleet now, accumulating several inches since his visit to the Shuster house, but beneath all the fresh white, it was slick as a slide. Visibility was a joke. The headlights barely illuminated a few feet ahead. The rest of the world was a whiteout.

It was a night to make a man realize just how alone he was.

He pulled into Whitney's drive and left Betsy running—she had a fresh fill of fuel, and there was no way to plug her in here. He heaped his arms with goodies, opened the cab to a hell-blast of cold and, in spite of the god-awful temperatures, whistled en route to her door.

He rapped. Once. Twice. When there was no answer, he poked his head in. "Whitney? It's me, Red."

He thought he heard a sound, but wasn't sure. He plopped down the groceries and wine, yanked off his parka and stove gloves. "Whitney?" he said, louder now.

"Here! I could use some help!"

Her voice was both muffled and distant. He fished the LED light from his pocket and took off. Past the French doors to the living room was a totally dark, biting cold hallway. Memories flew through his mind faster than speed dial. He'd first kissed Whitney in that living room, stole kisses and touches in every nook and cranny of the house—which was never easy. Her mom was regularly absentee, but her little sister loved to spy on Snow White—and then tell. And her grandfather always gave him The Look. Gramps seemed to think all teenage boys had only one thing on their minds. Which Red most definitely had.

The point, though, was that he'd been highly motivated to know the entire layout of the house. It didn't matter how dark the hall was; he hustled past the kitchen, bath and master bedroom, to the narrow stairs leading up. On the second floor, typical of a home built in that era, were two big bedrooms with a bath in between.

As he chugged up the stairs two at a time, he remembered the first day he met her, right after they'd moved to her grandfather's place. She was sitting on a cliff overlooking the ocean, crying her eyes out over her dad.

"Red? I'm up here in—"

"Yeah," he called back. "In your old room." It was

an easy guess, the instant he reached the doorway. His flashlight immediately highlighted the open closet doors…and on the carpet, lying on its side, an old aluminum ladder.

When he shined the beam up, there she was. All blue eyes and pale gold hair, framed in the attic opening.

"I don't want to hear a single word about how stupid I was to let the ladder drop."

"That never crossed my mind."

"And I wasn't waiting for you to come rescue me. I know you said you'd stop by later today, but you could have been tied up with anything in this blizzard."

All kinds of problems *had* come up. But he didn't waste time mentioning that wild horses wouldn't have kept him away, no matter how whipped-tired he was. "Let's get you down from there. Are you hurt?"

"No. Just cold. And bored. And exasperated. I can't believe I was so stupid as to kick the ladder over. I went up here to find the box, and I *did.* Only when I tried to carry it and climb down, everything was off-balance, and down went the ladder. I was thinking about jumping down. It's just that I couldn't avoid landing on the rungs. It's not *that* far a fall, but…"

"But you could have been hurt." She could easily have broken or sprained something, and then been stuck lying in the dark and the cold. The thought was enough to put hair on his chest. And he already had hair on his chest. Swiftly, he righted the ladder. "I'll get your box, but you come down first."

"I'd rather you took the box—"

He could hear a quiver in her voice. Not nerves. Cold. "*You* first. And for the record, I brought a hot dinner."

"Oh. That sounds wonderful. I'm really hungry, but…"

Trust her to be up there, cold and miserable, and yet still arguing. "How big is the box and how heavy?"

"That's just it. It's a wooden chest kind of thing. Not *that* heavy, but definitely bulky and awkward."

"Okay. I don't want to hear any more. If I got pictures in my head of you carrying something there's no way you could handle on a ladder, then I'd probably start swearing. I'd be that mad. Even thinking about it is making me crabbier by the minute. So if you just climb down, you can hustle in the living room where it's nice and warm. You can open the bottle of Bordeaux. And the Tuckers were cooking steak over the fire when I visited there, so I've also got a steak sandwich for you, rare—"

Her voice interrupted, sounding weak. "How rare?"

"Not still on the hoof. But close."

Her head disappeared and she turned around. Even wearing bulky clothes, her lithe, slim shape was more than evident. Cute butt. Long legs. The splash of blond silk on her dark sweater. He supported the creaky ladder with both hands, which meant that she naturally brushed against his body on the last steps down.

When she spooned right against his pelvis, she hesitated, went suddenly still as a statue. For him, the sudden sexual awareness was sharper than needles…which was not really a surprise. But until then, he had no idea if she still felt the crazy, wild desire that once ransomed both their lives. It was telling, he thought, that as soon as their bodies touched, she started spilling out words.

"I tend to eat lots of fruit and vegetables. You know. Doing the old, boring health food thing. Which means I haven't had steak in a blue moon. Much less a rare steak. Much less a rare steak sandwich."

"No kidding?" Regretfully, he had to let her go when

she reached the ground. She was probably looking for an excuse to bolt away from him. "The sandwich is in the living room, in one of those stay-hot containers. You'll see it. I'll bring your box from the attic."

That was easier said than done, but he managed, put the thin LED flashlight between his teeth, used it to locate the oddly shaped wooden box. The attic looked pretty much like everybody's attic. Broken rocking chair, a shadeless lamp, shelves and boxes of what-alls that no one wanted to throw away, a lot of dust and draping spider webs. Whitney's box was only easy to find because she'd pulled it close to the attic opening.

He could lift it. One-handed. Awkward or not, it wasn't five minutes before he hauled the infamous box into the living room. There—a feast for sore eyes—was the girl he'd fallen hook, line and sinker for way back when. She was sitting cross-legged on the couch, the way she always used to sit. And she was shoveling down the steak sandwich as if she hadn't eaten in days.

He set down the box, then plunked down beside her and grabbed a napkin from the cooler—just in case a little drool seeped from her mouth.

She tried to say something, and of course, couldn't.

"You know, no one's going to steal the rest of your sandwich. You don't have to inhale it. You can take your time."

She offered him a delicate finger gesture. Something she'd never have done in high school. Damnation, if he wasn't falling in love all over again. "You want some wine? Oh. I see you didn't open it. No time, right? Once you saw the steak sandwich, that was all she wrote. Try to remember to breathe in between bites, okay?"

He got another finger gesture. This time he laughed. In the bottom of the cooler was a corkscrew. A handful of paper cups had been stashed in there, too. Blizzards were no time to worry about dishes.

There was a second steak sandwich in there, but he figured he'd wait, make sure she didn't want another one. He wouldn't want to get between Whitney and her food.

"Don't try and talk. You'll get hiccups." Another glare from her, but she was still chowing down. Once he popped the cork and poured two paper cups, he offered her one. A couth kind of guy would undoubtedly have let the wine breathe, but he'd never managed to be very high-brow.

"While you can't talk, I might as well. At least until you get bored with my blizzard stories." He rooted for more stuff in the bottom of the cooler. Found sugar cookies, chips. "We still haven't found the little girl, but the whole town's alerted to search for her. Hey, north of town, you remember the castle people used to call Lands End? I heard someone wanted to buy it, turn it into some kind of pricey resort."

She started to speak, but he offered her a cookie. She had two hands full of food then, not counting the wine on the coffee table, which probably meant he had the floor indefinitely. "I'm living in the family house. You know. Where I grew up, where I never planned to live in a thousand years. And for sure, it's no place for a single guy. Three stories to keep up, for Pete's sake. But I can't beat the view. Damn, but I love the ocean...."

She raised a hand, as if wanting to ask him a question, but her mouth was full, so he guessed she was asking him to fill in the blanks.

"If you're asking me what happened, my dad died. A heart attack out of the blue. My mom and two sisters wanted to leave Tucker's Point as fast as they could pack, headed for Portland. They just all wanted more of a city life. Mom always claimed the big old house was a monster to clean. I never expected to live there, but when push came to shove, it was either sell it to strangers or have one of us care enough to keep it."

"Red." She'd swallowed, emptied the paper cup and lifted it for a refill. "I don't understand. When did you come back to Tucker's Point? Was it when your dad died?"

He shook his head. "No. My dad was alive and thriving when I came home. I left college a few months into my freshman year." And, yeah, he knew that could raise hurtful questions for her.

For an instant she stopped eating and just looked at him with a stunned expression. Not as if he wanted to pursue it, but he figured if there was any chance of clearing the air of old hurts, it had to start with him. "When I left school, I didn't have a clue what I was going to do. My dad always made a good living in construction, but I never thought I could get into it. He challenged me to think differently. He'd start arguments about how to do things, goaded me into telling him how I could do it better. Before I knew it, I took on some jobs, added some equipment. The bank still owns me. But I'm a lot more solvent than I was those first couple years."

"Wait." She stopped gulping down cookies, which wasn't a good sign. "I don't understand. Why did you drop out of school? Come home? What happened to football and basketball and your athletic scholarships?"

He poured another round of wine. Dixie cup volumes hadn't dented the bottle so far, but he had to hope she was as terrible a drinker as she used to be. Back in high school, a few sips of beer and she'd be curled up, snoozing in the passenger seat of his rusted-out Camaro. Someone—well, Russ Trumboldt, to be precise—called her a cheap date, meaning to be funny, and damn if he hadn't been forced to deck him. Nearly broke his hand. Got a reaming out from his coach.

But that was old history.

"I don't mind telling you, but not tonight." He leaned back. "I don't want to monopolize the conversation— and it's your turn. You did the Smith College thing. Then moved to Philadelphia. That's about all I know. Oh. Big job, someone said."

She hesitated, her attention clearly not on herself. She was looking at him. Looking at him differently. Looking at him…personally. Candlelight glowed behind her. The pale light struck him as an oasis on a dark night that stretched forever. This was their world.

That was how he'd always felt anywhere near her. As if the rest of the world was boring and irrelevant. Only Whitney mattered.

"Smith," he repeated. "You worked so hard to get in there. Was it everything you wanted?"

She averted her gaze, suddenly fussing with napkins and dinner debris. Once she answered, her tone seemed strange and overly cheery. "It was fantastic… but not exactly what I'd hoped for."

He cocked his head. "The way I remember it, you especially wanted Smith because it was such a respected school. You wanted your family to feel proud you could get in there. And even more, you wanted the kind of education that'd open doors for you. You always used to talk about wanting to make a real difference."

"Yeah, we both had those corny ideals in high school, didn't we? Wanted to make the world a better place. Wanted to really *do* something." She sighed. "Well, I started out really sure I wanted to do something terrific in American Studies."

"I hear a 'but'…"

She nodded. "But the women in the program that year were a lot more political and, um, angry than I was. Militant. I just didn't fit in. Changed majors, ended up with a pretty degree in Fine Arts."

"That's cool."

Again, she averted her eyes. "Yup…turned out great. I landed a super job with a design firm in Philadelphia— they're big, work with offices and large buildings. I have my own place, and I sure can't argue about the money, either. I do okay."

"That's great to hear." Which was true, except Red was getting a sick feeling in the pit of his stomach. Something was wrong. She'd said the right words, but something had to be seriously wrong with the job or her life, or she wouldn't be avoiding meeting his eyes. He stalled, grappling for a way to coax her into talking more, when she suddenly shook her head—hard, as if trying to shake loose some common sense.

"I can't believe it. Us. Talking like this, after all this time. As if we were still friends…"

She untwisted from the couch, lurched to her feet. There was no place to escape in a blizzard, but he understood that was what she wanted to do. Escape. From him.

Instinctively he leaped to his feet even faster—fast enough for his right knee to give out a knife-sharp protest. It was an old pain, not a new one; he didn't pay any attention.

"Whitney." He hooked her arm gently, but even that slightest touch caused her to whip around and almost lose her balance. He steadied her, placing both hands on her upper arms. Her face shot up, eyes meeting his.

It had happened before. Just like this. The night after their first date. It was dark. Her doorstep. He was thinking through his moves, planning to kiss her, believing she'd expect a kiss after that first date. He'd been practicing kissing girls since grade school, but when she suddenly looked up at him, it wasn't about high school moves anymore.

It was just about a guy and a girl.

His voice came out hoarse and low. "Whitney...we *were* friends. You were the best friend I ever had."

She frowned, as if confused. But it was there, just like before. Just like always. He was a bear next to her delicate figure. She had to look up to meet his gaze. But he'd never looked down on her. Ever. She made him feel a hundred feet tall, as if he were the one man who could protect her. The one guy she just might let cherish her.

"That's what I thought. A long time ago," she said, in a voice as raw as his.

"Because that's how it really was between us."

"Red. You're the one who cut it off. You broke us up. Not me."

"Not," he said thickly, "because I wanted to. I *never* wanted to."

And he'd waited as long as he could wait. His mouth came down on hers like a fighter jet coming in for a landing, fire-fast but soft, the total, sudden silence after there'd been noise.... The complete fadeout of everything else around them.

Her mouth was life. Her lips, soft as pansy petals. Her arms lifted to his shoulders, then to his neck. She made a sound, a song of longing, then closed her eyes and sank into him.

He remembered her innocence then. It was like now.
He couldn't run roughshod, let his hormones go, although his body certainly felt a rage of them. But she
communicated vulnerability, trust, the way she lifted
up, the way she melted into him. The way she kissed
back, with wonder, lips finding lips, finding tastes,
finding pressure, yearning for more. A little afraid,
but still needing more. Wanting more.

Wanting him.

And God knew, he wanted her. There seemed to
be a million pounds of clothes between them. Zippers
and bulk and buttons and layers on layers and nothing
easy...but he already knew her shapes, her textures.
The same scent, close to her skin, in the hollow of her
neck. The slender slope of her spine.

When he was in his teens, a lot of girls came on to
him because he was more or less the king of the high
school, the classic jock. Besides that, he was a lusty,
brainless teenager.

But the whole world changed with Whitney. He was
afraid she'd think she was just another notch. But it
was nothing like that with her. His desire for her was
a fire in his gut.

But more than sex, he wanted to *be* with her. He'd
never wanted to *be* with anyone like her, before or since.
It was a craving, just to see her in a hallway, to wait the
hours until he could finally rap on her door again, the
way nothing felt right until she was next to him, even
if they were only sipping vanilla shakes after a game.
Even if they were just walking to school. Even if it
was a Saturday morning, and he had to wait the whole
damned day until he could be with her again.

He'd forgotten. How unbearably fierce that loneli-
ness was, that hunger for her, that raw, hot yearning.

Now was no different than the past. Everything became right when he could touch her. Hold her. Get lost in her.

He pulled off his fleece, then her sweater. His sweater, then her silk long underwear top.

They both still had layers to go. His heart was chugging like a race horse, wanting to hurry, wanting her naked, wanting. Her. Now. Before this spell ended. Before anything could stop them. But fast wouldn't cut it. He wanted to love her like she'd never been loved. Like he'd wanted to love her all these years. Like he'd always loved her.

"Red."

He heard the buzzing noise. Didn't care.

"Red," she repeated, and framed his face in her hands. He opened blurry eyes, saw her wet lips, the flush in her cheeks even in the dim light. And what she saw in his eyes echoed how he felt.

Still, she pulled back when his mouth tried to claim hers again. "Your pager's going off," she said.

"I know. Damn it. I'm hoping it'll go away." He added on a groan, "It *has* to go away."

"Red."

Yeah, yeah. He straightened up. Sucked in some air. Kissed her fiercely, angrily.

And then started grabbing for his damned clothes.

"We're in the middle of a conversation here."

"Really? I've never heard that called a conversation before." It was a whispered attempt at humor. But he saw her just miss meeting his eyes. The spell was broken.

"Yeah, well, it *was* a conversation, Red. We were communicating just fine. There's just a whole lot more to say." The pager kept up the relentless buzzing. He still had one sleeve off his sweater when he snatched it, read the code, clicked on his cell and snapped, *"Red"* to the sheriff.

He listened, answered, "Yes," "Yes" and "Yes—" because those were the only answers he could give. But his gaze never left Whitney's face. Once he clicked off, he said, "People need transport to the shelter. Someone may have seen April, the missing kid. The storm's going to get worse before it gets better, not just because we're still due a half dozen inches, but because the wind's edging above thirty-five miles an hour."

She said nothing. But she hadn't stopped looking at him.

That was a hopeful sign, wasn't it? Wasn't it? It had to be.

He charged over, kissed her one more time, shot a frown in her direction. "Whitney, just give me a chance to finish the conversation, okay? I'm not sure when I can be back. But it'll be soon. As soon as I can. And if I can scare up a spare generator, I'll bring it."

CHAPTER FOUR

BY SIX THE next morning, Whitney had set up a mirror in the living room, leaning it against the side of the couch. She stripped down, and opened a package of towel-wipes—a godsend she'd discovered on previous travels. She didn't need the mirror to clean up. She needed the mirror to practice.

"It's fun, isn't it, Red?" she said to her image. "To still find some chemistry after ten years. No, of course I'm not bothered by the breakup, Red. I put all that behind me years and years ago."

The towel wipes were freezing. She burrowed in the duffel for her last set of clean clothes. Old gray cords. An Alpaca purple sweater with a tiny hole in the neck. A double pair of wool socks, Smart Wool, with a crazy bohemian pattern of colors. Down vest.

"Good grief," she continued. "Why would I still care that you threw me out like a weed? Flicked me off like a fly in the summer? Forgot me faster than a dream?" She searched for a scrunchie, couldn't find it, gave up and started brushing her hair. She abruptly remembered Red's hands, slowly shivering through her hair, the sweep of his kiss, the magic and lure of being close to him again.

She threw the brush across the room. It cracked against the far wall. The sound was enormously satisfying.

She grabbed a breakfast bar, then continued her monologue to the mirror with her mouth full. "No. Honestly, Red, I don't want to know why you broke up with me. You did. That's water way, way, *way* over the dam. We both grew up, have great jobs, made great lives. Well. You have a great job. I have a job I hate— but there's no reason you have to know that. I'll be gone as soon as the blizzard's over, so there's no point doing anything but enjoying each other's company. See? See my smile? See how I've got my pride on? I'm tough now. Really and truly. In fact, I've slept with zillions of guys since you…"

Okay. That last part was excessive. She couldn't pull off a lie like that. And the point was that now—unlike ten years ago—she didn't put a problem under the bed anymore. She still cared. That was reality. She still fiercely wanted to be touched by him, to talk to him, to be with him. That yearning was ten years stronger than it had ever been.

More of that crappy reality.

She was leaving in days. The best she could do was to make him think, *Boy, I'm glad I ran into her again. And I sure know why I fell in love with her.* It brought all the good memories back.

Or something like that. She could keep her smile on, and her pride intact, and express honest feelings to him without tearing herself up again. Without tearing him up, either.

And she was sick to bits of roiling this all up in her mind—and heart—again. Time to do something. Her gaze honed on the wooden chest across the room.

She hadn't opened her grandmother's box last night, but now seemed like the perfect time. She knelt down, pulled it closer to the light. The wood was old, probably walnut. Never varnished, but it still had a cared-for sheen. It was an odd size, not as big as a hope chest, but much too big for a regular jewelry box.

She tried the two tarnished brass hinges—they popped open easily, but the lid refused to open. There was no lock, no place for a lock, but there had to be some trick to getting into it.

She bent down, feeling slowly with her palms around the circumference of the box—when out of the blue she heard an odd sound. A high-pitched yip.

Her head shot up.

She couldn't fathom anything outside in this weather, but—unless she imagined it—it sounded like a dog. She stood up, listened again.

The sound didn't repeat, but she couldn't stop thinking that no pet would normally be outside in these conditions. She popped to her feet, yanked an afghan around her shoulders and took a quick hike around the first floor, looking out windows from all directions.

Most of the windows were iced over, revealing little more than daylight. The worst wind had come from the north, which meant nature had sculpted artistic mounds of snow, visible from the south windows. The kitchen faced south, the room comfortingly familiar with its red-and-white tiles and round table. From the back door, she could see a few bare patches in the yard. Her grandparents had put a fruit cellar in the ground, facing that direction, because that was the best chance of snow sweeping free from the cellar doors.

From the east—the downstairs bedroom and bathroom windows—she could see the Atlantic, still roiled up and furious, pounding relentlessly against the stone shore below. When she pushed aside the curtains in the living room, there was nothing in sight but a silent white world. No one was driving or walking. Big fat flakes were coming down, soft and white, covering the ice rink of a road and the earlier drifts.

Definitely no dog.

She returned to the box. She knelt down, and carefully felt every inch, every crevice, every seam. Then again. She was about to give up when apparently she touched just the right spot, and the lid popped open.

The contents made her breath catch. And then the tears came.

THERE'D BEEN ONE bad repercussion from reconnecting with Whitney. Once Red had kissed her—more than kissed her—there'd been no chance of his sleeping the rest of that night.

In principle, that was a good thing, since emergency problems kept tumbling in, one after the other. The sheriff paged him several times about the missing girl, April.

Both parents were out of their minds with worry. No one had reported seeing their daughter, but a neighbor two doors down had reported their dog missing. The pet was described as a copper-and-white mutt, dumber than rock, a runner who wouldn't obey anyone or anything, but despite his faults, the family adored him. The idiot dog had left via the dog door—in the middle of the worst of the blizzard.

Trouble showed up from other fronts. The school was now set up as the town's emergency center, with a kitchen, a gym full of cots, blankets and basic medicines, and a communication center was also up and running there. A tree fell on the McClelland house, poking a hole in their front window, requiring the family to be evacuated. Red made two trips, first for the two kids, then for the dad. By the time he'd deposited them at the school, Delaney reported another rumor. Old Mrs. Churnon had fallen, according to a neighbor. Since she was 100 if she was a day—and still refused to leave her house—Red had no idea how he was going get her inside his John Deere, particularly if she was injured. But he headed there, anyway.

He found her in her dining room. Fallen, just like her neighbor feared. But she'd scooched herself closer to the antique sideboard, and when Red barged in, he found her curled up in a heap of handmade afghans, her hurt ankle propped on a stool, and as far as he could tell, she was a quarter into a bottle of "sipping whiskey." She wasn't that hard to transport, primarily because he could lift her with one hand—she was lighter than air—but there was hell to pay when he tried taking away her bottle.

The stories kept coming, the way blizzard stories always kept coming—and got embellished—but by midafternoon, Red was wiped out. At the school, Delaney predictably made sure he was fed and caffeinated and had snacks to take with him.

They had a minor argument about whether he should bed down there; the school was warm, after all, with enough generator power to keep everyone reasonably comfortable and close to the communications center. Once Red's shift was over, though, he only had one thing on his mind. Getting back to Whitney.

He wasn't sure what to make of their last encounter, but he wasn't about to let it go. He'd never expected to kiss her, or that her response would be explosive. Soul-searing, he thought, even though he'd never say that kind of corny phrase aloud. But that's what it felt like when she kissed him back. When they were teenagers, she was his world.

He never thought he'd feel that again.

He never dreamed he'd even see her again.

There was no chance of leaving the school before three, and then he had to fuel and oil Betsy before he could take off. Outside, the afternoon had turned unexpectedly mystical. The temperature was still blister-cold, but for a few moments, the wind stopped and the snow quit, and it was just a virgin white world out there.

By the time he turned onto Route 1, he owned that white world. There was no sign of life anywhere. The trees were diamond-crusted. The landscape had swirls and whirls and whipped-cream tips, each drift a unique sculpture that never existed before, never would happen the same way again.

Which made him think of Whitney.

Which made him push Betsy's pedal into a burst of speed.

The school shelter had Mabel serving in the kitchen—and thankfully Mabel loved him, because she'd packed and wrapped hot meat loaf sandwiches, mashed potatoes, beans, brownies. He pulled into Whitney's drive, whistling as he grabbed the cooler, smacked on his hat again and hiked to the door.

He rapped, to let her know he was there. But then all the supplies he was carrying started to shift, threatening to tumble, so he used his elbow to twist the door handle and push in. "It's me, Whitney. Red—"

Hell. She was there. Of course she was there. Only place she'd be is by the kerosene heater.... But she had the wooden box open, and when her face lifted in his direction, a river of tears tracked down her cheeks.

"Hey. What's this?" He heeled the door closed,

dropped the cooler of food, yanked off his jacket, pretty much crashed across the room.

She tried to speak. Couldn't. She closed her eyes tight, as if to force back any more tears, and tried swallowing. Swallowed again. "I'm fine."

"Yeah, I can see how fine you are." He swooped an arm around her, not trying to start anything. He just plain needed his arms around her, while he looked wildly around the room, trying to figure out what had upset her. But nothing was out of the ordinary, except for the old box, and contents from that were strewn all over the coffee table.

He took a second look at the stuff. On top of the heap was a short veil, yellowed with age, so fragile he figured it'd fall apart if he touched it. Stacks of letters had been tied up with ribbons—one of the stacks was open, so Whitney must have started reading them. A high-heeled shoe had tipped out of the box. Red. Still inside the box was something silky—looked like lacy lingerie to him. A long, silky nightgown thing. A scent infused all the contents. A perfume. Nothing he'd ever smelled before. Obviously it was musty, the scent faded...but it was flowery. Nothing like Whitney had ever worn. Nothing he'd ever smelled before.

"Okay." Until she could talk, he could only try to fill in some blanks. "The contents of the box...that's what upset you."

She nodded. Hard.

"It was your grandmother's. Isn't that what you told me? That your mom and sister ran across some old records or journals or something, and there was a reference to this box in the attic...."

She shook her head no, then nodded yes. Finally, she sighed, lifted her cheek from his shoulder. "This all started when my mom found some journals in an old dresser of my grandmother's. When my grandmother first got ill, she made entries about getting to the box in the attic, burning it before she died, before anyone saw it."

"Which made your sister and mom so curious they couldn't stand it."

Whitney nodded, combed a hand through her hair, fumbled on the table for a tissue to blow her nose. "I'm sorry you found me crying."

He didn't waste time telling her not to be ridiculous. "So…what does this stuff mean? That made you so sad?"

"Apparently my grandmother was married twice. The first time to a man named Stan. She adored him. He adored her. The trousseau, the lingerie, was from their one-night honeymoon. The day after…he went to Vietnam. He was drafted. So they both knew he was going."

Red guessed what the bad news was. "He didn't make it home?"

"He didn't make it home." She had to blow her nose again. "But that's only part of it. She was pregnant. From that one night. The thing was, they'd eloped. Their parents didn't know. Their parents already violently objected to their relationship, because they were both 'too young.' Not counting that Stan had a high number in the draft pool."

"Which meant he was bound to get called up for Vietnam."

"Yes. When she found out she was pregnant, she wrote him. She'd just sent it off when she received notice from the Army that he was killed in action." A new flood of tears sparkled in her eyes like diamonds. "Red, she was pregnant with my dad. And I don't know ex-

actly what happened then. Apparently she never wrote
about Stan in her later journals, because my mom didn't
know about Gram's first husband from reading those.
So all I could do was piece together what happened."

She kept trying to quit crying.

"I guess," she said, "that she knew my grandfather,
Jack. They were friends. And it's not as if she *had* to
be married, in those times, but she wanted a man who
loved children, who'd be an active dad. A man she didn't
have to lie to. So they got married within weeks of her
Stan dying. Made out like my father was premature.
Never told anyone. She made all the history with Stan
disappear. No one knew about it. But she wouldn't have
kept these things if she ever really stopped loving him."

"You think—" Red grappled for something to clarify what had upset her most "—that she never got over
him."

"I'm positive she didn't." One heave of a sigh, and
she started pulling it together, looked at him. "I don't
doubt she loved my grandfather. I saw them together all
those years. They had a wonderful marriage. Still. Loving and being in love are two different things."

He said carefully, "And some people never forget
their first loves."

Weird, but the room suddenly went silent. Even the
propane heater stopped its soft hiss. Candles stopped
sputtering. He stopped breathing for just that second.

Maybe she did, too.

Out of the complete blue, she suddenly said softly,
"No."

"No what?"

"I missed you, Red. For a long time. And it hurt when
you broke it off. For a long time. But I don't want to
know why. Not anymore."

He didn't hear a door slam. Except in his heart. To-night he'd come here, hoping to spill the whole thing, why he'd broken it off, what had happened. "Why don't you want to hear?"

"Because whatever you did ten years ago…however I reacted ten years ago…there's no way to wear that size shoes again. We wouldn't do the same things, say the same things, feel the same things."

"That's true," he said, but his throat felt thick, and his heart started this heavy thud thing. He'd just been so sure those wild kisses had meant something to her. He'd thought, if she still cared, that she'd want to know why he'd called off the relationship. If not, well…maybe that volatile embrace had only ignited forest fires for him.

She suddenly rubbed her eyes, stood up. "I need a few seconds to clean up," she said swiftly.

"No sweat. Like I said, I brought dinner."

"I can't say I'm hungry…."

Yeah, right. That lasted until she returned and saw the meatloaf and the brownies. She dove in, although as soon as she'd swallowed enough to ward off starva-tion, she said gently, "Red. I'm sorry."

For not loving him? For not thinking those kisses knocked desire right out of the park? "For what?" he asked, as if he wanted to know.

"For being…thoughtless. The crying, the spill-out. If I hurt your feelings…"

"Hey, you didn't." He was pretty sure if he pulled the knife out of his heart, he'd bleed out. But she didn't need to know that. "You had quite a surprise handed to you."

She nodded. "It was. First, to find out that my grand-mother had been married before. To the father of my dad. And then…I'm not sure what to say to Jane and my mom. I could tell them there was a box, but it had been destroyed by mold or mildew or something. Or tell them the truth."

"Which do you think?"

"I don't know. I don't want to lie. But my first instinct is to do what my grandmother wanted. It was her secret, that she chose to keep. And in that journal my mom found, my grandmother clearly intended to destroy the box before she died or anyone found it." She motioned with a brownie.

"What?"

"Put tape over my mouth, would you? I've been talking about nothing but me. Tell me about the storm, the adventures today. Any news of the little girl? I hope no one's been hurt."

She cleaned up the food and collected the debris in the cooler—after he took out a Thermos to share. The contents were hot coffee, with a pinch of whiskey for a warmer. Donated by the emergency crew, he told her. She knew half of them from high school.

"They were always good guys," she recalled.

He relayed some of the day's tales, got her laughing at the story of Mrs. Churnon—who she remembered. And the McClelland family rescue. Then how the whole community was still hanging on for any rumor about the missing April.

"Everybody who comes into the shelter, we ask. I still think she's holed up in someone's house. Anyone would have let her in. And they might not have been able to tell authorities where she was, with the power outages and everything."

"And this is the second day. Darn scary. No word at all?"

"Nothing. The only news was about some dog missing in that general area."

"Really? I thought I heard a dog earlier."

Once the minor chores were done, he'd crashed on one side of the couch—the side that had had a bad spring for as far back as he could remember. But now, he came to full alert. "You saw a dog?"

"No. I was sure I heard a bark, but I went from window to window, looking for a dog or tracks or any sign of movement." She shook her head.

"Well, there's no reason to think there's a connection between the kid and the dog. But she loves the dog, apparently. Went over to their house to visit it quite often. She wanted a dog, had been begging for one for ages, and I guess that got more intense after her parents told her they were splitting up. Still. The dog's a total mutt and already has its own family." He relaxed again. Or attempted to look relaxed. He tried out a tone easier than butter to ask her, "Hey. You never said. Is there a guy waiting in the wings? Fiancé, guy friend, whatever."

"Don't, Red."

"Don't what?"

She settled on the couch, too—but on the opposite side. Red figured she was trying to make sure no serious body parts could accidentally touch. The couch was older than the hills. Possibly older than the start of the country. But it was a long sucker.

"I've slept with half the men in Philadelphia. Found a lot of great guys, but I'm not married. Collected three or four kids out of wedlock." She smirked. "See? You don't want to ask me questions where you don't want to hear the answer."

Man, she was touchy. He tried pouring her another mug of hooch-flavored coffee. "I've got an idea. This time you ask *me* a question, so I have the chance to get all crabby about it."

She didn't want to grin, but she did. And then she cocked her head and turned serious. "I was confused about what you told me yesterday. You said you started working with your dad in the construction business—when you left school your freshman year. But why did you leave U of M? Something must have happened?"

"Oh, yeah." He was ultrawary of bringing up any heavy material in the memory department, but he sensed—hell, he knew—that Whitney was vulnerable. At least vulnerable about the two of them. She wouldn't have turned so touchy if the past was easy for her to talk about. And this was history he had trouble getting past himself.

But he tried. Sat up, parked his feet on the floor, elbows on his knees.

"When I started at U of M, right from that first semester, I practiced with the team." He didn't have to say the football team. She knew. "I didn't expect to play. They scout out QBs from high schools, but it's pretty rare they let a newbie play, especially that first year. Too much to learn. High school ball is way different than college ball."

She waited while he chugged down a gulp of coffee. She'd always listened.

"But the third game out, the quarterback got the flu. Puked his guts out in the locker room because he didn't want to tell Coach, didn't want to be benched. But he was sick as a dog. Anyway, Coach put me in. I got my first shot at some glory, threw a pass that turned into a touchdown."

She shot him a big thumbs-up with a grin to match it.

"Okay. That was the good game. But the next game—the following Saturday—the ace quarterback was in the hospital with pneumonia by then. Coach had

only let me play the week before because we were playing a Podunk team—but this second game was more
competitive, so he put the backup QB in. That's how
it should be. Nothing weird. In fact, I had no idea why
Coach gave me that shot the week before. But I found
out. The backup QB was beyond lousy. He had speed
but no brains, no sense for the game. Right off, we lost
two scores, and then he caused a fumble because of a
rotten pass. Coach benched him. Put me in."

Any other girl would have made him hurry. He knew
how tedious it was for nonplayers to hear the blow-by-
blow. But damn. Whitney'd always listened. She knew
the game. Probably because he had always loved football so much he couldn't stop talking about it.

"So I get in there. Guards should have been close, but
they bumbled, weren't where they were supposed to be.
I'm stuck with the ball, nowhere to throw it, their big
boys coming right at me. So I had to run with it. Two
guys took me down, both bigger than horses. Well, *one*
took me down. The other fell on top of him. Just for the
record, I kept the ball."

Her stocking foot gave him a short kick. Her smile
was rueful, impatient.

"I'm telling you as fast as I can. But this isn't the fun
part. I know how to take a fall. But it was just the way I
was hit, the way I went down. Nobody's fault. But my
right knee and ankle were both broken."

Her expression changed immediately. Her hand shot
out to touch his shoulder. "How bad?"

"Bad. The knee was a mess. Ended up at John Hop-
kins for a total reconstruct. The ankle was just a basic
break, but by then it didn't much matter. That was the
end of the athletic scholarship. The end of competitive
sports for me altogether. When my dad picked me up,

I had casts and crutches and an attitude. Nobody could live with me. Surprised my mom didn't beat me over the head."

"Aw, Red." Her whisper was as soft as a caress.

"My dad never said anything. Just let me stew and do nothing and swear all over the place and watch stupid television. When the casts came off, that was another hell. I'd lost all muscle tone. It was like learning to walk all over again. And it all hurt, which was fine with me, because I wanted to be mad at something. But by spring, my dad came in one day, just told me to come with him. Put me up in a dozer. Pointed me at a cement wall that needed taking down. He said, 'go have fun.'"

"Did you?"

"I beat the cement wall to smithereens. Went back to my dad. He gave me another project, this one with a back hoe, digging a hole for a new massive swimming pool. He stayed around while I did that one. It had to be right. I knew how to work the dozer, but not the back hoe so much. Dad never asked me if I wanted a job. You knew my dad. He didn't talk much. He just let me take out a lot of anger and frustration and loss and all that crap. By working. And then…"

"Then what? What happened?"

"End of that summer." Red shook his head. "Hard to talk about. Even now. Dad and I came home after a really long, really hot day. We'd poured on the coals. Wrapped up a good job, put the check in the bank. Put our feet up on the back porch, and Dad offered me a beer—like he hadn't had a fit my whole life about not drinking underage. He popped the top on his and fell over. Like that. One minute happy. I mean we were both tired. But he was still *happy*. I know damn well he loved working with me. We'd never been so close. I

almost laughed, thought he was playing some joke—
until I realized he wasn't moving. Wasn't breathing."

He had to quit talking. That was all he had to say,
anyway. And Whitney said nothing for a moment, just
looked at him with something so big and bright in her
eyes that he had to look away. Maybe that's why he
didn't see her move. She'd never been much on athlet-
ics, except for gymnastics. When she launched herself across the couch, she wasn't exactly flying—she
was looking right at him—but she did kind of a slow
catapult.

Straight into his arms.

She said fiercely, "I *hate* that story, Red." And then
she kissed him. "I hate it about the injuries." Another
kiss. "I hate it about it screwing up all the goals and
dreams you had." Another kiss. "I hate it that you were
badly hurt and I never knew." Another kiss. "I hate it
that your dad died. That you lost him and he lost you.
It's an awful, awful story and I hated every single word
of it."

He had the oddest feeling that he was being seduced.
Since all she was talking about was hate, hate, hate,
that seemed unlikely. But between kisses, her down
vest sailed across the room, then her purple sweater.

In spite of all that aggression on her part, he probably could have stopped this, considering that she was
moving slowly. Her vest did a slow sail. Those kisses
of hers were melding soft, melting slow.

He figured he had two choices. To either put a serious stop to this, make sure she was doing something
she wanted to do.

Or he could try to catch up.

Back when, she was the one with all As and he was
the one who had to work hard for a C. Still, this was

a no-brainer. And years ago, he'd understood instinctively that sometimes she needed something from him that had nothing to do with IQ.

Apart from which, he could peel off clothes way, way faster than she could.

CHAPTER FIVE

WHITNEY KNEW SHE was going to get hurt…and didn't care. Maybe she'd come home hoping to affirm how over him she was. Instead, she seemed to be falling all over again.

But right now, that just didn't matter. This wasn't about her. It was about him, thinking about how his whole world had crashed his freshman year, losing his dad, losing his dreams. She hadn't been there for him then. His choice. But she wanted to be here for him now, even if it was only for a short time during a blizzard, even if she never saw him again.

Maybe she'd never mattered enough to him before.

But he'd mattered to her. He still mattered to her.

Her mouth picked up a tremble. Too much kissing, too much pressure. Too much promise. Clothes stuck and bunched and got in the way. Chilly drafts assaulted bare skin from all directions. But she assaulted those drafts…and so did he. Every stroke, every nuzzle into his neck, his shoulder, against him, created a blast furnace of heat.

He found her breast, cupped it, groaned as if he'd just discovered hunger. That discovery inspired him to explore some more. Even if the couch required him to be a contortionist, he somehow managed to trace the shape of her right breast with his tongue. Then her left. And then he simply nuzzled his face between the two,

rubbing his cheek against them, his lips, his tongue...
it was a deja vu. But not. He'd always been relentlessly
crazy about her breasts.

But he was so much more man now. The look in
his eyes was no longer boyish and impatient. It was
shiver-provoking. The fire in his eyes burned with
knowledge—knowledge that he knew how to please
her. Knew how to wring every second of desire and
torture from these moments. Knew where and how to
touch, in the ways that would make her go wild. Always
had. Always would.

Sounds surrounded them. Laughter. Groans. Cries.
Yearning moans.

Scents intensified her awareness. The pumpkin and
lemon candles. Dust. The shampoo he'd always used,
nothing sweet, just a scent she always knew as his. His
skin, healthy, warm sweat.

And then there were the textures. His textures. The
callouses on his hands. The tough muscle in his upper
arms and shoulders, smooth, taut, unyielding. His chest
hair, just enough to splay through her hands, to feel
that crisp hair fold around her fingers. The throb of his
Adam's apple. The wet-satin of his lips. The impossibly hard, warm, sleek feel of him...right before he
stroked, tested and then entered her on a single long,
sweet plunge.

She closed her eyes on a gasp of breath. They'd been
so young before. There'd been need and desire and excitement, but nothing like this. This was the two of
them melding together. Playing off each other's yearning. Coaxing each other's vulnerability.

Skin against skin, heartbeat against heartbeat.... She
came first, let loose a soar of a cry.

Then Red.

And then all she was conscious of, for a long time, was the warmth and weight of him, the precious stroke of his hand, the tenderness in his gaze. He moved, only to shift the bulk of his weight, and to pull something around her so she wasn't cold. She didn't move at all. Couldn't imagine wanting to move again in this lifetime.

The lemon candle went out. The pumpkin burned down halfway. Shadows played on the wall; slow, soft shadows, of his hand stroking her back, her cheek.

"I hate to admit this," he said finally, "but I'm falling asleep."

"It's okay."

"I don't *want* to sleep. It's just that I've been up so many hours that—"

"Red. Close your eyes. Let go. There's no reason you can't sleep right here."

"But I want to talk to you. Not to waste time sleeping. Whitney—I didn't tell you about losing the scholarship and all that past history to make you feel sorry for me."

"Tough. I feel terribly sorry for you. And I'm extra sorry about you losing your dad."

"I remember when you lost yours. When you first moved into your grandparents' place. I didn't know who you were, but I remember seeing you. Sitting on the rocks over the beach. Just looking at the ocean. So beautiful. So impossibly sad."

"I adored my dad. But I could never please him. When he died…it was like I'd lost any chance to finally do something that he'd be proud of me for. I mean, I never doubted that he loved me…" Maybe she should have expected it, that being with Red would bring old memories to the surface. She'd probably said the exact same things to him years ago.

"But he was a fisherman. Rough and tumble, in a way you could never be." Red brushed the side of her cheek. "But I always thought you were wrong about him, Whitney. I think he loved you for yourself."

"I know he loved me. He just never felt a connection. When I came home with a report card, top in my class, he gave me a big hug. When Jane soloed on a sailboat, he threw her a party." She shook her head. "It wasn't his fault. He just kind of saw me as an alien."

"Well, hell. I always thought you were an alien, too."

Her eyes widened, and then she thwacked him solidly with a couch pillow. His grin was full of devilment. It was the thing he'd always done. Make her able to laugh at herself. Shake her out of her serious side.

"Hey," he said suddenly.

"What?"

"I missed you, Snow White."

She froze. Not because of the cold. Not because she minded his teasing. But because, back in high school, he'd turned that tag kids used to call her behind her back into something endearing, cherishing. The kids thought she was a prude. Too goody-goody to have any real fun.

"When you first asked me out," she said slowly, "I was more than surprised. All the girls chased you. You had a reputation for going out with any girl you wanted. And I had a reputation for never giving in. I always figured the kids must have laid a pretty big bet for you to ask me out."

"Yup, they did." He admitted it, meeting her eyes, then added quietly, "But I didn't take it, Whitney. In fact, I threw a punch to the guy who suggested the bet."

"You never told me that." He'd never told her a lot of

things, she thought, and suddenly felt a stab of hurt. It was awful, what he'd been through his freshman year.

But she could have been there for him. That was their plan—to go to the same university, to stick together, the two of them, together forever. A romantic, stupid plan, maybe. A plan that might not have worked. But he was the one who'd shut it off, the spring before. Not her.

"What?" he asked suddenly. "What are you thinking?"

She shrugged, tried to make her voice light and easy. "We're talking as if it were all yesterday. As if we were still two green-behind-the-ears kids who were wildly in love."

"I *was* wildly in love with you." He must have seen skepticism in her eyes, because he tensed, lifted a hand as if to touch her cheek.

His pager went off. She heard it, knew he had, too.

"You don't believe me?" he asked. "Whitney? You *had* to know how much I loved you—"

His pager buzzed again. Darn it, it wasn't as if either of them could forget they were in a blizzard. Whitney knew his being part of the emergency team had to take priority. People's lives could be at stake.

He started to say something else to her, but when the pager went off for a third time, he made an exasperated sound and lurched off the couch. Buck naked, he stalked over to his parka, dove in the pockets for the device. He half turned, as he took in the message, giving her a view of his delectably tight butt. When he turned back, though, she already knew he was leaving.

"I have to go." His voice was a low growl.

"You haven't had any sleep."

"Mr. Verdan took out his snowblower. Thought he'd tackle the first couple of layers while the wind wasn't blowing so bad. Something happened. He's trapped in the blades."

"Oh, God."

"The three on the closest team are all called in. Doesn't matter if anyone's off shift or not. Chances are the storm'll be over in another twenty-four hours— except for the cleanup. Hell. Where are my damned socks?"

He was pulling on clothes fast and furiously. Missing buttons. The sweatshirt askew. And the socks, of course, were right where he'd hurled them off the couch.

She pulled an afghan around her shoulders, started helping him, scared up his mittens, then his snow hood. Her heart wanted to curl up in a fetal position and do a coma thing for a while. He was so right about the storm being over in another twenty-four hours. Blizzards and tornadoes, no matter how horrible, never lasted forever.

She'd be leaving then.

She had no excuse in the universe to see him again.

When he opened the door, he was still grumbling and swearing under his breath. The cold poured in on a blast of icy air, but he still turned back, turned to her, smacked a bruising-hard kiss on her mouth. "I'll be back. As soon as I possibly can."

And then he was gone.

It was as if someone stole her sunshine. Her smile faded the instant the door closed, and over the next couple hours, she pulled on clothes, straightened everything, cleaned up as best she could. By the time she curled back on the couch, hoping to sleep, her mind refused to stop racing, her heart beating to an anxious treadmill.

Regrets? None, she told herself. Only…it was just like before. She'd felt close to Red, closer than she'd felt with anyone, ever. Loving him couldn't possibly be wrong. But he'd left her life before, and she had no reason to believe it would be different this time. What he called "love" seemed to be terribly different from how she defined it.

She'd punched the couch pillow several times, turned and turned again, refixed all the blankets and covers… and when her eyes finally closed, she heard a yipping sound.

The sound seemed to be coming from the kitchen.

This time she didn't waste time opening her eyes. She'd bought into that nonsense last time, but now she knew better. It was an old, creaky house. The wind could make sounds that appeared human or animal. Nothing new. Nothing interesting. If she were going to be afraid of something, it'd be her feelings for Red— not fear of imaginary critters in a snowstorm.

Until she heard three more yips.

She yanked off the covers, thinking this was all Red's fault. She wasn't sure how he was responsible, but he was. She grabbed a flashlight, stalked out of the cozy warm living room to the freezing cold hall, stomped into the kitchen.

She spotted them immediately—the two grimy intruders huddled on the floor behind the table. Or sort of behind. Their heads and faces showed in the light. One—a midsize copper-and-white mutt—was wagging his tail hard enough to knock down mountains. Clearly he didn't mind being found. But the little one—it had to be April. The missing child. She was wrapped up in gunny sacks, the kind potatoes or onions were stored in sometimes, with dirt streaks tracking her tears, her blond hair hanging in tangles under a filthy hat. She was shivering so hard that her features were blurred.

"Holy camoly." She herded them both out of their hiding place, out into the hall, into the living room close by the heater. So many things needed doing that she could barely figure out which was first. Warmth. Water. Food. Reassurance. And Whitney needed answers to a zillion questions.

Yes, the little girl was April Shuster. "But I didn't know it was snowing that hard. I wasn't looking around at first. And then I did, and everything was a whiteout. I couldn't see the street. I couldn't see anything. But then Copper…" Clearly her name for the mutt. "Copper found me, and I found him, so we stayed together."

"Honey, you've been out since Sunday night? Two nights?"

April nodded. Even though Whitney had immediately wrapped her in covers, her teeth were still chattering. Red had left her a Thermos of coffee, and she urged the child to take a sip. Maybe coffee was the worst choice, but at least the liquid was warm. Whitney scrabbled through her supplies, searching for bread, peanut butter, water bottles.

"We're really hungry, though. We've been eating peaches. And pears. And beans. But we're sick of those. And Copper doesn't like any of them."

"Peaches?"

"Yeah. In jars. You know. Like when you can stuff in the summer."

Whitney did know. The picture started to come together. They'd hidden in the fruit cellar. And after her grandfather died, apparently no one remembered to make sure the fruit cellar was cleared out. The gunny sacks might not be fancy, but they would have at least added layers on top of her hat and jacket.

"But April—how did you get in the house here?" The

girl was still gobbling the peanut butter, the dog was gobbling the second sandwich. Whitney made a third, then took one of her wet towels from the package and started a serious swipe of April's little face.

"I just opened the back door. I guess I could have done it before. But I just assumed it was locked. And I didn't know if it was okay. But Copper and me, we really, really, *really* got hungry. And maybe we were getting a little scared."

The door was unlocked. All this time the door was unlocked.

"Whitney?"

"What, honey?" With the first layer of grime off, she found big blue eyes. Chapped lips. A heart-shaped face.

"Copper and me. We had to go to the bathroom in the fruit cellar. Because it was too cold outside. We couldn't help it."

"Don't worry about it. It's not a problem."

"But I also broke one of the jars. There's broken glass near the ladder stairs." Her face was still lifted so Whitney could keep cleaning it. "I didn't mean to break it. There was this tool to open jars on the top shelf. But I didn't do it right the first time. And I dropped the jar."

"There's another no sweat, April. I could care less about a broken jar. I'm just glad you weren't hurt."

"I was really cold, though. My dad says fruit cellars in the ground never get as cold as freezing, if they're made right. So maybe it wasn't freezing, but it was *freezing.* Even with all the stuff I had on and all the sacks I made beds and blankets out of and even with Copper sleeping next to me, I was still cold."

"I'll bet you were." It could have been so much worse, Whitney knew. She started cleaning the little girl's hands. "We have to find a way to tell your dad and mom that you're here and safe."

The sweet smile disappeared. "They won't care if I'm gone."

"Oh?"

"All they talk about is divorce, divorce, divorce. And all they care about is fighting. They fight all the time about who's meaner, who's the worst person." April sighed. "I feel like a towel."

"A towel?"

"You know. Like something in the bathroom that's just always there. But nothing anyone cares about. I don't matter to them anymore."

"April, I'm positive that you do. They've been looking high and low for you. They've got the whole town searching."

"Maybe. But if I really mattered to them, they'd be together like they used to be. They'd be a mom and dad like they were."

"Maybe they can't do that."

"They can. They don't want to. But I go to dad's place and he doesn't have the right kind of peanut butter. And he doesn't get me to school on time. And I go back to mom's, like Sunday before school? And she wasn't even there and I didn't know where she was. That was the thing. No one knew where I was. Nobody cared. So I left."

"Did you have a plan for where you were going?"

"I had *two* plans. I'm not dumb, you know. The first plan was to go to the library. Because there's a sign there that says it's a safe place. And in the kids' section there are bean bags and couches where you can lie down if you want."

"And the other place?"

"I was going to go to Christina's house."

"She's your best friend?"

"Well, yeah. Otherwise why would I go there if I didn't know her?"

"How far to Christina's house?"

"A ways. Her mom and dad moved to Bangor a couple months ago. Bangor is a little ways from here."

"Yes, I'd say so." Whitney watched the little girl's eyelids start fluttering. She was exhausted, but she didn't want to stop talking. After lapping up a bowl of water and two peanut butter sandwiches, the dog had crashed in a coma at her feet. April, though, snuggled into the covers, and even when her eyes closed, she still kept on.

"We used to have fun all the time. We'd go to movies sometimes. And we'd skate in the winter, the three of us. Mom took me crabbing in the summer. Dad'd take me to the library. But now Mom has to work, so I have to go to a babysitter after school, like I'm a *baby*. And when she gets home, she's too tired to do anything. And I'm supposed to see my dad only at these certain times. It doesn't matter if I want to play with a friend that Saturday. It's Dad time. And I *want* to be with my dad, but not when it's like going to the doctor. You know. Where you have to make an appointment and then you go there, and you still have to wait because he's busy."

Whitney wanted to listen—and she desperately wanted to contact Red, or anyone, to let them know April was with her. The child was talking with her eyes closed—and still had her eyes closed when Whitney guided her to the bathroom, then back to the nest on the couch.

"Here's the thing," April said as Whitney pulled off her shoes and started zipping her into the sleeping bag.

"They tell me all the time they love me. But that's not how it is. When they're fighting, I could sleep on the kitchen table and they wouldn't notice. I could eat all the ice cream. I could fall on my bike and be really hurt. I try to be good. I try and try. It doesn't matter."

She let out a deep sigh…and was gone, out like a light. Whitney finished tucking her in, feeling a heart full of empathy. Their situation wasn't identical. April was hurt by her family having so much on their minds that they stopped *seeing* her.

But Whitney remembered feeling invisible—remembered trying so hard to be a good girl, to do the right things. Yet she could never seem to measure up to what people wanted from her.

It was why Red dropping her had hurt so much. She mattered to him. She'd been so sure. She'd never thought *he* would drop her like a hot potato and never look back.

Her heart flashed back to making love with him, just hours ago, in downright uncomfortable conditions—not pretty, romantic circumstances. Yet he'd made her feel treasured. Cherished. Uniquely wanted, by him. With him. With each other.

What was she supposed to believe? What she felt in her heart? Or what she rationally knew he'd done to her in the past?

And darn it, she had no time to think about this right now. She had to find a way to let April's parents know that their daughter was safe. It hadn't mattered before that her cell phone was dead—if there was no other way, she could chip the ice off the rental car, hope the car started and try recharging her phone that way. But there had to be other things she could try.

She scrounged around the house, found empty cabinets, a naked linen closet, but finally, on a shelf in the laundry room, an old red stadium blanket. She yanked on a jacket, hat and gloves, and grabbed a hammer and tacks. Her first step outside, the wind slapped her face so sharply it stung her eyes. She couldn't last long out here, and she was sure no carpenter. She did what she could—a messy, uneven job—but she managed to hammer the red blanket to the frame on the door.

By the time she got back in the house, her fingers were numb, her cheeks were apple-red and her eyelashes felt frozen solid. She was shivering too hard to get her jacket off.

For just a few minutes, she sank down by the couch, her back to the heater. Her charges were both fast asleep, the mutt at one end of the couch, April at the other. She just wanted a few minutes to warm up, get some feeling back in her hands.... She had no memory of dropping off, until a rap on the door startled her awake.

She'd been curled up on the carpet with her head on the couch next to April. Her muscles felt cramped and stiff, but at the sound of the knock, she bounced to her feet. Instinct ruled over sense.

She ran to the door and hurled it open, an exuberant *"Red!"* already out of her mouth...when she abruptly realized that it wasn't Red at all.

CHAPTER SIX

THE STRANGER LOOKED dumbfounded when she greeted him with wide open arms, but she dropped them quickly, and once he started talking, that initial embarrassing moment eased. It just never occurred to her that anyone but Red would stop by.

The man wasn't particularly tall, but he had thirty years on Red, eyes that were a soft, kind blue, and a naturally reassuring smile.

"I'm Frank Hart, miss. I'm an extra on the auxiliary team. Saw the red blanket. Figured you were sending an SOS."

"I was. I am. The missing girl—April Shuster—she's here. She's safe, she's okay. Come in, out of the cold. Where's Red?"

"He got caught up—a store in town, the roof caved in, debris all over Oak Street. It had to be cleared right away, because it was blocking access to the school and health services. So Red's Betsy is on that. I've got my Massey snowblower, so I can pretty much get anywhere, but I can't clear away debris the way Red's equipment can. He'll get free at some point, but while I was doing my side of Pine, thought I'd trek this way, make sure his section was covered. So you found April?"

"Yes. She's here. Sleeping." She motioned him in.

Frank entered, but only far enough to shut the door. He pulled off his hat and unbuttoned his jacket, but he seemed determined to park on the front door mat and not intrude any farther. He spotted the two sleeping bodies on the couch, shook his head.

"Her parents have been beside themselves."

"So I heard." She relayed the story of how April and the dog had holed up in the fruit cellar, eating from jars of fruit and vegetables. "She's dirty, and she was really hungry, but overall, I think she was amazingly resourceful. She managed to keep herself warm enough and safe. I can't see any sign of illness or harm."

He stepped closer quietly, assessing the girl, the dog, the room and then turned back to her.

"I guess I can take her to the school shelter. Afraid it won't be the most comfortable trip in my tractor—"

Whitney interrupted without thinking. "I think she should stay here."

Frank raised his eyebrows in question.

"I know. It's not my right to say. But she's really unhappy about her parents divorcing. That's why she ran away. And I think it'd be better if she knows, before she leaves here, where both of them are. What's going to happen to her. And besides, she's really attached to the dog."

The older man hesitated. "Whitney? Ms. Brennan. You really know she should go to the school, don't you? You don't have food or running water here. And there're liability issues."

"I know. I know. I'm in the wrong. But I have make-do food for a couple of days yet, and even though I can't get her clean, I can keep her warm. And she'll be able to stay with the dog for a little longer." She tried her most soulful eyes on him. "You don't really want to wake her up in the middle of the night, do you? Drag her out in the cold? Take her to that huge school, when we don't even know where her parents are right now?"

He sighed. "Anyone ever tell you you've got a soft heart?"

"I'll be happy to hand her over when it's time. But… she was unhappy and scared, and she won't be while she's with me. I just—"

"Ayuh. You got a soft heart. I get it." He sighed. "All right. I'll radio in to the school pronto. Make sure the parents know she's safe first off. And then the next volunteer this way can bring you more food—and dog food to boot. Last weather report claimed the blow and the snow will both stop by late this afternoon. Of course, a lot of cleanup before people can get back to their houses or get supplies. But it won't be that long before power starts coming back. We're on the right end of the storm, finally."

Her heart clutched. Of course, she knew the storm couldn't go on forever, but she assumed she'd have another full day. And with all the work Red had been doing, he had to be beyond exhausted. It hit her heart like a blow—what if she didn't see him once the roads were cleared? She had to get home, to her job. She had to communicate with her family. It wasn't as if she didn't have to hightail it out of here as soon as possible.

Mr. Hart was yanking on his hat again, pulling out his gloves. He glanced at the little girl, then back at her. "She's lucky she found you."

"More like I'm the lucky one."

"Ayuh. I know Red. Remember you two in high school. Girls flocked after him, but you, you were the only one with sweetness in you, and he never looked at a soul after he found you. I knew Red's dad. He saw the same."

Her cheeks flushed. "Good grief. I can't believe you'd remember either of us."

"Well, my son was two years younger than you two. So I was around the school a lot. And you know Tucker's Point. Once the 'summer complaints' are gone, we get to huddle back into our own little community and watch over each other."

She'd forgotten that Mainers used "summer complaints" to describe the tourists.

"Frank…when Red's dad died, where did his mom and sisters go?"

"Oh, now. She bolted for Portland before his stone was set in the ground. Couldn't bear the idea of another Maine winter alone, as she put it. Both she and the younger girl wanted more of a city life." A wry grin creased his cheeks. "She calls him all the time."

"Red?"

"Ayuh. She always did. If he doesn't answer on a first ring, she's likely to call the whole town until she locates him. He's good to his mother, very good, but he doesn't jump when she calls. It's like all family. There's always one that drives the rest crazy."

"That's so true," she murmured, thinking about her sister and her mom. But she'd never thought of Red having female relatives who badgered him. Red always seemed so easy with family. With everyone. She'd never seen him lose his temper, or talk anyone down. It just wasn't his way.

"Well, here I am gossiping, and I need to be back on the road. If someone isn't heading in this direction in a matter of hours, I'll come back myself, make sure you've got those extra supplies before long. Not to worry. I don't suppose there's a chance you might move into your grandparents' house?"

She felt an odd lump in her throat. "I love this old house."

"It's a sound one."

"But I have a job in Philadelphia."

"I understand. Just hard for me and the missus to think about strangers living here. Our grandfather, he loved the ocean. As did your father. I guess for some the sea renews a soul, and for some, it's just salt water."

She chuckled. "If that isn't a Maine saying, it should be."

After she closed the door and watched his red tractor back out of the driveway, she stood there for long minutes, feeling oddly bemused and restless. She didn't know Frank. But she did. The core people who lived here always seemed to accept each other. Watch out for their neighbors. And she'd never thought about it, but what he'd said was true. The people who loved out here were those who valued the sea, who took strength from it. A storm was just a storm. It didn't take away from the natural wonder of the ocean.

She spun around, absently rubbed the back of her neck, thinking that somehow, she'd finally figured it out.

She had to see Red, for certain, before leaving Tucker's Point.

She'd waited for him before, a long time ago...and he never came through. But this time, she wanted clear answers from him.

And she wasn't leaving without them.

PREDAWN, RED staggered into the school, so tired he could hardly put one foot in front of the other. Inside was a world of warmth and quiet. He passed by the gym where cots were filled up with storm refugees. The only

bright lights in sight came from the cafeteria kitchen—
where, of course, he immediately headed.

A lone body stood near the sink counter. Mrs.
Bartholomew—or Mrs. B, as kids had called her for
generations—was the retired school cook who invari-
ably manned the kitchen in times of crisis. In looks, she
was a Mrs. Claus clone, plump and round, with wild
white hair and pink cheeks.

She was a good cook, but tart. Like he'd done dozens
of times since first grade, he found a tray of cookies
cooling on the counter…and she slapped his hand with
a spoon before he could steal his first bite.

"That's beyond cruel," he told her.

"You were a wicked little boy, and here you're grown
up and you're still a thief."

"Hey. Only of cookies. Your cookies."

She scowled when he stole another one, but she didn't
slap him this time. "You've got circles under your eyes
bigger than craters. Do you really need an eighty-two-
year-old woman to tell you that you seriously need
sleep?"

"Nope. I knew that. I just can't quite fit in rest yet.
I need a special care package from you."

"I didn't just fall off the turnip truck, you know."
Mrs. B paced over to the far stainless-steel counter,
where she had assorted boxes taped up. "Dog food,
enough for two days. Kibble, but also two soup bones
and a rawhide toy. Then for the little girl, mac and
cheese—it'll stay warm through lunch. Peanut butter
and banana sandwiches. Cookies. An apple and a peach.
Milk and juice boxes. Then for Whitney—bless her
heart for looking after those two. Such a sweet one.
Good to know she's back here, but I wish she'd stay.

And I wish you'd had the brains to marry her when you had the chance."

Thankfully, she had to take a breath, so he could get a word in. "I never had the chance."

"You're an adult. You make the chance. Don't give me excuses. And the point being that I made a little tenderloin for her—not fancy, can't cook that fancy in a school kitchen, but I fussed a bit with some rubbings and a little orange tarragon sauce—"

"All this, with everything else you're doing?"

"Why do you think there are so many ovens in a school kitchen? Don't answer that. If you had a brain, you wouldn't have asked. Point is, there's enough for two. I hope she eats it all, but conceivably there's enough for you. And I was doing a warm winter lemon cake, so I cut a few pieces ahead for a nice dessert. No salad. There's no more fresh food until we're over this storm. But I'm guessing you could scare up a bottle of nice wine, if you thought about it."

"I already thought about it."

"What you need is sleep. Quit gallivanting around town. The snow'll wait now. No one asked you to kill yourself."

"But I need to take the food and supplies—"

"No, you don't. I heard three others offer. But no, you wouldn't have anyone going there but you. What you're forgetting, though, is that you're going over there with bags under your eyes and whiskers and the same clothes you've been wearing all day. Ask me, that's no way to set up a nice dinner, but what do I know? I'm only eighty-two."

"Can I kiss you on the cheek, or are you going to hit me again?"

"Get out of here. I have a breakfast to put on for some

seventy people in a couple hours. You think I have time to chitchat with you all morning?"

He risked his life and another tongue lashing to give her a thank-you kiss on the cheek, then packed up his loot and headed back outside.

The cold and wind were getting old. The slap of icy air gave him a temporary brace of energy, but he knew he couldn't keep on much longer without sleep. Still, Whitney and the little girl—and apparently a dog— needed food. And he needed to see Whitney.

Even if he was exhausted to the point of coma, he needed to see Whitney.

Betsy had been plugged in and fueled, but she still did a lot of gasping and groaning, turning onto Route 1. She'd had enough of battling the elements, too.

He'd heard the whole story from Frank, about April and the dog and how Whitney had taken them in and asked for help with the flapping red blanket. Frank told him about how pretty Whitney looked—even prettier than when she was in high school. How she'd missed the town and her grandparents' house. How she'd given the girl the couch to sleep on, and she'd been more or less bedded down on the floor when he'd come by. How she'd run to open the door and was apparently planning to put her arms around him—except that she wasn't ex- pecting Frank, but obviously someone else.

Red dwelled on that story, replayed it in his head a few more times.

He'd listened hard to the weather before taking off. The wind was supposed to disappear, go on to terror- ize Newfoundland and the upper Atlantic coast. By the dinner hour, power would hopefully be restored on the south side of town. Snow was still drifting down, but it was the last sputter of the storm's bad temper. Drifts were still a menace, some fifteen feet or higher, swirling in roads, burying doors, snugging up to every crevice and corner. The town couldn't be plowed out in a day. Probably not for several days.

But Route 1 would be cleared first. Fresh food and gas would start coming on regular schedules. Businesses would reopen. Dentists could start drilling again, and teachers would soon be stuck with their herd of cabin-fever-stricken kids. And everyone who wanted to—including Whitney—would be able to get out of town, to get to airports or work or wherever they needed to go.

She'd be able to leave him.

Unless he could find some way to make her stay.

WHITNEY NEVER EXPECTED to go back to sleep, but she'd curled up on the couch with April and must have dozed, because a sudden sound woke her. For a moment she couldn't move, between the weight of the dog on her feet and her arms tangled around the little girl.

But she didn't need to move, anyway. It was a nice dream, finding Red standing there. Smiling. "Don't move. Just sleep," he said softly. "It's still really, really early. I brought food and supplies, but nothing that won't wait."

Apparently she drifted off again, because the next time she opened her eyes, Red was still there. Lying on the carpet with a jacket for a pillow and an afghan covering him—more or less. He was sleeping on his stomach, as if he'd crashed that way and never moved. His cheek was developing a noticeably scratchy beard. He looked drawn and exhausted.

He looked adorable.

"Whitney?" April, still spooned against her, turned wide awake in a flash. She whispered, "Is he lost, too?"

"No, honey, he came to bring us food and supplies."

"What kind of food?"

"I don't know, but I'm guessing it's something he thinks you'll like."

April frowned. "Is he going to take me away after that? Can't I just stay right here? With you?"

"Let's wait until he wakes up. Then we'll all talk about what needs to happen next, okay?"

For a while, though, it was obvious a tornado couldn't wake him. Whitney and her adopted household all roused. The humans used the bathroom, the dog had to be let out, then in, a toothbrush created for April, then a cleanup. After that, she rummaged in the containers Red had brought in, gave the dog kibble and then the soup bone. She and April investigated the people food.

Once April found the mac and cheese, she turned into a deliriously happy girl—which was about when Red finally woke, shook himself like a growly bear and honed in on the fresh Thermos of coffee faster than a hound for a bone. April gave him a wide berth, parking next to Whitney on the couch, clearly anxious about what was going to happen to her.

But Red seemed to sense that, pulled over an ottoman and plunked down with his hands wrapped around the Thermos mug. He brought up one touchy issue at a time. "I talked to the family that the dog belongs to, April. They did a lot of thinking about this. They love their dog. And they don't really want to give him up. But if your parents agree—and you all need to be sure about this—the folks think you might need Copper more than they do. Especially as he seems so attached to you."

"I do need him. A *lot*. And he loves me."

"Okay, we'll see what your parents say. Right now, we have something else we need to talk about."

April was no dunce. She answered the question before he could ask it. "I want to stay here. Forever. With Whitney."

Red exchanged a look with her, but quickly faced April again. "That's not one of the options we have," he said gently. "Both your parents have been crazy with worry. They were thrilled to hear you were okay. Your mom doesn't have power yet and she isn't likely to for another day or maybe two. But your dad's apartment got power back a few hours ago."

"So you're saying I have to go to my dad's."

Red shot another look at Whitney, but he didn't duck the problem. "April, right now I want to hear what you want."

"I don't know. I'm just tired of divorce. If I go to Dad's, he'll have to work, so he won't have time for me. And now that Mom's working, she doesn't have time for me, either. No matter what I do, I can't make them happy. No matter how good I try to be, nobody really wants me there. Nobody laughs with me anymore."

"That sucks," Red said.

"You're not kidding. It sucks, sucks, sucks."

"I wish I had some answers," Red admitted, and then turned to Whitney. "Any ideas?"

It took a second before she realized he was talking to her. Watching him with April was jerking her heart strings. They hadn't discussed the child's situation ahead of time; neither knew her, neither had any kind of power over what would happen in the child's life—nor should they. But Red seemed to instinctively feel protective of the child the way she did. Neither wanted to just drop April off in a situation that made her so unhappy.

"April...I do have one idea." She sat on the floor, next

to Red. "When you first see your parents, I think you should tell them why you ran away. What you wanted."

April considered this. "I guess what I wanted was to get their attention. I thought maybe they'd get back together if I did something…big."

Whitney nodded. "I understand. But here's the thing. You told me your mom and dad couldn't seem to quit fighting. Maybe they won't get back together, maybe they can't. But everything would get better if they could stop fighting, wouldn't it?"

"Oh, yeah. Way better," April agreed.

"So you could be a little sneaky. You could tell them that you ran away to get their attention. But then you figured out running away was a bad idea. It didn't fix anything. It just got you in a bigger mess. And you know that now. So you want to talk about what's bothering you. And you want them to talk to you. Instead of just pretending everything's okay."

April frowned, considering.

Whitney said, "You could do it like this. You could say, 'I won't run away anymore. If you two don't run away, either.'"

"Oh. *Oh*. I can do that. I get you now. You're saying like I ran away for real. But they've been running away, too. Even if they didn't run out the door and hide, like me. They're just running away from talking to me. And talking with all of us together."

"You got it."

Red's pager went off. The call was from April's mom—the sheriff had allowed her to use the emergency line so she could talk to her daughter. Initially April froze, didn't want to talk to anyone but Whitney and Red, but they coaxed her into it. And while she huddled in the old rocker with the dog and Red's cell phone, all curled up...Red got this look in his eyes.

A look that worried her.

The dog lifted his head, as if sensing something monumental was about to happen. But it was only Red, hooking his arms on Whitney's shoulders, pressing his forehead to hers.

"You were terrific with her."

"I didn't really know what to say."

"Yeah, you did. You looked at her and tried to voice how she was feeling, how she was hurting."

His appreciation gave her a warm glow, but she was still troubled by how he looked at her. Red had never been much for analyzing heavy, deep feelings, but his grave expression suggested that's exactly where his head was. Gut-serious, heart-serious issues were on his mind.

"I'm going to end up having to take April back right now, aren't I?" he asked, but it was a rhetorical question. They both guessed how the phone conversation was going to go between April and her mother.

"I'm guessing yes. If I were the mom and my child was missing, I wouldn't want to hear any excuses. I'd want my kid in my arms right now."

"I need to talk to you, Whitney."

"And I need to talk to you, too."

"It can't happen until we're alone. So I'll take her back. But I need to know that you won't leave. Until I get back here. Until we have that talk."

"How long are you planning to be gone?"

A clutched frown creased his forehead. She could see it in his face. "I don't know. I want to say I'll be back immediately. But I can't swear what'll happen when I take her home. My plan is to be no longer than a couple hours, max. But I have no way to be sure."

"Of course you don't."

April skipped over between them, full of information after talking with her mom. Mrs. Shuster had been moved into town—to a bed-and-breakfast on the south side that now had power. So Red was going to take her there—with the dog, at least temporarily—and her dad was going to be there, too.

The child was beaming at this turn of events. Whitney hugged her, but over April's head, she looked straight at Red. Her voice was barely a whisper. "Red... that one time. There were no strings."

"There are for me. And there's something I need to give you."

"I don't want or need anything."

"What are you two talking about?" April lifted her head. "It's okay to take me back to my mom now. Can we go?"

"Yup. Get your jacket and stuff on. I'm taking you and Copper. Leave whatever else you had here."

"Copper could be worried about this," the little one said gravely.

"Just Copper's worried, huh? Well, I'll stay with both you and Copper when we get there and make sure everything's cool." But he looked at Whitney the whole time he was helping April gather up her gear, find her boots, untangle her hair from under her hat.

"Whit." Again his voice turned slow and soft. "The reason I shut us down was stupid. I didn't know that then, but I know it now. I'm just asking you to stay until I show you something."

Once he left with April and the dog, Whitney paced the living room like a caged cat. She was the one who'd initiated their lovemaking. She knew that. But that didn't explain anything he'd said or done. How he looked at her. How he was with her. What "thing" he could conceivably want to show her.

She hadn't trusted her heart since leaving Tucker's Point ten years ago, and it seemed that coming home had brought her to the same precipice. He could so easily break her heart…again.

Too anxious to sit, she waited until the sun came up. Within an hour, it had climbed the horizon and shone blindingly bright on the snowy landscape. The temperature was still bitter, but she went outside in stretches to start working on her rental car. Beneath a thick frosting of snow, the whole car was encased in ice, but once she managed to open a door, she started the engine, ran defrosters and heat, plugged in her cell phone.

No one was on the road yet. There were no signs of movement anywhere. She could see two massive drifts still blocking Route 1, but a few swipes with a serious snowplow would fix that, so if that was the worst of the road blockage, she'd be able to leave before long.

The thought put a lump in her throat the size of a mountain.

She headed for the door—she had to go inside, her hands were frozen—and to her shock, found the overhead light glaring in the living room.

There couldn't be power. The electricity had been shut off all these months. Red, she thought. He must have done something. Or maybe the emergency team had a way to test the power in the whole grid? She didn't understand it, but once she found water running in the kitchen sink, she couldn't care less about the why. The water was cold, but it was still running water. She could do some serious cleaning now. Run her grandparents' antiquated vacuum in the living area. Brush her teeth. *Really* brush her teeth. Wash her face and hands and body with real soap and water—and she didn't care if she got frostbite; it felt *so* good to be clean again.

After all that, there was still no sign of Red.

From the front window, she saw lights, then heard noise. Snow plows. Two of them. Dealing with the drifts on Route 1.

She layered up again, to start filling up the trunk with all the clothing and belongings she'd brought with her. She hesitated when it came to her grandmother's wooden chest.

Gram had chosen to keep her first love a secret all these years. No different than Whitney never sharing what had happened between herself and Red.

That thought put another lump in her throat, but she kept moving. The only thing she planned to leave in the house was the propane heater, because she had no real use for it in Philadelphia. Her energy flagged by mid-afternoon, but slowly, unexpectedly she seemed to be building up a fresh head of steam.

Maybe she was dog-tired, but her temper seemed to pick up a whole *chimney* full of steam.

She never got mad. She hated getting mad. She was thinking about prom night, ten years ago, as if it were yesterday. She recalled exactly where he'd taken her after the prom. What he said when he'd severed their relationship.

She hadn't demanded solid answers then, hadn't fought him. She was too stunned, had never seen it coming. And later, she was certain he'd change his mind. She'd waited and waited for him to call, positive that he would at least give her some explanation.

And here she was, waiting and waiting and waiting

for him. Who knew if he'd come? Who knew if he just assumed she'd wait around—like she had before. Like she'd just be there for him—like she had been before.

CHAPTER SEVEN

SHE'D LEFT. RED just knew it. A bunch of roads had been cleared; power was back through the whole grid; she was way overdue for her job, had clients expecting an office proposal this week; she couldn't even call to let them know why it was late. And like everyone else in Tucker's Point, would probably kill for a hot shower. And another hot shower. And maybe even a third.

He turned onto Route 1, glanced at his reflection in the rearview mirror and winced. The right side of his face... Well, the eye wasn't completely swollen shut. And once the bandage had been taped on, the bloody goose egg was covered up. There was one advantage to showing up at two in the morning. By daylight, he was undoubtedly going to look a whole lot worse.

For the first time since the blizzard began, he was driving his four-wheel-drive pickup instead of Betsy. The truck had a blade in front, so he'd be able to clear out her driveway—and take her with him, if she'd come. But that was assuming she hadn't already left. After all these hours, she must have thought he wasn't coming. She must have thought... Hell. He didn't know what she'd thought.

He only knew what he'd been thinking about. What he wanted. What he needed. For her and with her.

His jaw tightened the instant her driveway came into view. Her rental car had been dug out, and she'd shov-

eled the walk and driveway herself. It looked as if she
was well prepared to take off any second—but at least
she was still there for now.

He parked fast, tucked the locked leather satchel
under his arm and charged toward the house. She must
have been watching for him, because she yanked open
the front door before he'd even reached the porch. With
a quick glance, he noticed she was wearing cords and a
quilted down jacket, her hair tidied up in a hair band.

She definitely hadn't been sleeping. She not only
looked ready to fly, but the gleam in her eyes was all
hot-blue fire.... At least until she caught a glimpse of
his face.

"Good grief—what *happened* to you?"

Since she motioned him inside—he hadn't been sure
she'd let him in—he did his best to look pitiful. "I was
trying to be a knight in shining armor, only it didn't
work out. This lady saw her road had been plowed, and
immediately tried to get out. She not only got stuck, but
her car careened into a snow drift, and her two kids
were in the backseat...."

He set down the satchel on the coffee table. For him
it was a little like an elephant in the living room, but one
crisis at a time. The sharp fury in her eyes was starting to fade. She swooped closer to get a better look at
his face. "You had to get stitches!" she accused him.

"I know. Five. And they sting like a..." He swallowed the term he was thinking of. "They sting. A lot.
Anyway, the two kids were screaming and crying—
they were all scared the car was going to turn over.
Which it could have. I got everybody out, pulled the
car out of the drift. And then... I can't even explain
what happened. I walked around the back of the car,

just to check what kind of damage there was. There were trees there, and a chunk of snow crashed on my head. I guess it was mostly ice. Sharp ice. Who'd have thought ice could cut like that? And the only part of the story that really matters is this—Whitney, I love you. I've always loved you."

She scowled at him, backed away as if he'd suddenly developed bad breath—when he knew perfectly well that he'd cleaned up and brushed his teeth before coming here.

Her right forefinger shot up. She started shaking it. In his face. "I *thought* we were in love. I *thought* you were the most important person in my world. And that you felt that way about me. We had *plans.* We were too young to get married, but we were both headed for U of M. You had that terrific athletic scholarship. I had fancy grades. Between the two of us—"

He backed up, not avoiding the finger she was shaking in his face, but to ease closer to the leather satchel. "Whitney. That was all true."

"And suddenly you blew me off."

"No. It wasn't *suddenly.* It was prom night. After the prom. We'd left the dance, went to the bluffs, just sat on the rocks for a while. Talking. Just talking. You told me about the scholarship you'd gotten from Smith." He plunked down on the couch, fished the small brass key from his jeans.

She frowned, as if just noticing the satchel—or as if she didn't understand why he was sitting down, but she abruptly sat, too. "That wasn't news, Red. You knew I was accepted at Smith months before that."

"Yeah. But that was a dream. A pipe dream. Something you really wanted, but never thought you could have. Until the news about that full academic scholarship came through. And that made everything different, because that put us on two different planets. U of M was the only school I could get into. Because I never had close to your grades."

"So what? We were both happy with the plan!"

"No. *I* was happy. But I always knew you were sacrificing because of me. Your dream was to have a bigger life, starting with an Ivy League education. And here's the thing, Whitney. I was wrong. Dead-wrong."

She bowed her head. When he couldn't see her expression, his pulse started thumping in time to his panic.

"Look," he said. "That's how I thought then. That if I loved you, I'd do what was right for you, no matter what it cost me. I know it's corny as hell. But I wanted to be your hero. You always felt like the odd one in your family. No matter what you did, you couldn't please them. That was a big thing for you."

"I remember."

Red clawed a hand through his hair. Maybe she remembered, but her voice was vague and distracted, as if she was thinking about a grocery list.

"So that's why I thought it mattered. I wasn't like your family. I loved you for yourself. I didn't want to change anything about you. I cared about your goals and dreams. I didn't want you to be anyone but you."

He waited for her to respond, but her head was still bowed. He pushed the words out faster. "I get it. That I was wrong. I should have asked you what you wanted. Instead of just doing what I thought was the right thing. And the reason I know how stupid that was…was because I lost you. Whitney, for God's sake, you're giving me a heart attack. Talk to me!"

She immediately lifted her head. He saw the tears brimming in her eyes.

"Wait. Don't cry. Let me explain some more."

Her lips parted, but she had to swallow before she could speak. Her hands were filled with the contents of the leather satchel. Letters he'd written to her, but never sent. A small candle that smelled like white camellias. A white shell comb she'd worn in her hair on prom night. The heel of a shoe—she'd broken it on one of their first dates. A snapshot from a mall photo booth—her looking beautiful, him looking like a lovesick calf. An overgrown, lovesick calf. A vial of sand, from the dunes where they always went for privacy. A handful of ribbons—she was always tying back her hair with ribbons, always losing them. A red leaf, pressed in a book; it was a fall day when he'd kissed her the first time…they'd been ambling through the crunchy leaves, holding hands, talking nonstop about nothing, and then he'd stopped. And kissed her. And his whole world changed.

"See?" he said desperately. "That's what I wanted to show you. That I had a box, like your grandmother had…"

Her eyes met his. It was going to be all right. He could breathe again; he could see it in her eyes, in the way she looked at him. They were both making soft, huge promises about the future.

She lifted her hands, took his. Ten years had passed. Okay, maybe it was just ten seconds, but it was a *long* ten seconds before she leaned over and kissed him. It was an eyes-closed, velvet-soft, honey-sweet kiss.

At least the first one was.

But she leaned back for a moment, still holding on

to him, still looking at him with that fierce expression. "When I saw what was in my grandmother's box, do you know what I thought?"

"What?"

"That I understood. How she could go on and have a good life with my grandfather. But her first love was everything. I understood, Red, because that's exactly how I've always felt. You weren't just my first love. The love we had together was…incomparable. Heart-filling. Precious. More precious than anything in my world, then or now."

He whispered, "Exactly. I locked up everything I still had of you. Kept it closer than a secret. I can't lose you again."

"Ah, Red. I'm beginning to see that we never lost each other. We just didn't know it."

He reached for her. The world wouldn't survive another second if he didn't get his hands on her, his lips on hers, his body folded against hers. He bent his head, offered a kiss, soft and long and slow. Then hunkered down for some serious kissing. Wooing kisses. Treasuring kisses. Kisses of promise, of trust, of loving awe for each other.

Eventually, he figured, they'd have to worry about the inconsequential, irrelevant things. Jobs, rental cars, where she wanted to live. After that, they'd have to worry about a few consequential things, like where she wanted to raise their kids, and how many of them she wanted. Oh. And what kind of ring she'd like.

That question was likely to come up extremely soon.

But for this night, there were only a few hours of blizzard left. It was their world for now, with nothing that could intrude on these hours together. She was going to be stuck with a lot of tenderness, he was afraid. He'd had ten years of tenderness pent up, and this seemed just the time, just the night, to let it all loose.

"I love you, Red," she said fiercely.

"And I love you more than anything in my world, always will," he promised her, the vow in his voice as real as the one in his heart.

* * * * *

For Marsha Zinberg

LAND'S END

Barbara Dunlop

CHAPTER ONE

"I BET YOU'RE sorry I broke up with the six-feet-two rowing champion," Tessa Ambroise called to Emilee Hiatt as the two women hauled a sea kayak up the concrete stairs to the rocky peninsula at her seaside family home. It was Emilee's first day in Tucker's Point, but Tessa felt no compunction at putting her friend and former college roommate to work.

"Please don't tell me you're having second thoughts," Emilee called back as they reached the top of the stairs.

"I'm not having second thoughts," Tessa assured her, just like she'd assured herself each day for the past six months.

"Good," said Emilee. "Because Colton Herrington took a well-earned hike right out of your life, and he can stay there."

"I'm sure he's found someone who can keep up with his high standards," said Tessa. She didn't have a single doubt that the who's who of Boston debutantes had lined up the second her diamond ring hit his palm.

"What I'm truly sorry about," Emilee continued as they leveled out on the narrow peninsula, "is that you won't move back to Boston."

"I can't move back to Boston." The winter wind blew the sea spray up from the rocks, dampening Tessa's brown hair and whisking her ponytail against her cheek.

"Sure you can. There's no one to keep you here anymore. I mean, I'm not saying I'm *glad* that your great-aunt passed away. But she was ninety-three years old."

Tessa missed her aunt dearly, but Sophie had been ill for several months, going rapidly downhill those last few weeks. In a way, it was a blessing that the end came quickly. Her heart had given out in November. According to the doctor, she'd died peacefully in her sleep.

"I've got a thousand things left to do here," Tessa pointed out. She was currently going through the nooks and crannies of the sprawling basement, discovering family treasures that had been in storage for decades.

"Don't you rich families have people to do that for you?"

"We're not rich. Well, maybe a little bit rich," Tessa amended. "Or, at least we were once."

"Rich people never think they're rich." Emilee switched hands, settling her grip around the stern of the kayak as they approached the stone boathouse.

"I am going to need a job," said Tessa.

The upkeep of Land's End estate was expensive. And what might have started as a family fortune two hundred years ago had dwindled over the generations. The Ambroises were now land-rich but cash-poor.

Tessa couldn't help but glance up at the castle. The imposing twenty-six-room stone mansion had been built by her several-times great-grandparents nearly two centuries ago, and had guarded the harbor from its perch ever since. Right now, it was backlit by the setting sun, its two-story wall dark in the shadows, a turret bracing either end. In some ways, it was beautiful. In others, it was an albatross.

"Maybe Colton could have helped me clean out the basement," she mused.

"Manual labor?" Emilee snorted. "Colton Herrington wouldn't dirty his hands in your basement."

Tessa didn't believe that was true. She'd seen Colton step up to help his neighbors with manual labor, not to mention the movers who'd delivered the new sofa set to his penthouse. Not that he had a lot of call to undertake it. Unlike the Ambroises', the Herringtons' rapidly growing fortune ensured assistance was always readily available.

It was the kind of wealth that showed. Everything about the man oozed class and breeding. Tessa had noticed it from the first moment she'd seen him, emerging from the waves of Nantucket onto the beach where she'd been reading on a folding chair. He'd moved through the sunlight, tall, bronzed, impossibly handsome, confident in every step he took.

"He might not get his hands dirty often." Tessa felt a certain loyalty to her former fiancé. "But he was a gentleman through and through."

"And wasn't that just the problem?" Emilee asked, an edge to her tone. "He'd have 'gentleman-ed' you into the loony bin."

"True enough," Tessa conceded.

That was the crux of the problem between them. Colton set ridiculously high standards for himself. And his level of perfection always left her feeling inadequate. So much so that she was embarrassed to admit it, and spent an inordinate amount of energy hiding her flaws. It was hard to spend so much time around a paragon of all virtues. His attention to detail had made her jumpy, and not in a good way.

Now, she pulled hard on the wide oak door that led to the ground floor of the boathouse.

"To be fair," she found herself defending him, "he was exceedingly organized."

She knew that if he'd been in charge of the operation, Colton would have had a twelve-man crew combing the basement of Land's End, retrieving Tessa's great-aunt's paintings and sculptures from the rest of the junk that had gathered down there over the decades.

"Was he like that making love?" Emilee asked, maneuvering to one side as the door groaned open.

Tessa didn't understand the question. "Exceedingly organized at making love?"

"Yeah, organized—and all staid and fastidious like he is in real life?"

"No," Tessa lied, moving into the dim space. The words *organized* and *staid* seemed unnecessarily critical.

"I can tell when you lie," Emilee warned from behind.

"Well, maybe a little bit organized," Tessa allowed. Her mind jumped involuntarily to their lovemaking before she quickly banished the compelling memories.

He might have been more organized than your average guy, but his brand of organization was *effective*. Colton was an amazing lover. One might even say perfect. Where Tessa— Well, Tessa was more impulsive and chaotic. Not that Colton had ever complained.

Gripping the kayak with one hand, she hit the light switch on the wall, illuminating the bare bulbs affixed to the ceiling. The aged stone walls and concrete floor absorbed most of the light. The boathouse was cold and musty, having been closed up since October. She knew she should've moved the kayaks up from their beach racks a couple months ago, but somehow it had never reached the top of her priority list.

But now, with snow and high winds predicted for the coming week, the first real storm of the winter brewing off the coast, she needed to batten down the hatches.

"Organized lovemaking," Emilee pondered out loud. "So, what are we talking about? Only on Thursdays? Only in the bedroom?"

"He was just really, really good."

"Oh, I can see how that would be a problem."

Tessa struggled to put her feelings into words. "It was as if he'd sat down, drafted a perfect plan and then executed it."

"Oh, now you've got me curious."

"He always had to shower beforehand," Tessa admitted. "And shave, and brush his teeth."

"I'm not so sure that's a bad thing," said Emilee as she hoisted the kayak's stern onto a rack against the wall.

"Turn that thought around," said Tessa. "I always felt like I also had to shower, shave, brush and floss."

Emilee grinned as she dropped her arms, her tone going mocking. "I'd ravish you, baby, but you have hairy legs?"

"More like, I'll meet you in the bedroom in half an hour. I bought you a lavender silk nightie from Giselle's. There's some new spearmint toothpaste on the counter."

Tessa stopped. It was the first time she'd owned up to any of it out loud.

Emilee's eyes had gone quite round. "Please tell me you're exaggerating for effect."

Tessa wished she was. "When you think you're in love, you let these things slide. But when you start looking back…"

"It's like he wanted a perfect princess."

"I'm never going to be a perfect princess."

"I did tell you so."

"That you did," Tessa agreed as she stepped back from the kayak rack to survey their work.

From the first time Emilee had met Colton, she'd insisted he was too uptight for Tessa. But it was hard for Tessa to see past his gorgeous body and dazzling smile—not to mention the flashy BMW, his sky-rocketing business empire and his elite circle of well-read, influential friends. If a woman were to write a checklist of the perfect husband, Colton would hit on every feature.

Emilee rubbed her damp hands against the front of her skinny jeans. "Personally, I like spontaneous."

"Stop," Tessa barked, feeling a budding tingle at the thought of sex with Colton. "It's been six months for me."

"You haven't slept with anyone since Colton?"

"Of course I haven't slept with anyone since Colton. Who would I have slept with since Colton?"

"I don't know. *Anybody?*"

"Tucker's Point is a small town, Emilee. I grew up with most of the guys around here. I'm not about to have a one-night stand and kick-start the gossip loop."

"All the more reason to come back to Boston with me," Emilee immediately put in. "Come back for New Year's. We'll watch the fireworks, go to a wine show, stuff ourselves with triple cheese pizza. I'll even set you up with a nice guy to kiss at midnight."

"You don't know any nice guys."

Emilee was doing an internship with a celebrity man-agement firm that specialized in sports teams. The men she knew were mostly footloose and narcissistic, criss-crossing the country from game to game. They defi-nitely didn't restrict themselves to the home team.

"I work with hot guys. I'll set you up with a hot guy."

"The guys you work with will get me into the tabloids."

"True enough. But it would be 'star pitcher Tom Macbey spotted at midnight kissing an unidentified woman.'"

Tessa couldn't help but laugh at the truth of that.

"What do you say?" Emilee cajoled.

"I can't come to Boston for New Year's."

It was tempting, but Tessa had work to do. She knew her brother, Barry, was needed at his medical practice in Atlanta. The two didn't contact each other very often. They'd never been close, and now they led very different lives. But they'd had to make some decisions about Land's End now that Sophie was gone. Closing the house up for a few years seemed to make the most sense.

"So when?" Emilee pressed.

"Maybe later on in January."

"I'm going to hold you to that."

Tessa glanced around the boathouse. "Well, that's the last of the stuff we'd left on the beach. Let the wind blow."

Job done, she led the way out, pushing the heavy door closed and latching it behind them. The breeze was picking up in the early evening, the temperature flirting with the freezing point.

Waves broke with a roar against the huge rocks that surrounded the narrow finger of land that jutted out beyond the protected harbor. The Ambroise property was at the edge of the seaside town of Tucker's Point. Fishing boats were moored in the gloom of the marina near the center of town, while B and Bs and small inns dotted the beachfront on either side, their lights coming on as the sun settled completely behind the hills.

Historically a sleepy fishing village and tourist stop, Tucker's Point had recently become popular with successful entrepreneurs. Lone eagles, they called themselves, businessmen and women who could work remotely from anywhere in the world. They'd escaped the bustle of New York, Chicago or Boston for the bucolic atmosphere of Maine.

"I've given myself a craving for triple cheese pizza," Emilee observed, fastening the top button of her brown leather jacket and turning her back to the wind and restless ocean.

Comfort food sounded like a great idea to Tessa. "You want to go out or order in?"

"How's your wine cellar holding up?"

"There are still about a thousand bottles down there." Tessa had recently toured the temperature-controlled room set in a far corner of the original basement. It had been years since anyone had stocked it, but it would take many years more to drink their way through the existing bottles.

"Then let's order in. We'll build a fire in that big old stone fireplace, get a little drunk."

"So, we won't hang Sophie's pictures tonight?"

Emilee playfully grasped Tessa's shoulder. "You've got to stop working so hard. Take a break. We'll hang the pictures in the morning."

Tessa was itching to see how the haunting portrait of three women on a widow's walk would look bracketed by the copper candle holders. They'd been crafted by her grandfather. But Emilee was here on vacation. So it was only fair to do something besides work.

IN HIS OFFICE atop Herrington Tower in the heart of downtown Boston, Colton Herrington scrolled through the property photos his Vice-President Rand Garvy had forwarded to his email account.

"You're positive they're planning to sell?" he asked Rand without glancing up.

The place was as picturesque as Tessa had once described—twelve lush-lawned acres in the sleepy little seaside village of Tucker's Point, Maine. Most of the photos had been taken in summer, a few of them in the fall. The grounds were undeniably beautiful, the view of the ocean spectacular and the small castle perched in the middle of the property was, well, interesting.

It had obviously been patched together over the years, one turret original, the other newer, slightly larger, giving the place an off-balance appearance. Though it had probably been quite grand in its time, the stone had aged, all manner of foliage creeping its way up the facade, obscuring the architectural details. Rand had discovered the foundation was deteriorating, and the roof needed replacing.

"My guy in Atlanta talked to her brother," Rand replied, dropping into a chair on the opposite side of Colton's desk.

It was nearly five o'clock, and the offices of Herrington Resorts had grown quiet.

"Barry Ambroise?" Colton confirmed.

"Barry Ambroise. He says they're in the final stages of rezoning, and they'll be putting it on the market as soon as the paperwork is complete. He's been working at it for a while now."

"She never said anything to me." Colton remembered that Tessa loved her ancestral property. He couldn't imagine her wanting to sell. Then again, perhaps he hadn't known her as well as he'd thought.

"I guess you never truly know what's going on in another person's life."

"We were engaged," Colton pointed out.

"And then she backed out."

There was no arguing with that.

When Colton had asked Rand to check out her brother in Atlanta, he hadn't even thought of Land's End. He'd been curious about her family.

With no plausible explanation for why she'd suddenly broken off their engagement, he'd wanted more facts. They'd been happy, deliriously so. He'd never met such a smart, sexy, funny woman.

They'd debated, sure. But they always resolved the issue. Normally, it had just taken a little more information for her to see his side. She was great that way, always willing to come at things from a new perspective.

He'd found himself wondering if she was battling other pressures, maybe secrets he didn't know about. He'd discovered her great-aunt was ill. But that didn't seem like any kind of explanation. So he'd looked into her brother next, not really sure what he was expecting to find, but unable to simply let it go.

"You know you're behaving like a stalker," said Rand.

Colton frowned at his friend. "I'm simply gathering additional information."

"You're not going to find any by examining her house."

"You don't know that," Colton countered.

"She changed her mind, Colton. It happens."

"It doesn't make sense." As far as Colton was concerned, it didn't make any kind of sense at all.

Not that Colton was particularly proud of investigating her. It hadn't been his first course of action. He'd spent more than a month getting on with his life, trying to forget about her. But he couldn't seem to get closure. Their relationship felt like an unfinished race. His boat was in the lead, his muscles pumped. They were stroking in unison toward the finish line, when someone inexplicably blew the horn to scratch the event. And now he needed to find out why.

"It makes sense to her," Rand offered in an undertone.

Colton turned his attention back to the computer monitor, letting his mind run with the pictures in front of him. "Look at the line of the beach."

Rand rose and moved around the desk, looking over Colton's shoulder. "What about it?"

"It's a perfect setup—swimming, boating. And the land is almost level." Once the plan had formed in his mind, Colton knew exactly what he wanted to do.

Rand stilled. "I don't like the sound of that."

"We'd have to truck in sand, maybe create an artificial reef. But remember what we did in Spain?" He referred to a Herrington Resort they'd developed five years ago.

Rand sucked in an audible breath. "Tell me you're not serious."

"I'm completely serious."

"Stalker behavior, Colton. Off the charts."

"It doesn't matter how we found it." Colton spoke to himself as much as to Rand. "The point is, there's a real opportunity here."

"Now you're deluding yourself."

Colton gestured to the screen. "Tell me *that* isn't perfect. Give me one good reason why we shouldn't explore putting a hotel on this beach."

"Permitting would be a nightmare."

"I already checked it out," Colton countered. The Tucker's Point civic website was surprisingly comprehensive. "We're golden up to seven stories, and we can modify the waterfront."

Tucker's Point was historically a fishing village. It had been revitalized in the past few years, becoming more of a tourist town, but their land permitting system was likely left over from its days as a working harbor.

"Okay, forget the hotel. You're out for revenge, or you're out to win her back. Either one of those things will end in disaster."

"I'm out to build a new resort."

"That's a flat-out lie."

Colton enlarged one of the photos. "Look at this. I've thought it through."

"For all of *what?* One day?"

Colton ignored the jab. "Marina here, behind the point. A swimming beach here, main guest tower back there, golf out the back and along the cliffs. Put a clubhouse at the southern tip, and a restaurant, pool, fountain feature in the middle…."

"Colton."

"It's an hour and a half from an international airport. Several of the restaurants in the town center are four-star or higher. Sure, they're boutique, but it's a place to start. And the town is chockablock with funky arts stores and antique shops."

"Have you seriously convinced yourself this is about the property?" Rand demanded.

"It's all about the property." Colton was willing to accept that it was over between him and Tessa. He might not like it, and he might not understand it, but he absolutely accepted it.

Rand braced a hand on the desk. "Listen to me. I'm your closest friend."

Colton resented Rand's tone. "And I'm your boss. No matter how it happened, we're in on the ground floor of a prime beachfront property. It hasn't even been listed yet. It's priced at residential zoning. And we said we'd look at the East Coast next."

"We also said we'd look at the West Coast next. And we said we'd wait two years before starting a new development."

"Opportunities like this don't come along every day."

"It's about the girl."

"It's about the land. The girl is incidental." Colton was enough of a businessman to keep the two separate.

Rand straightened. "You won't win her back."

"I don't want her back."

If she'd asked to come back a few months ago, he might have been willing to reconcile. But wanting to understand why she'd broken things off was a long way from wanting to rekindle anything.

"You'd bulldoze her home?"

"It's falling apart."

"You want to make her hate you?"

Colton refused to care about Tessa's opinion of him one way or the other. "We'd be first into the local market. You know as well as I do what that can mean."

"A leg up on the competition and a serious boost to the bottom line," Rand acknowledged.

"We've never built a resort from the ground up."

Of the thirty-four properties owned by Herrington Resorts, half had been built by his grandfather. The other half had been purchased from rival companies. It would be immensely gratifying for Colton to finally create something that was completely his own. Not that there was anyone around to be proud of him.

"Have Lily book the jet for tomorrow morning," he told Rand. There wasn't a moment to lose on this.

"Tomorrow is New Year's Day."

Colton hesitated, drawing in a sharp breath of impatience. "Okay, set it up for the second. You haven't used my name?"

"Barry only knows you're a resort developer."

"Good."

There was a beat of silence between them before Rand broke it. "Let me say it again, Colton. This is a mistake."

"Let *me* say it again, Rand. It's about the property."

Though he might ask Tessa a couple of clarifying questions while he considered the purchase, Colton would never let his personal life interfere with business. He'd buy or not buy the property based on merit alone. Tessa was absolutely incidental.

"I CAN'T BELIEVE you were serious about moving it up here," Emilee called from the bottom of the east staircase, raising her voice above the whine of the power buffer's electric motor. The women had spent the past three days exploring the castle basement.

Tessa was in the great room, a canvas drop cloth on the floor, giving a final polish to a replica suit of armor created years ago by her great-grandfather. She'd hauled it up in pieces from the basement and assembled it near a front bay window where the light was best.

Tessa shut off the buffer and turned, pulling her safety goggles onto her forehead. She was slightly out of breath, her right arm aching from her shoulder to her wrist. "It used to be up here when I was a kid. It's one of my earliest memories."

Emilee walked into the room, circling the armor suspiciously. "It certainly makes a statement."

"There aren't many houses that could pull this off."

"You definitely need the large room."

"And the stone walls help."

Emilee came to a stop in the middle of the room, gazing around. "You ever think of modernizing the decor, rather than going with extreme retro?"

"My great-grandfather made this." Tessa ran her fingertips across the shiny breast plate. The edges were etched with scrolls and swirls that mirrored the designs on the shoulders and arms.

"I hope he didn't use it."

"He was born in 1914."

"You're the history major, but that was after the Renaissance, correct?"

Tessa rolled her eyes. "Very funny."

"I'm just wondering why he felt the need for a suit of armor."

"It's art."

"That's debatable."

"Well, it's staying."

"We both know I have to go back to Boston tomorrow," said Emilee. "But I'm a little afraid of leaving you alone here. Next thing, you'll put that boar's head above the fireplace."

"It's hardly moth-eaten at all," Tessa teased.

They'd both groaned in disgust when they'd found the mounted taxidermy tucked away in the basement.

Emilee held up a warning finger. "I draw the line at dead things."

Tessa laughed. "Me, too. But I also found some terrific pottery vases this morning. I remember now that my mom made them. For a long time, we kept them in the kitchen."

"Let me guess, you put them back, too?"

"She used pearlescent mauve-and-peach glaze. They look great in the breakfast nook."

"You do know you're reconstructing your childhood."

"That's not what I'm doing. I'm recreating the castle's glory."

"You're harkening back to a time when you felt safe and happy."

"I'm perfectly happy as an adult."

"Maybe so, but you should think about selling some of this instead of wallowing in it. I bet you could get good money for it online."

"Maybe the boar's head. If anyone would actually buy it. But most of this is great stuff. I'm going to save it for my own kids."

Emilee assumed a mock expression of shock, gazing pointedly at Tessa's flat stomach. "Is there something you're not telling me?"

"I'm talking about someday. *Someday,* I'll have kids."

"And you think they'll want to live in a museum?"

"It's sure better than that new monstrosity next door."

Tessa's best childhood friend had grown up in a classic Tudor mansion on the next property. Sadly, the family had moved to Seattle during high school, and the new owners, the Biddles, had leveled the house, building a stark, white, geometric glass-and-stucco contemporary that looked like a cross between a warehouse and an aquarium.

"They must get amazing views out of that place," Emilee observed.

"I get amazing views from my bedroom."

"Sure, you do. Through narrow, blurry, leaded glass. I'm talking panoramic—"

A sharp knock sounded on the front door.

Emilee stopped, tone dropping to a whisper. "You suppose the neighbors heard us talking about them?"

Tessa glanced out the window, seeing a black sedan parked in the driveway. "That doesn't look like the Biddles' car."

She stripped off the goggles and set the power buffer down on the drop sheet, raking back her sweaty hair as she headed for the door.

She pulled it open. Then her stomach dropped to her toes as she came face-to-face with Colton Herrington.

CHAPTER TWO

COLTON WATCHED TESSA'S expression go from astonished to annoyed, then to remote. Remote was the one he remembered, and the one he hated. Given a choice, he'd laugh with her or make love to her. Not that either of those were going to happen. But he'd still much rather argue with her than face her indifference.

It took a long moment, but she finally spoke. "What are you doing here, Colton?"

"I'm here to see Barry."

"Barry's not here," came her immediate answer. Then her eyes narrowed. "Why do you want Barry? How did you meet Barry?"

Rand stepped smoothly into the conversation, offering his hand. "Hello, Tessa."

She blinked at him, seeming as surprised to see him as she was to see Colton. "Rand?"

"It's nice to see you again," he offered pleasantly.

"What are *you* doing in Tucker's Point?"

"We expected your brother to be here already," Colton felt compelled to explain. "Did he talk to you—"

"Is this a joke?" Emilee Hiatt appeared beside Tessa's right shoulder, her tone both accusing and demanding.

"Yeah," Colton drawled, annoyance blooming inside him. He'd never been crazy about Emilee. "We flew all the way from Boston to be funny."

Tessa squared her shoulders and crossed her arms over her chest. "What's going on here, Rand?"

Rand glanced to Colton, obviously looking for direction.

At the same time, a sports car turned off Beech Tree Road, pulling noisily into the short driveway, drawing everyone's attention.

"Here's Barry now," said Rand, obviously relieved.

Colton didn't think it was worth either explaining or arguing while Barry quickly parked and exited his vehicle, so he stayed silent. He assumed Barry had already told Tessa there was a potential buyer. But the fact that the potential buyer was Colton was obviously going to be news all around.

"When did you meet Barry?" Tessa repeated to Colton.

"I'm meeting him now," Colton answered.

"You know what I mean."

Colton noticed her tight expression. "I haven't met him before today."

"I'm so sorry." Barry bustled forward, his black overcoat pulled tight against the light flakes of snow. "My flight was delayed. Tessa, sweetheart." Wasting no time, he pulled her into a hug. "How are you? It's so great to see you."

"I'm confused," she answered, pulling back, glancing at Colton and then back to Barry.

"I know. I know. I should have called, but I thought… Why don't we all step inside?" Barry gestured to the open doorway with a welcoming arm.

Tessa didn't look at all happy at the prospect of inviting them inside, while Emilee looked positively irate. But the two women grudgingly stepped aside, and Colton walked with Rand into the grand entry hall of the castle.

The castle was dated, but still quite impressive. The stone on the curved walls had aged to light gray. The hallway was illuminated with sconces, and two ornate pillars flanked the entrance to the great room. As Barry gathered their coats, Colton followed Tessa into a huge and equally impressive room with beams arcing across a high ceiling. His attention was snagged by a massive stone fireplace and a freshly polished suit of armor.

The hardwood floors were well-worn but highly polished, reflecting the daylight that made its way through the recessed windows. Colorful area rugs brightened the floor, delineating several furniture groupings.

"Coffee?" Barry asked brightly, gesturing to the sofa and several armchairs that surrounded the fireplace. Then he turned to Tessa. "Is Matilda around?"

"They're in Oregon for the holidays," Tessa answered. Their housekeeper, Matilda Booker, and her husband, Milton, always visited their family over Christmas and New Year's.

Barry frowned. "Oh. Of course. How could I forget?"

"We don't need coffee," Colton said, waiting for Tessa and Emilee to sit.

"Forget coffee." Tessa's hands went to her hips as she stared at her brother. "What the hell is going on?"

"Let's all sit down," Barry suggested.

After a long, stubborn moment, she dropped her arms and sat in one of the big armchairs. There, she pulled her wool-sock-covered feet beneath her jeans. Colton couldn't help but note how disheveled she looked in a loose, blue-plaid flannel shirt. Her ponytail was messy and there were traces of dust on her hands.

"Tessa," Barry opened with a smile, as they all got settled. "I have very good news."

Tessa gave a fleeting, suspicious glance at Colton. "I'm listening," she said to her brother.

"These two men." He glanced expectantly at them.

"I'm Rand Garvy," Rand quickly put in.

"Good to meet you." Barry turned to Colton.

"He's Colton Herrington," Tessa all but shouted. "My ex-fiancé, Barry."

Barry glanced to Colton in confusion that seemed to be turning to consternation. "What's *he* doing here?"

"He's the buyer," Rand explained. "We are absolutely interested in purchasing the property. Everything I told you is factual."

Colton couldn't tear his gaze from Tessa as she paced across the floor. It had been months since he'd seen her like this. Come to think of it, he'd never seen her like this—cheeks flushed, hands gesticulating, blue eyes blazing, glaring at him as if she'd like to attack.

"*What* do you have to say for yourself?" she demanded of him.

"I want to build a resort," he answered simply. "Well, I'd like to look at the possibility of building a resort. Here. In Tucker's Point."

"You can't build a resort here," she snapped.

"We're working on the zoning," said Barry.

Tessa turned on her brother. "What zoning?"

Barry seemed to regroup. "The land zoning. Listen, Tessa, I know you didn't expect Colton. It surprised me, too, of course. But this is good news. You should be happy."

Her tone turned incredulous. "Happy about *selling Land's End?*"

"We talked about it, the cost of the upkeep, the—"

"When? When did we—"

"Tessa," Emilee interrupted, coming to her feet to place a hand on Tessa's shoulder. "Perhaps Colton and Rand could excuse themselves for a few minutes so you and Barry can talk?"

Tessa filled her lungs with air. "That would be good."

Emilee turned to them, tone firm. "Can I show you two gentlemen outside, maybe around the grounds?"

Colton would have preferred to stay and support Barry in the argument, but there was no way he could reasonably do that.

"We'd love to take a look around the grounds," he agreed, keeping his voice even as he rose to his feet.

"Don't bother with the tour," Tessa said tightly. "There's absolutely no point."

"No harm in looking," Rand put in. "We'll give the two of you some time to talk."

Rand looked about as excited as Colton felt about leaving Barry alone with Tessa. They'd both expected Tessa to fight against selling to him. He hadn't expected her to fight against selling at all.

THE FRONT DOOR opened then closed behind the trio, a burst of cold wind swirling into the room.

Tessa glared at her brother.

"Why don't you sit back down," he suggested.

"I don't want to sit back down."

"Do it, anyway."

"Have you lost your mind?"

He crossed one leg over the other, stretching his arm along the back of the sofa, looking every minute of his five years older than her. "We talked about this, Tessa."

"Talked about what? When? I never agreed to sell Land's End. I certainly never agreed to sell it to Colton

Herrington. Will you *imagine* for a second how I felt when he showed up at the door?"

"I didn't make the connection. I spoke to his representative in Atlanta, then I spoke to Rand Garvy. Nobody mentioned a Herrington."

"No kidding."

"It doesn't matter," said Barry.

"How can it not matter? He's my *ex-fiancé.*" Not that she'd agree to sell Land's End to anyone. So, she supposed, in some ways it was a moot point.

"We can't afford to keep it," Barry offered reasonably.

"We don't owe any money on it." The occasional mortgages, taken out by previous generations, had long since been paid off.

"That's not what I mean. You know we can't afford the upkeep."

"We're managing," she countered.

"We're not managing. This place needs..." He glanced around the big room. "Well, everything. The roof, the walls, the foundation. The castle is nearly two hundred years old."

"Only the original section."

"Yes, the original section. The others are barely over a hundred."

"It's our home, Barry." Tessa didn't understand why he was springing this on her.

"It *was* our home. Times change, Tessa. Do you have any idea what the property is worth now?"

"You want to turn our children's heritage into liquid cash?"

His expression turned stony. "We don't have children."

"But we will. Someday, we will. And Land's End belongs to them every bit as much as it belongs to us."

"Are you suggesting we move back here, the two of us? Maintain the house, keep up the yard, cover the expenses?" he challenged. "Are you actually planning to *live* in Tucker's Point?"

"What's wrong with Tucker's Point?"

Barry rolled to his feet. "I have a medical practice in Atlanta. I'm not coming back to Tucker's Point."

Her shoulders drooped. "So, because you don't want to live here, I lose my family home. Is that it?"

"Do you have to be so melodramatic?"

She gestured around the big room, full of her childhood treasures. "You'd cash it all in? Just like that? Put an end to what everyone else built?"

"I'm not going to blow the money on women and liquor. I'm going to expand the medical clinic. Not to pull out the morality card, Tessa, but I'm saving the lives of children."

"Well, that was a low blow."

"You're the one who accused me of cashing it all in."

She pointed to the half-polished suit of armor. "You remember that? Great-grandpa made that."

He gazed at the shining suit and a nostalgic smile grew on his face. "It's a little hard to forget."

"I found it down in the basement. You should see all the stuff that's down there."

He nodded to Aunt Sophie's painting and the brass candlesticks. "I see you've pulled some of it out."

"It's nothing short of treasure. It's bringing back memories I didn't know I had." She dropped into the armchair across from him. "We can make it work, Barry. Maybe we have to close up the house for a while, just pay the taxes, but we don't have to sell. Not yet. Not to *him*."

"We can't base a decision on the buyer, Tessa. That's completely illogical."

Tessa didn't find it illogical at all, but that wasn't her strongest point, so she let it drop. "I'm saying I don't want to sell, period. This place is too important to sell."

Barry sat down again. "It needs work. It needs work soon. It's not just a matter of closing the doors and turning off the heat."

"Why are you dropping this on me like a bombshell?"

"I thought we'd agreed."

"When did we agree? At what point did that conversation take place?"

"Two years ago, when Sophie gave me her power of attorney. She understood the financial drain. I told her then that I was looking at rezoning."

"Two years ago?" Tessa parroted back in astonishment.

"Yes."

"Nobody told me."

"*I* told you. You said we couldn't move Sophie. I said that was fine while she was alive, but we'd have to make some hard decisions for the long term."

"I didn't think you'd sell before she was cold in the ground."

"I didn't expect to get serious interest this soon."

His words took Tessa's thoughts back to Colton. Colton was here, at Land's End. She knew breaking up with him had been absolutely the right thing to do. No matter how much fun they'd had together, she was always battling a sense of inadequacy that made her jumpy. His circle of friends and business colleagues—

they all operated so effortlessly in the upper echelons of Boston.

Tessa was constantly struggling to measure up. As a child, she'd learned her instincts didn't always lead her down the proper path. And she simply couldn't spend the rest of her life analyzing every choice she made and every word she uttered, for fear of embarrassing Colton.

But breaking up with him had also been the hardest thing she'd ever done. There were things about him that she desperately missed—his insight, his sense of humor, his ability to rush fearlessly into any situation and bring it under control. And, of course, his lovemaking.

She didn't want him here, reminding her of everything she missed. She didn't want to see him. She didn't want to talk to him. She wanted him gone, and as soon as possible.

"I'm not going to agree to sell," she stated with conviction. "And you know you can't sell the estate without my agreement."

"Tessa, think about what you're saying."

"I have!" she shouted.

Barry held up his hands in surrender. "Fine. I can see you're not going to agree right here and now. No problem. But Colton Herrington is here today. It's my house, too, and I'm showing him around."

Tessa opened her mouth to protest, but Barry talked right over her. "If he's not interested, fine. Then we've got some more time. If he is interested, we can fight again in the morning."

"You're staying over?" Tessa found herself asking.

Barry tipped his chin toward the big window where snow was sticking to the trees and the grass. "I think I'd rather travel in the daylight tomorrow."

"I'm determined to change your mind about this," she warned him.

He smiled patiently. "And I'm determined to change yours."

COLTON STOOD NEXT to the rotund boathouse on the spit that stretched from the tip of Land's End out into the bay. They'd already walked the length of the rocky beach, across the expanse of lawn and around the back of the castle to the narrow strip of woods that gave privacy from Beech Tree Road. Now they squinted through the falling snow, gazing at the ocean and the picturesque town around the bay.

Tessa's childhood property offered everything Colton could have dreamed of in a seaside resort. Sure, it would take a lot of work to get it there, but he could already picture the final result. It was going to be spectacular. He made up his mind to do whatever it took to complete the purchase.

"What do you think?" asked Rand from beside him.

"The beach will take at least six months to upgrade," he responded, mindful of Emilee listening. If he seemed too enthusiastic, she'd probably tell Tessa and Barry to jack up the price.

"We'll need dozens of truckloads of sand."

"She told you she won't sell," Emilee interjected.

"She'll listen to reason," Colton responded, not even remotely sure if that was true.

Tessa was usually very reasonable. But every once in a while, she'd inexplicably dig in her heels, and dynamite wouldn't blast her from her position. He could never figure out why. There was certainly never a pattern to it.

Once, he'd bought her an emerald necklace, surpris-

ing her with it when he'd picked her up to attend a char-
ity event. But she'd flat-out refused to wear it. It wasn't
as if it was overly expensive. And it looked fantastic
with her dress. There wasn't a reason in the world that
she should have refused. But she had, and no amount
of logic had been able to sway her.

As his mind wandered further, he couldn't help but
remember taking her home that night, back to the small
apartment she'd rented with Emilee since they were
students. Tessa's goodnight kiss had nearly blown his
mind, and he'd tried to talk her into coming back to his
place and spending the night. It was only twenty minutes away. His car was waiting, and they could have
made love and slept in each other's arms.

Again, she'd inexplicably refused. He'd spent the
next three days frustrated and plotting to get back on
her good side. Which he had. That weekend, they'd
dined on his balcony, enjoying a five-star meal created
by his chef, candles, white tablecloth, six courses and
an award-winning bottle of California wine.

It was the night he'd decided he would propose, the
night he'd realized they were made for each other.

It had taken him two weeks to get everything ready,
finding the perfect diamond, having it set in platinum,
writing and rehearsing his lines. He'd picked her up in
a stretch limo, dressed in a tux, spiriting her to a private
dinner in a rooftop room at Andantina's. There, he'd
gotten down on one knee as the Fourth of July fireworks
went off outside the window. She'd looked so incredibly
beautiful that night, in a sparkling red gown, her hair
upswept, crystals dangling from her ears and her neck.

Then again, she looked equally beautiful today, in
blue jeans and a flannel shirt. It was hard to believe,
but over the past few months, he'd forgotten exactly

how beautiful she was—even without makeup, even without designer clothes, even when she wasn't flashing that million-watt smile.

"It's ironic," said Emilee.

Colton blinked himself back to the present. It *was* ironic. For a second, he had to assure himself Emilee couldn't read his mind. He shifted in his dress shoes, realizing it was getting very cold as the sun slipped down in the sky.

"What's ironic?" Rand stepped in to ask.

But Emilee was looking at Colton. "They've been predicting a storm for days now. It hasn't materialized. If we'd waited a little longer, you could have helped us move the kayaks."

Colton narrowed his eyes in puzzlement.

"We were hauling the kayaks into the beach house, and Tessa mentioned that you could have helped."

Something in Colton's chest tightened. "Tessa was talking about me?"

Emilee stared hard at him, scrutinizing his expression. "What are you really doing here, Colton?"

He didn't miss a beat. "Buying some property for Herrington Resorts."

"Don't you dare mess with her head."

"Excuse me?"

Emilee took a step closer, wrapping her leather coat more tightly around her in the freshening wind. "I know you, Colton."

"You barely know me at all."

"I know enough. You're used to getting everything you want in life. You use people and situations like pieces on a chess board."

"Barry was the one who decided to sell." Colton resented the implication he'd somehow orchestrated this.

He was taking advantage of the opportunity, sure. But he wasn't some mastermind.

"I'm not talking about the property," Emilee continued. "I know that you walk away from women. Women don't walk away from you."

"You're making assumptions." Emilee had no idea who'd walked away from whom in his past.

"I'm making observations," said Emilee. "And I read the gossip columns."

"A bastion of accuracy on my personal life," he scoffed.

"They're close enough."

"What exactly are you saying?"

"I'm saying, don't let your ego make you hurt Tessa."

"I'm not here for Tessa."

No matter how beautiful she was. No matter how much he missed her. She'd made her position abundantly clear, and he had no place in her future.

He admitted to himself that Emilee was partially right. He normally did get what he wanted in life. But one of the reasons for that was that he didn't waste his time on lost causes. Tessa was a lost cause.

Emilee tossed her hair in the gusty wind. "I think you're here to convince yourself it was your decision to split up. And that means you'll have to convince Tessa she still feels something for you."

"Does she still feel something—" Colton snapped his jaw shut, angry with himself for asking.

"You're not good for her."

"That may or may not be true. But I'm here to buy some land. Full stop. Tessa and I are over."

Emilee looked as if she was going to say something more, but Colton's phone rang inside his coat pocket and he took the opportunity to step away.

"Hello?"

"Mr. Herrington? Captain Parker, here."

"Captain." Colton acknowledged his airplane pilot.

"Sorry to disturb you, but we've just been advised they're shutting down a runway due to the snow."

"Right now?" asked Colton, glancing at the cloud-filled sky. Flakes had been falling when they'd arrived, increasing in intensity, but it didn't look like anything serious at the moment.

"It's getting thicker by the minute out here. We've got a half-hour window to get off the ground before they close the airport to private traffic. Can you get here in time?"

"Not a chance." They were an hour and a half away. "How long will they restrict traffic?"

"They're saying at least twenty-four hours."

"Are commercial flights still getting out?"

"They are. Jack tried to get us some hangar space, but there's nothing available. We can wait it out here, or we can meet you back in Boston."

"You better take the window," said Colton. He didn't want to risk storm damage to the company jet, or risk marooning it in Maine. There were other executives who had it booked for the next few days. "We'll grab a commercial flight tonight."

"Would you like me to call Lily?"

"Yes, please. Have her email me the details when she's got them."

"Will do. See you back in Boston, Mr. Herrington."

"Have a safe flight."

"What's up?" asked Rand as Colton ended the call.

"Airport's closing to private traffic. The boys have to take off in the next thirty minutes."

Rand glanced at the sky. "It must be worse down the coast."

"Sounds like it is. Lily's going to book us a commercial flight."

"My toes are getting numb," said Emilee.

"Do you suppose it's safe to go back inside?" Rand asked her.

"It might never be safe for you two," Emilee retorted.

Colton tucked his phone back into his jacket pocket. "My money's as good as anyone else's."

He scanned the beach one last time. Tessa's place or not, this was exactly what he needed—a comprehensive and complex project to occupy his mind.

He was going to get over her. There'd never been any doubt about that. But keeping himself busy for the next few months was a very good strategy. By the time he was finished here, he'd never have to think about her again.

WHEN TESSA SPOTTED the group heading back to the house, she decided the best tactic was to stay out of their way. Barry had the right to show Colton or anyone else around the castle whenever he wanted, but Tessa sure didn't need to stand around and watch.

But first, she zipped up the stairs to her bedroom, quickly made the bed, straightened the clutter on her dresser and checked the en-suite bathroom for embarrassing undergarments. Sure enough, there was a lacy bra sitting on the counter and a pair of purple panties dangling over the edge of the hamper.

After tidying up, she took the back staircase to the basement. There was plenty of work for her to do down there. Hopefully, by the time she was finished, Colton and Rand would be long gone, far away from Tucker's Point. She took a narrow hallway to the wine cellar.

In addition to hundreds of bottles of wine, the room was stocked with old crystal decanters and a multitude of stemmed glasses, along with silver serving trays and small glass plates. Successive masters of the Ambroise castle had carried on a tradition of wine tastings in the cellar on special occasions. Though no one had done it in years, there remained a massive maple table in the centre of the room. It was surrounded by leather stools for guests, plus an imposing armchair at the head. The chair was first used by Payton Ambroise, who built the castle, to preside over ceremonial occasions.

Tessa started with the serving trays, working her way through the collection, setting aside any that were familiar, planning to choose a couple of them to move upstairs. At one point, she heard her brother's voice in the distance. She froze, tempted for a wild moment to duck out of sight beneath the table. But the voices faded, and she breathed a sigh of relief. She glanced at her watch, decided four in the afternoon was late enough and hunted down a corkscrew.

She chose a Spanish merlot, flagged Gran Reserva. No point in skimping on quality on a day like this. She polished a cut-crystal glass and twisted the corkscrew into the cork. It came out firm and plump, and the aroma of the wine wafted into her nostrils. She poured the ruby liquid into the glass and let it breathe for thirty seconds. It was a compromise for the first few sips, but she'd drink slowly, letting the flavors open up along the way.

"I wondered where you'd gone," Colton's voice rumbled unexpectedly from the cellar door.

Her pulse jumped to attention as his footsteps echoed on the uneven stone floor. He moved toward her and she looked behind him as he advanced, watching for Emilee or Barry. But they didn't appear.

"Did you lose the tour?" she asked.

Colton came closer, and her heartbeat quickened. "The tour lost me."

"They're probably back upstairs," she offered as airily as she could manage, pointing the way as she took a bracing swig of the wine.

"Probably," he agreed. But instead of leaving, he came to a halt, too close, gazing down at her.

Her physical reaction to him was frustratingly familiar. He'd always been incredibly attractive, fit, sexy. Her attraction to him had never been in question.

And she didn't dislike him. She mostly admired him. Trouble was, her own flaws seemed magnified when he was around. Right now, his regard made her self-conscious about her appearance. He was pristine, and she was dusty, even frumpy.

She made a shooing motion with one hand, hoping to end the encounter. "You don't want to miss seeing the kitchen."

His gray eyes seemed unusually dark in the dim light. "I'm not interested in the kitchen."

"The view is to die for." She attempted to pique his interest. "It's my favorite part of the house."

"Why's that?"

She decided being contrary was her next best defense, reminding him of one of her flaws. "It's where we bake the cookies. Big, sweet, gooey cookies. Probably about a million calories each. I eat them by the handful."

Colton was meticulous about exercise and nutrition. He'd never be so weak as to chow down on chocolate chip cookies. She couldn't count the times that she'd smiled and agreed with him that they should skip dessert at The Grille, when in reality she was desperate for a taste of crème brulee or a slice of decadent chocolate cake.

"The kind that will make you fat and weak," she added for good measure.

She took another sip of her wine, noting the way his eyes followed the motion. She imagined he was thinking it was early in the day for drinking. Too bad for him. She liked a little buzz in the afternoon—especially this afternoon.

"Want some?" she taunted, canting a hip out to one side.

He was silent for a long moment, but she could see the hesitation in his eyes.

"Sure," he answered.

"Yeah, right," she scoffed.

He reached for a glass, then lifted the bottle, pouring a good measure.

"That glass is probably dusty," she pointed out.

He glanced suspiciously at the crystal. But then he shrugged and took a drink.

"Well, well, well," she singsonged.

"What?"

"It's not even five o'clock yet."

He shrugged. "It's not a hard-and-fast rule."

The words took her by surprise. "You have rules that aren't hard and fast?"

"Sometimes." He took another drink, and she realized he was being deliberately contrary.

She'd taunted him, and he was responding by being disagreeable.

It was her turn to shrug. What did she care if he drank wine in the afternoon? Until she'd started dating Colton, she'd certainly had nothing against a pre-predinner drink. She finished her glass and poured some more.

His brows drew together. "Trying to get drunk, Tessa?"

"Trying to get numb, actually."

He didn't seem to have an answer for that. Though he did finish his own glass and helped himself to some more.

She felt as if she were in a ridiculous game of chicken. Normally, she acquiesced to his desires. Not because he was a bully or had a temper, but because his perspective was usually best. Often his perspective wasn't fun, but it was always commendable.

He set the bottle back down with a thud. "Can I ask you something?"

"Why not," she breathed.

"That emerald necklace."

"What emerald necklace?"

"The one I bought for you last April. Don't pretend you don't remember it."

"I remember it," she allowed.

In retrospect, it had been one of the first warning signs. Maybe if she'd listened to her instincts back then, things would never have gotten so far out of hand.

"What was wrong with it?" he asked.

"Nothing." It was a beautiful necklace. Any woman would have been thrilled to get it.

His lips compressed. She could tell she'd disappointed him. Luckily, she didn't have to care anymore.

She temporarily set her glass down. Then she braced her hands on the maple table, boosting herself up to sit on it. Telling herself nothing he said or thought mattered, she crossed her ankles and lifted her wineglass to her lips, taking an unconcerned sip.

"So, why wouldn't you wear it?" he pressed.

"I don't want to have this conversation," she said boldly. The alcohol was making its way into her circulatory system, taking the edge off her anxiety.

"Well, I do."

"Then have it by yourself."

He tipped back his glass, draining the wine. "What is the matter with you?"

"Absolutely nothing."

"You never used to be this contrary."

"I was. I just never let you see it."

He paused, peering at her as if her hair was gradually turning orange. "What was wrong with the necklace, Tessa?"

"You don't want to know."

"Yes, I do."

She shook her head in refusal.

"Don't tell me what I want or don't want," he insisted, leaning closer.

"Okay," she capitulated, deciding the quickest way out of this conversation was to give him what he'd asked for.

She started to take a drink but realized her glass was empty. She reached for the bottle, but Colton beat her to it, pouring another measure into her glass.

She waved it between them. "I want to go on record as answering this under protest."

"So noted," he intoned.

She squared her shoulders. "Fine. You made me feel like a dress-up doll."

He drew back. "What? I thought you felt pretty."

"I felt like a plaything that you'd decided to dress up and show off."

He went silent, looking confused. "Because I bought you a necklace?"

"You also bought me the dress and the shoes."

The outfit had been gorgeous. It had reminded her that his tastes were so much more refined than hers. His unlimited budget was one excuse, but Tessa knew it went deeper than that. Colton's instincts would always take him in exactly the right direction. Hers couldn't be trusted.

He relieved her of her wineglass and set them both down, propping a hand on the table beside her. His voice went cold and deep. "Let me get this straight. The problem that night was that I bought you too many presents."

"That wasn't the problem," she snapped.

He moved in close. "Then what *was* the problem, Tessa?"

Her hands balled into fists. For some reason, the weeks and months of frustration that had built up inside her head burst from her lips. "If I could explain it to you," she all but shouted, "we never would have broken up!"

They both went stock still, as if neither could quite believe she'd used that tone. Tessa sure couldn't.

A slight creak of the table beneath her seemed to boom in the silence. The air went thick, first warm, then cold, before Colton finally spoke.

His voice was calm, controlled. "Is that so?"

"Yes," she ground out. "That is so."

He was silent for another long moment. "Okay. Then explain it to me now."

"I don't know how."

"Figure it out," he said softly. "And I'll give you back your ring."

She scoffed at the absurdity of his statement, sliding down from the table to plant her feet on the floor, all but elbowing him out of her way.

He stood his ground, crowding her, their bodies almost touching. His index finger went gently to her chin, and he repeated the words. "Explain it to me now, and I'll give you back your ring."

CHAPTER THREE

COLTON WATCHED TESSA'S back as she marched out of the wine cellar, and realized his words had been foolish on so many levels. He'd asked her to come back. He'd sworn to himself in a thousand different ways that he wouldn't stoop to that. She'd made her choice. He shouldn't even contemplate *taking* her back, never mind asking her back. He certainly had no interest in a woman who didn't want him.

As her footsteps faded away, he started for the door himself. He'd go upstairs and make a show of checking out the kitchen. Then he was getting out of here.

He was absolutely going to buy this place. He'd offer whatever it took. But then he'd level the wine cellar. He'd level the castle. He'd erase any trace of Tessa and this ridiculously embarrassing episode in his life.

The value of Land's End was in the property—its view, its location, the spectacular beach and the funky little town that would appeal to upscale tourists. There was no value at all in the aging castle.

He wound his way through the cluttered basement to a narrow staircase that led to a first-floor hallway. He could hear voices in the great room and followed them to find Rand, Barry and Emilee. Tessa was there, too, but she was completely focused on buffing the suit of armor in the windowed alcove, ignoring everything else around her.

"There you are," Rand opened. "I just talked to Lily."

"Great," said Colton, moving toward the entry hall where he'd hung his overcoat. "Let's get out of here."

"She can't get us a flight," Rand called behind him. Colton stopped and turned. "That's ridiculous."

It was hardly the height of tourist season. And Herrington Resorts was an exceedingly good customer of most national airlines. That generally bought them some consideration when they had to travel on short notice.

"The storm's worse than expected," said Rand.

"But commercial traffic is still going."

"They've delayed or cancelled most of the flights."

"Get us on one that hasn't been cancelled."

Emilee was working on her laptop. "There's a weather warning from Canada to New York. But I have a flight in the morning that still shows as on time."

"Lily is looking into hotels for tonight," said Rand.

"So, we're staying in Tucker's Point? That's the plan?"

"That's the plan," said Rand.

Colton didn't want to stay in Tucker's Point. He was itching to get all the way out of town. He'd made up his mind to buy, and anything else could be done long distance.

"Why don't you come and take a look at these," suggested Barry. He had unrolled some diagrams on a large dining room table.

"They're the original survey drawings, and some geological information," he explained. "You can see the current building footprint and the potential for other development."

Tessa glanced sharply at her brother, but she didn't make a comment. She didn't look Colton's way at all, turning her attention back to the armor.

"Let's take a look," Rand suggested. "Lily's going to call as soon as she has something set up."

"Why not?" Colton figured he might as well have something other than Tessa's animosity to distract him. He made his way toward the table.

Barry had produced three sets of surveys, each one updated as additions to the building had been built. Colton could see that the original castle was about half of the current building. Extra bedrooms had been added in the early 1900s. A second turret had been tacked on in the fifties. And the kitchen had been updated and expanded in the seventies.

"What are the current height restrictions?" he asked Barry.

"The permitting framework doesn't specifically address height. Honestly, you'd probably run up against complaints about the impact on the view if you went up more than about four stories at the north end, here." He pointed to the space beside the castle and the pier.

"What about the south side?" asked Colton. "Is there a difference?"

"The hillside park overlooks the water to the north. But on the south, the terrain behind us is swampy, and the grade of the hill is too steep for development. There's no view to obstruct."

"How close are you on the rezoning?"

"The committee met last month. There's no specific opposition, except that they don't want light or heavy industrial. Retail or tourism sailed through without a challenge. As I understand it, the decision is being incorporated into the official community plan."

Tessa appeared at the table, glaring at them all. "It's three simple words," she enunciated carefully. "*I won't sell.* Why is this so hard for you people to understand?"

"Tess, not now," said Barry.

For some reason, Colton had an urge to defend her against her brother. He only just stopped himself from speaking up.

"This is a waste of time," she told them.

"It's my time to waste," Colton responded evenly, silently admonishing himself for his ridiculous gut reaction.

Tessa didn't want his help. And Barry was the one on his side, anyway.

"I'll never say yes," she told Colton.

The air thickened between them, and he wondered if she was referring as much to his offer in the wine cellar as to the land sale.

"You haven't heard my offer," he told her.

"I've heard enough."

"Tessa," Barry interrupted. He took his sister's arm and tugged her to one side.

Again, Colton reacted with his gut, tamping down an urge to step between her and Barry.

"Let go of me," she warned.

"We have to keep our options open," he hissed as they moved away, almost out of earshot.

"No, we don't."

"I can't make you sell," Barry whispered. "You're right about that. So, what's the harm in them looking? What's the harm in them thinking about it? We'll make a deal, or not, sometime in the future. But don't screw this up now."

"I know what you're doing," she grumbled in return.

"What am I doing?"

"You think you can change my mind by inches."

"I think you're missing the big picture."

"I think *you're* missing the big picture. You want a quick financial win over—"

"Can we talk about this later?"

Tessa's jaw clenched. Colton had seen that look a few times in his life. Once she got it, he couldn't budge her. At least this time he could see some kind of logic behind her intransigence.

"Fine. We'll talk after they're gone." Her glance went to Colton and her expression faltered. She seemed to realize he had overheard.

Rand's phone chimed.

"Lily," he informed Colton as he pressed the talk button.

"Can I get a copy of these?" Colton asked Barry, moving the conversation along.

"Of course you can."

Tessa rolled her eyes and marched away, Emilee joining her in the alcove by the armor.

"How is that possible?" Rand was saying into the phone, drawing Colton's attention. His expression told Colton something had gone wrong.

"Well, what are our options?" Rand paused. "You have got to be kidding." He turned to look out the window.

Colton followed his gaze, realizing the falling snow was almost impenetrable now, blowing sideways across the lighted front drive.

"It doesn't look good out there," Barry observed.

Tessa and Emilee had obviously noticed, as well. Both were staring out the alcove window.

"The car's getting totally buried," said Emilee.

"I don't think you're going anywhere tonight," Barry put in.

Colton hated to agree with him.

"I guess it is what it is," Rand said into the phone. His look to Colton was resigned. "Okay. Thanks for trying."

"What is it?" Colton asked as Rand signed off.

"Not a hotel room for a hundred miles. She said the interstate is still open, but side roads are almost impassable."

"You're welcome to stay here," said Barry.

"What?" Tessa's shocked voice echoed across the big room.

TESSA'S BOOTS SQUEAKED against the snow of the castle's driveway as she made her way toward Beech Tree Road. She didn't know what she expected to find there, proof that it was safe for Colton to drive away? Maybe a lighted vacancy sign on the B and B around the corner. Something, she realized, *anything* to tell her that Colton would be leaving Land's End tonight.

She'd woken up this morning, clear in her purpose, feeling as though she'd finally had a real direction in life. Land's End was that direction. Since Sophie passed away, Tessa had been working her way through the castle, rediscovering its magic, understanding why it was such an important place to her ancestors.

She might have broken up with Colton, but that didn't mean she couldn't see a marriage in her future. She'd love to have kids, to raise them here, to teach them about her wonderful parents, about Sophie, about the great-grandparents and all those before them who'd come here, made a home, turned it into a thing of value and artistic beauty.

She rounded the curve in the driveway, coming up to the edge of the road. Her nose had grown cold. A dense stream of snowflakes blew sideways along the road, silhouetted against the streetlights. A few cars had left tracks in the snow, but those were quickly filling in. It was incredibly quiet, everything muffled.

Tessa drew a deep breath of the chilled air, trying to clear her brain. For a moment, Colton's face flitted through her mind. She fought it, but then gave up, letting her thoughts roam free.

He'd said he'd give her back her ring. Why would he say that? What did that mean? Did he still *have* her ring?

Not that she wanted it back. No way, no how. He was a fun, smart, sexy, sophisticated guy, but there was no way she could spend the rest of her life trying to live up to his impossible example.

She wasn't perfect. She was so very far from perfect, and no matter how hard she tried, she couldn't seem to get anywhere near it. She'd given up a long time ago, and she had no desire to try again.

She could still remember her mother telling her she had to set an example, that the Ambroises were a prominent family in Tucker's Point and beyond. It might've been all well and good for other little girls to run and shriek on the beach, to play in the mud, to argue or cry in public, but it wasn't okay for Tessa.

Barry never seemed to have a problem with his role in the community. He'd achieved good grades, participated in the right social organizations. He'd never been great at team sports, but his success in ROTC and his talent at golf made up for it. And when he got into Harvard Medical, her parents had been over the moon. Tessa, on the other hand, got mediocre grades in high school, hadn't played sports. Instead of winning medals and trophies, she'd packed as much fun as she could into her teenage years, even lying about spending the weekend at a friend's beach house in Nantucket to take off to Florida for spring break.

"Tessa?" It was Colton's voice behind her.

She closed her eyes, pretending she could will him away.

"Tessa?" he repeated, closer this time.

She gave up and opened her eyes, blinking across the quiet street. "You do know that *you're* who I'm escaping from out here?"

He drew up beside her, also gazing at the falling snow. "I guessed as much."

"That begs the question of why on earth you'd come after me."

"I was worried."

"About what?"

"That you'd fall in a snow bank and freeze to death." He glanced up and down the street. "Now I'm worried that a car will slide out of control and mow you down."

"There are no cars out here."

"Not at this precise moment. But it is a public road."

"I can take care of myself," she felt compelled to point out. "I'm a grown woman."

"We got seats on a flight to Boston in the morning."

"Early?" She'd be more than willing to sleep in if it meant Colton would be gone before she came down to breakfast.

"First thing."

"That's good."

"I'll be out of your hair in no time."

"That's also good." She glanced curiously up at him, wondering about the turn of phrase. "Does that mean you're not interested in Land's End?"

A small smile curved his lips. "I'm still interested in Land's End."

"Why? There must be a hundred properties for sale along the Eastern Seaboard. Why here? Why mine?"

Again, he looked around them. "I like it here. It feels peaceful."

"So, you want to ruin it by building a monster resort?"

"It won't be a monster resort. Have you ever even stayed at a Herrington Resort?"

"No."

"They're intimate, boutique class, very tasteful."

"I'm sure they are."

"I can't believe I didn't take you to the Classic." He referred to the chain's flagship hotel in Boston.

"I drove past it once," she admitted. "Right after we first met. I was going to check out the lobby, maybe have a coffee, but I couldn't find parking."

"They have a valet," he pointed out.

"I didn't want to spend the thirty dollars."

The Classic was both exquisite and expensive. She couldn't help but wonder what he would have thought of the Bayou Side Inn where she'd spent spring break, four girls in a room. The parties rang through the halls all night long. It was crass and tacky, but harmless and a whole lot of fun.

"You should come back inside," said Colton.

"I'm fine."

"You're getting cold."

"I'm not cold. In fact, I'm thinking about going skinny-dipping."

"Don't talk nonsense."

"Why not? I like to talk nonsense."

"Tessa, what's the matter with you?"

She raked her damp hair back from her face. The snowflakes were melting into it, making her even colder. "There's nothing the matter with me. There's a hot tub on the back deck of the castle. I'm going to strip down and get in, turn on the music, turn on the colored lights, maybe open another bottle of wine."

"In the snow?" he asked with a touch of surprise.

"In the snow."

"Naked."

"Buck naked."

"With a houseful of people, including Rand."

"They're welcome to join me if they want," she shot out cavalierly.

"Over my dead body."

"Getting naked in the backyard too tacky for you, Colton?"

"I'm not about to let my vice-president see you naked."

Truth was, Tessa wasn't about to let Rand see her naked, either. But she wanted to shake Colton up. It served him right for invading her life like this.

She turned on her heel. "You guys can do whatever you want. I'm having a hot tub."

Colton snagged her arm, turning her back to him. "What's gotten into you?"

"I'm angry," she answered honestly, shaking off his grip.

"Well, this is a funny way to show it."

"You don't get to tell me how to be angry."

He studied her expression, no trace of emotion on his face. "I wouldn't dream of it," he answered levelly.

Then he shook his head and started down the driveway.

For some reason, his cool reaction angered her even more. Did anything shake him up? Anything?

She impulsively reached down, grabbed a handful of icy snow and shaped it into a compact ball. She took aim and threw hard.

It splatted into the back of his head.

"What the—" He turned to glare at her.

Her hands were wet and freezing, but she was already shaping another missile. "Is this a better way to be angry, Colton? Is this okay with you?"

She threw the second ball, and he ducked out of the way.

"Have you gone crazy since you left Boston?"

She scooped up another handful.

"Stop it." He stepped forward.

She let it fly, half formed, before he could get to her. The loose snowball smacked into his chest.

"You want to fight me?" he demanded.

"I don't know."

What *did* she want? Some kind of emotional reaction from him, maybe? For him to do something that wasn't perfectly controlled?

He grasped her right wrist. "I promise you, I'm a bigger, badder snowball fighter than you'll ever be."

"Go ahead," she taunted defiantly. "Give it your best shot."

"No."

"Why not?"

"Because I'm not going to hurt you."

"They're snowballs, Colton, not rocks."

He stared at her for a long moment. Then he reached to the ground, took a scoop of snow and, before she realized what he was doing, dropped it down the front of her shirt.

She gasped from the cold.

He gave a satisfied smile.

She leaned down. He didn't stop her as she scooped her own handful of snow in her left hand.

She gazed at it, all white and icy. Then she took in

Colton's smug expression and pushed the snow into his face.

He snagged her wrist, pinning both hands by her sides. "That wasn't nice."

"It wasn't, was it?" she agreed. "And what are you going to do about it?"

Shout at her? Toss her in a snow bank in retaliation? Would he finally lose some of that control?

He leaned in. "This."

To her shock, he captured her cool lips with his own. It took only a second for familiar heat to burst between them. His lips parted hers, delving deep. It had been so long. It had been too long. For a moment, she let herself sink into the mind-blowing sensations of Colton.

Her wrists still trapped in his hands, his arms went around the small of her back, bringing her body up against his. He was so solid, sturdy and strong. She'd never had a single doubt that he could solve any problem, take on any foe, keep her completely safe in any circumstance. His strength was one of the things she'd loved most about him.

It was compelling, just for a few moments, to let herself feel it all again. She let her curves mold against him, returning the kiss, swirling her tongue with his, tasting what she'd desperately missed.

When he pulled back, she was slightly dazed.

"What was that?" he asked gruffly.

They were still tight together from knee to chest.

"Sexual attraction was never our problem," she breathed, even though she knew her reaction had gone way beyond sexual attraction.

"What was our problem?"

"Let's do it," she offered, answering his question in

a very oblique, roundabout way, knowing there wasn't a chance he'd agree. "Right here, right now."

"Do what?"

"Have sex."

He jerked back. Now *there* was an emotional reaction.

"In the *woods?* In the *snow?*"

"Why not?" she asked

"Do you actually need a list of reasons?"

"I guess I don't."

She wasn't disappointed. She couldn't really have sex with Colton, in the woods or anywhere else—at least not anymore. Though there was a time when she'd have done it in a heartbeat.

TESSA AND EMILEE had braved the snow and climbed into the hot tub, setting a tray of cheese and a bottle of wine on the ledge beside them. Tessa knew there wasn't a chance any of the men would come out on the deck while they were half-naked. Which meant she was safe from Colton for the time being.

"How're you doing?" asked Emilee, concern in her tone as Tessa poured the wine.

"Totally and completely blindsided," Tessa admitted.

Muted, colored lights flashed beneath the water. Steam rose into the night, while huge flakes fell steadily from the sky, melting in the water or clinging to the leafless maple trees around the deck.

"Did you know Barry was even thinking about selling?"

"He reminded me that we'd talked about it, at least in really general terms, a couple years ago, when Sophie gave him power of attorney. I'd completely forgotten about the conversation, but he's been working toward it ever since."

"Weird about Colton." Emilee studied Tessa's expression.

"Very weird about Colton," Tessa agreed.

"You've been alone with him a couple of times," Emilee ventured.

"I have."

"Did he give anything away? What's he really up to?"

Tessa shifted under the water. "You mean aside from trying to talk me into selling him my house?"

Emilee lifted her glass of wine. "Yes. Aside from what he's making obvious."

"He offered to give me back my engagement ring."

Emilee sputtered. "Excuse me?"

Tessa trailed her fingertips through the water. She knew her decision to break it off was irrevocable, but just for a moment, just for a second, she'd let herself imagine it could all work out.

"Was he serious?" asked Emilee.

"I have no idea."

Not that it mattered. Tessa couldn't let herself go back to the uncertainty, the stomach-churning double-check of everything she thought and did. Why couldn't Colton be flawed? Maybe if he were a little more human, she'd have a fighting chance of keeping up.

"Did you consider it?" asked Emilee.

"No. Not then. But I had a bad moment when he kissed me."

Emilee sat up straight in the water. "He *what?*"

"He's a good kisser, Em. He's always been a good kisser."

"I don't like where this is going." Emilee's tone was dire.

"It's not going anywhere," Tessa assured her. "I didn't break up with him because he couldn't kiss."

"You know, when you commit to someone for your entire life, there shouldn't be any compromises."

"You're preaching to the converted."

Tessa told herself to quit dwelling on Colton. She reached for the tray and popped a cube of cheddar into her mouth. Then she followed it up with a sip of wine, realizing she was starving.

It occurred to her that a good hostess would have offered her guests some dinner, or maybe lunch, or anything, really. Then again, Colton and Rand were Barry's guests. She decided that he could worry about their comfort.

Emilee seemed satisfied by the answer. She relaxed back into her molded seat. "What do you think of Rand?"

"For what?" As a real estate purchaser? Rand wasn't buying Land's End. It was Colton who owned Herrington Resorts.

"I don't know." Emilee shrugged. "A fling, maybe."

Tessa was puzzled. Okay, *shocked* was a better word. "You think I should have a fling with Colton's vice-president?"

Had Emilee lost her mind? Sure, that would slam a lid on *any* possible future for her and Colton. But it seemed unnecessarily drastic, and rather mean-spirited.

"Not for you," said Emilee.

Tessa noticed that Emilee's cheeks were flushed, her smile secretive. She waggled her sculpted brows.

"*You* and Rand?"

"He's got one sexy smile, and a kick-ass sense of humor. You can't be that funny without being smart."

"You don't mean here. Not tonight."

"No." Emilee waved away the idea. "I was thinking maybe back in Boston. A date or something. I didn't really mean a fling."

"Wow." Tessa tried to wrap her head around the idea.

"Would it be too weird for you?"

"No. Well, a little. But not too much. I mean, I'm not planning to even come back to Boston for a while. Why would I care? No. It's fine. Sure. Go ahead."

"You do realize you're protesting way too much."

"I'm not. At least I don't mean to be. You took me by surprise, is all."

"It took me by surprise, too." Emilee tasted her wine. "Mmm. That's good."

"You're thinking about Rand, aren't you?"

Emilee responded with a sassy grin.

Suddenly, the hot tub motor clunked to silent. The lights went out, and the entire estate went black.

"Oh, that can't be good," came Emilee's disembodied voice, as the water settled to still.

"The power lines get weighted down with the snow," Tessa explained. "It'll probably come back on in a few minutes."

"Should we just wait?"

Tessa heard the sound of the back door opening, about twenty feet from the tub.

"You okay out there?" Colton called through the darkness.

"Fine," she responded to him.

"You need a flashlight?"

"Just put an oil lamp on the garden box. We'll be

able to see." She turned back toward Emilee, unable to make out anything in the black night.

There was movement near the door, followed by the faint glow of a match. And then the lamp ignited, spreading a pool of yellow light across the snow-covered deck.

"That okay?" asked Colton.

"That'll work," Tessa acknowledged. She could see Colton and the door quite clearly, and she could just make out Emilee and the wine bottle.

"You need me to carry something?" he called.

"The kayaks," Emilee deadpanned.

"Told you he was like that," said Tessa. Emilee's earlier criticism of Colton avoiding manual labor was just wrong. He helped out wherever he was needed.

"What was that?" he called.

"We're good," Tessa called in return. "But we're not decent. So, go away."

There was a slight pause, before Colton muttered something, then the back door banged shut behind him.

"I didn't like the sound of that," Emilee observed.

"The sound of what?"

"The way he shut the door."

Tessa wasn't following. "How did he shut the door?"

"There was a distinct level of sexual frustration in the bang."

Tessa peered at the indistinct, gray outline of her friend. "You have got to be kidding."

"He's here for you, Tess," Emilee stated with quiet authority.

"He's here for my house."

She'd allow for the possibility that he was doing it to spite her. He'd been pretty annoyed when she broke things off, and Colton didn't take disappointment very well.

"Maybe it is revenge," she allowed. "Maybe he saw an opportunity to get back at me, and he's taking it."

Emilee shook her head. "You need to be very careful."

"I'm not going to sell him my house."

The top layer of the water was cooling with the persistent snow. Tessa lowered her arms and slumped down so that her shoulders were further submerged.

"I meant about the other."

"I'm not going to turn back into his dress-up doll, either."

"Glad to hear it."

"He'll be gone in the morning, Em. And Barry will give up. And life will go back to normal."

"And what's normal?"

Tessa had to smile at that. "I haven't figured it out yet."

"You should come back to Boston."

"I'm having fun here. Well, maybe not today, exactly, but this is such a great place, and I love everything I'm rediscovering. Sophie had a library set up in the north turret. There are some books there that came over in the 1800s."

Emilee tipped her head back, gazing up at the blackness of the back castle wall. "You can't spend your whole life going through your family's junk."

"I don't think it'll take quite that long."

"Next you'll buy some cats and start wearing outlandish clothes. The neighborhood children will be afraid of you."

Tessa laughed. "I don't think the Biddles are planning on having children." She sure couldn't picture

Sherry and Jack Biddle tolerating noisy, messy hooligans invading their obviously well-ordered life.

The back door reopened.

"You two coming in or what?" Colton asked.

"The water's cooling off," Tessa said to Emilee, draining her glass of wine. "You want to go inside?"

"On our way," Emilee called to Colton.

CHAPTER FOUR

THOUGH POWER FAILURES in Tucker's Point rarely lasted more than a few hours, Tessa knew they should stoke up the great-room fire to try to hold the house's temperature. Since the castle had existed long before electricity and oil furnaces, there were also fireplaces that would heat the kitchen and many of the bedrooms.

Dressed now in jeans and a chunky sweater, hair still damp, with sneakers on her feet, Tessa wrestled a three-foot log in from the utility room. Milton always made sure there was an ample supply of wood within easy access of the great room. The big rounds were heavy, but they held a fire for hours and hours. It was well worth the effort.

She turned sideways to fit through the doorway, knocking the jamb as she maneuvered. Luckily, the castle was almost indestructible.

"For goodness' sake," came Colton's annoyed voice. "Just ask for help." He lifted the log unceremoniously from her arms.

"I don't need help," she pointed out.

"This thing weighs forty pounds."

"I carry them all the time."

"You shouldn't." He crossed to the fireplace, setting the log in the empty wood box.

"I'm perfectly capable—"

"Rand," Colton called into the dining room where

Barry and Rand were discussing the property plans by lamplight. "Let's load up the wood box."

"Sure thing." Rand reacted immediately.

It took Barry a split second, but then he followed. He hesitated, seeming torn between doing the manly thing and protecting his surgeon's hands.

Colton opened the big glass doors on the front of the fireplace and stuffed the log in on top of the bed of coals.

"Feel better?" she asked, brushing stray bits of bark from her sweater sleeves into the wood box.

"Much."

"I'm not a maiden in distress."

He scowled. "You're not a lumberjack, either."

Tessa struggled not to smile.

"What's funny?"

"I was just thinking the age of chivalry might not be dead."

His expression relaxed ever so slightly. "You got a dragon you need me to slay?"

"I've got a suit of armor you can borrow." She glanced across the room. "Then again, it looks like it would be a bit snug."

He turned to follow her gaze.

"No, no," came Rand's raised voice, obviously aimed at Colton as he maneuvered his way into the great room carrying two logs. "Don't bother to help. We've got it under control."

Barry followed with a single log.

"I'm busy flirting with the princess," Colton drawled.

Tessa couldn't help but bristle at the word *princess*.

"You'd better not be," called Emilee as she entered from the staircase on the opposite side of the room.

She'd dried off and dressed in a pair of skinny black

jeans and a shimmering gold blouse. Her high-heeled ankle boots were gold leather, polished to a shine. She'd applied some makeup, and her hair bounced like a blond halo around chunky hoop earrings.

Rand came to a stop and stared at her for a long minute.

"He's not flirting," Tessa answered Emilee, realizing her conversation with Colton had somehow fallen into a familiar, teasing pattern. "He was worried I'd break a nail."

"I'm worried you'll break your back," Colton countered.

"Anybody else hungry?" Emilee asked.

Tessa glanced at her watch and realized it was nearly seven o'clock. The power had been out for over an hour, so it looked as if it wasn't going to be a quick fix. She took the opportunity Emilee had offered.

"Follow me," she instructed Emilee, scooping up a lighted oil lamp, leaving the men behind as she headed for the kitchen.

"You were flirting," Emilee asserted under her breath. "I saw the expression on your face."

"Me?" Tessa countered. "Look at you. Pretty put together for a snowstorm."

"I want Rand to remember me."

"Oh, he's going to remember you all right."

They rounded the corner into the big kitchen. Tessa sat the oil lamp down on the center island and hunted for some matches and candles. They were easy enough to find, and she placed several around the counters and into the breakfast nook. Then she pulled out a stack of bowls and a handful of spoons.

"First rule of a power failure," she told Emilee. "Don't let the ice cream melt."

Peering into the dark freezer, she located several tubs of gourmet ice cream. She loaded butter brickle, coffee fudge, pecan praline and French vanilla onto the island. Emilee hopped up on a stool, snagging a bowl and a spoon.

Footsteps sounded as the men made their way into the kitchen.

"Help yourself," Tessa offered, feeling her way to the back of the freezer.

"Did we miss the dinner part?" asked Colton, the humor in his voice laced with concern.

Now, there was the Colton she knew and— Nope. That wasn't what she meant. This was the Colton she *remembered.*

"What's the matter?" she tossed over her shoulder. "You don't think that's balanced? Not enough green in this meal? Wait. Here we go, mint chocolate chip. That's as green as you can get."

She closed the freezer door, turning around to plunk the tub of ice cream down with the others. With a mocking grimace in his direction, she peeled back the lid and scooped herself a generous portion.

"That's the best you can do?" he asked. "On an empty stomach?"

They both knew Tessa had a sweet tooth. Sugar messed with her mood, and she always regretted overindulging. But she didn't care tonight. She needed to remind herself that Colton might be sexy and funny, but he was also exacting and obsessive. There was no better way to bring that home than to push his buttons.

She met his gaze, putting a spoonful into her mouth and making a show of enjoying it. "Yes. I've gone over to the dark side."

"You should have some fruit, maybe some cheese."

Barry made his way to the refrigerator. "I'm sure we have options—"

"We need to eat the ice cream," Tessa insisted.

"It's delicious," Emilee put in staunchly.

"I'm game." Rand took the seat next to Emilee and helped himself to a bowl.

"Why are you doing this?" Colton asked Tessa.

She took another bite. "It's melting."

"Who *cares?* Don't poison yourself. Let it melt."

She spun the carton around, moving it so she could see the ingredients list in the lamplight. "Cream, sugar, cocoa, milk solids, corn syrup, whey protein, guar gum, carrageenan, peppermint flavor. Nope. No poison."

"You're behaving like a child."

She stuck out her tongue at him, which she knew would be stained green.

Colton immediately rounded the island, cupping her elbow. "Excuse us."

"Hey," Tessa protested.

"Hey," Emilee echoed.

"This'll only take a minute," Colton assured everyone, firmly moving her from the stool and angling them toward the doorway.

Since Barry was hardly the confrontational type, and since Rand worked for Colton, nobody made a move to stop them. Not that Tessa was worried. If Colton intended to give her a lecture on nutrition, he could save his breath. She wasn't listening to a word of it. She was a grown woman, and she could eat ice cream for dinner if she darn well pleased.

"This is the problem," she began as he urged her around the corner of the hallway.

"No," Colton argued. "*This* is the problem."

Before she could wonder what he meant, her back

was against the cold stone wall and he was kissing her hard and deep. Intellectually, she fought it. But hormonally, she capitulated almost instantly. There was nothing tentative about his actions. His body was pressed firmly against hers, his arms around her, mouth open, tongue probing.

His hands went to her hair, smoothing it back, cupping her face, his touch achingly familiar. She braced her hands on his shoulders, telling herself to push him away, but somehow she gripped him hard instead. His muscles were shifting steel. His thighs were rock hard. She should have felt trapped, flattened against the wall, but she didn't. Instead, she felt inexplicably warm and protected.

Finally, he pulled back, drawing in a very deep breath. "I love peppermint."

"You love spearmint," she countered before she had a chance to think about it.

"*You* love spearmint," he corrected. "You told me so. I've always preferred peppermint."

"But—"

He kissed her again, and the question that had formed in her mind about toothpaste immediately disappeared.

After long minutes, he drew back again.

"Are you angry with me?" she asked, all but breathless.

"Yes."

"I don't care," she lied. She hated that she did care.

"No kidding," he chuckled low.

It didn't make sense, but she couldn't seem to stop herself from wanting to please him, or maybe make him proud. For some reason, his opinion of her still mattered.

"I'm eating ice cream for dinner," she reiterated.

"You'll regret it."

"I'll regret it more if I don't."

"Throw the damn ice cream away. I'll buy you some more when the power comes back on."

"It must be nice to have unlimited money," she blurted out.

He touched a finger to her chin, searching her expression. "Who are you, and what have you done with my Tessa?"

The wall suddenly felt hard and cold against her back. Now, she felt trapped. "I'm not *your* Tessa."

"Isn't that what I just said?"

She wriggled, pressing her palms against his chest, forcing some space between them. "This is me, Colton. I eat ice cream for dinner, and I proposition men in the woods."

He drew sharply back. "What men?"

She hadn't meant it that way. "Well, you most recently."

"And who did you proposition before that?"

She slipped away to the side. "You're like a dog with a bone."

He stopped her with a hand on her shoulder. "Because I care about your safety?"

"I'm trying to say I'm not perfect."

He gazed at her, the confusion obvious in his eyes. "You were perfect to me."

"No. You were trying to make me perfect. You failed."

"Is that why you left me? Because I failed?"

Tessa had to think about the question for a moment. "If you'd failed, I probably wouldn't have left you." She paused. "Then again, if you'd never tried, I probably wouldn't have left you, either."

His gaze narrowed. "Now you're talking nonsense."

She brushed his hand away. "Yet another one of my flaws." She determinedly started back down the hall. "I'm going for ice cream. You want some?"

COLTON AWOKE THE next morning to a raging blizzard and the cancellation of his flight to Boston. The entire Eastern Seaboard was being battered by what people were calling the storm of the decade. The power was still out in the castle, and the phone lines were jammed and mostly unusable. What little information they could get told them the monster storm was expected to make its way slowly northward over the next two days.

There was a little girl named April missing in town. Colton would have offered to help in the search, but emergency authorities were asking citizens to shelter in place. They currently had the manpower they needed with their trained volunteers. There was little for him and Rand to do but wait it out.

By midmorning, Barry had convinced Colton that Tessa would eventually agree to sell the property. Much as she might claim she loved it, and much as she might have stars in her eyes about living here and possibly raising her own children, the upkeep was simply too costly. The repairs needed on the crumbling castle were extensive and expensive. They'd cost more than the building was worth. Barry asked Colton to have a little patience while he reasoned with her, and he assured Colton he wouldn't entertain any competing offers while they worked through the deal.

Colton was satisfied with the arrangement. At least he should have been satisfied with the arrangement. But he couldn't seem to stop himself from feeling guilty about Tessa. Not that her emotional state was in any way his concern. She'd made it plain as day in conversation after conversation that their romantic relationship was history.

All she wanted to do was fight with him. Well, she also seemed to still like kissing him. She came at it with fire and passion, exactly how he remembered. But now, even their sexual attraction felt like some kind of a duel, as if she were proving something to herself or to him.

Why on earth would she want to make love in the woods? Who made love in the woods? Teenagers, maybe. But that was only because they didn't have homes or cars. Not that he wanted to make love in a car. It was cramped and uncomfortable, not to mention there was no plumbing.

Tessa had gone crazy. It was the only explanation.

Just then, she walked into the great room where Colton was watching the storm through the main window.

"I found a radio," she announced to Barry who was at the dining table typing on his laptop. "It'll save our phone batteries."

Emilee and Rand were traipsing through the room, having volunteered to reload the wood boxes in the second-floor bedrooms. From what Colton had overheard, Emilee was holding the door while Rand carried the wood.

"Batteries?" Barry asked Tessa.

"Plenty," said Tessa, taking a seat across the table from her brother.

She raised the antenna and began fiddling with the knobs, finding static, then music, then finally voices on a news station.

She set the radio at a precise angle on the table and sat back to listen.

Colton made his way to the furniture grouping next to the fireplace. Half listening to the news report updating the ongoing search for April, he retrieved his phone and began scrolling through his emails, triaging those that were most important. He was trying to conserve battery power, but Lily needed information and decisions from him on several issues.

A knock sounded on the front door.

All three of them glanced at it in surprise.

"Emergency crews?" Tessa speculated out loud as she came to her feet.

Barry showed no signs of going to the door, so Colton stood, as well, following her to the front entry. It might be emergency crews checking on them, but there was no telling who might be on the other side of the door, and for what reason.

Tessa was dressed in loose khaki cargo pants today. They rode low on her hips. She'd topped them with a snug navy long-sleeved T-shirt. She looked ready for action, or ready for yard work, and he struggled to picture her in an evening gown. He knew she looked great in them, but these clothes suited her, as well.

In the echoing entry, she dragged open the heavy door. Outside, a man and a woman were both bundled in fur coats and hats, covered with a thin layer of snow. Obviously, they'd been outside for a while.

"So sorry to barge in," the woman opened in a high-toned voice.

"Sherry?" Tessa asked, stooping slightly to peer at the woman's face beneath the fur ruff of her hood. Tessa's voice conveyed surprise and a hint of trepidation.

"The power's out at our place," the woman stated, breezing into the foyer without waiting for an invitation, causing Tessa to step rapidly out of the way. The woman was quickly followed by the taller man behind her.

Colton immediately stepped forward, planting himself half in front of Tessa, squaring his shoulders, as much a bouncer as a greeter as he offered his hand to the man. "Colton Herrington."

"Jack Biddle," the man responded, shaking Colton's hand.

"Sherry and Jack are my neighbors," Tessa informed Colton, obviously sensing his distrust of the couple.

Jack peered closely at Colton, maintaining a grip on his hand. "Are you *the* Colton Herrington?"

"I'm sure there are a few of us around," Colton replied noncommittally, removing his hand from Jack's grip.

The recognition of his name wasn't unusual, but Colton hadn't expected it under these circumstances. Here in the little town of Tucker's Point, off the beaten track, in coastal Maine of all places, he'd anticipated anonymity.

Sherry interjected in a staccato rhythm, her voice slightly shrill. "I thought we were going to *freeze to death* last night. I hope you people still have a fire going. We saw smoke coming out of your chimney before we went to bed. And then this blizzard. I can't believe they haven't fixed the problem yet."

"We have a fire," Tessa told them, her tone polite but even. "Please, do come in."

Colton was pretty sure he detected a note of sarcasm in her final words as she pushed the door shut behind them. It seemed to clank with a level of resignation.

"Herrington Resorts?" Jack pressed Colton for information.

"Yes," Colton admitted, wishing he'd left his last name out of the introduction.

He'd prefer to have visited Land's End anonymously. The last thing he needed was a competitor figuring out that he was interested in this property. He had Barry's word that he wouldn't look at other offers, but nothing had been signed yet.

Jack immediately snagged his hand again, pumping it enthusiastically. "Well, well. Let me say, it's a *great* pleasure to meet you." Jack's smile stretched a mile wide. "I'm a senior agent with Faust and Michaels, wealth management."

Colton felt his jaw tighten. Being marooned by the storm was bad enough. Being discovered at Land's End was slightly worse. And the last thing he needed today was an impromptu sales pitch from a financial company representative.

"Have you heard of Faust and Michaels?" Jack asked him in what was obviously the opening of a much-practiced pitch.

"Why don't we go inside," Tessa interjected brightly. "Can I take your coats?"

Colton silently thanked her for the distraction and immediately took advantage.

"Here, let me help," he told Sherry.

Without waiting for her response, he deftly peeled the glossy black coat from her shoulders.

"Do you have a hanger?" she asked, glancing dubiously at the row of coat hooks along the wall. "It's genuine mink."

"Tessa?" Colton wasted no time in jumping on the opportunity for a temporary escape. "Can you help me find some hangers?"

He relieved Jack of his coat and strode into the great

room, making a purposeful beeline for the hallway that led to the stairs. Barry glanced up at him curiously as he passed, but didn't make a comment.

Colton made it to the cool, dim second floor. He paused while Tessa caught up.

"What was that all about?" she huffed as she came to the top. "There are plenty of hangers downstairs."

"Jack was about to launch into a sales pitch."

"Just say no."

"Sometimes it's not that simple." Colton didn't want to have to be rude, and Jack came across as exceedingly persistent.

"I bet you're tougher than he is," Tessa put in.

"Back in Boston, he'd never even get an appointment."

"I take it back. It's Lily who's tougher than he is."

Colton drew himself up, speaking with mock indignation at the suggestion his assistant was somehow protecting him. "Hey."

Tessa grinned, obviously pleased at his reaction to her joke.

"Are they your friends?" he asked.

"They live next door." She started down the hall. "They moved in a few years ago, leveled a heritage house and built a glass-and-steel monstrosity. They seem to like Barry. But they thought Sophie was dotty, and I think they still consider me an annoying kid. Maybe they're waiting to see if I get rich before they decide to be cordial."

Colton followed. "You know, I was very sorry to hear about Sophie."

He realized his condolences were coming far too late. There was really no excuse for that. He should have contacted Tessa as soon as he'd heard. Though neither of them spent a lot of time talking about their families, he knew she'd loved her great-aunt.

"She died peacefully." Tessa pushed open one of the bedroom doors.

"You must miss her."

"I do." Tessa's voice was soft.

"It was good of you to take care of her this year."

"I was honored to have the time with her."

Colton hesitated, but saw no reason not to speak his mind. "So, you'll stay here by yourself, then? Is that the plan?"

He suddenly realized they were in Tessa's own bedroom. It was one of the nicest rooms in the castle. The floor was covered in a thick burgundy carpet. Her curtains and quilts were gold, and she'd decorated the walls with fabric hangings instead of paintings. It softened the room, making it feel warm and welcoming.

A small fire burned in her fireplace, flicking against the stone hearth and a pair of cream-and-rose-striped armchairs.

She disappeared into a walk-in closet, her voice hollow and echoing back. "Are you about to tell me this place is too big for one person?"

She was acting as though he'd been critical, which he hadn't. At least not yet.

"This place is too big for twenty people," he responded honestly.

She returned with two coat hangers. "Well, I happen to like it."

"Why?"

"Do I need a reason?"

"You don't need a reason," he allowed, finding himself quite curious. "But I bet you have one."

She glanced around the bedroom as if she was remembering snippets of her childhood. Perhaps there'd been a dollhouse in the far corner. Or maybe she'd used the padded bench seat to experiment with makeup. Had she whispered secrets with friends, fought with her mother, written in a diary?

He wished he was allowed to ask her those personal questions. But he wasn't. That moment in his life had passed. He realized now that he should have tried hard to get to know this part of her life while he'd had the chance.

"This was your room when you were a little girl," he ventured.

"It was," she admitted, her expression going less guarded as she cast a gaze around them. "Somehow, since Sophie's death, the memories are fresher."

"Good memories?" he prompted, curiosity growing. "You know, you never talked much about your family."

"You never talked much about yours."

He felt a sharp spike of emotion. "I stopped talking about my father the day he walked out the door."

"Colton." She'd pressed him for details a few times while they were dating, but he'd always put her off.

"Leave it."

"You had your grandfather."

"My grandfather was busy running the hotels. Mostly, I had nannies and drivers."

"Poor little rich boy?"

"Something like that. But we're talking about you. There was no reason for you to stay quiet."

Pain flashed briefly in her eyes, but she blinked it away. Then she gave a little laugh. "It's because I always thought you'd like my mother's version, where I was a perfect little girl. And I couldn't quite bring myself to tell it."

"You're not making sense," he pointed out.

"I was a hellion."

"I don't believe that for a second."

"Okay, I wanted to be a hellion. But my mother wanted me to be perfect. So, I did both." She ran her fingertips along the back of a striped armchair. "Sometimes I was her version of me, and I knew those were the stories you'd like."

"I'd have liked any stories," he told her honestly.

She gazed at him, eyes opaque, for a long moment. "I ran too wild, yelled too loud and got dirty a lot."

He found himself smiling at the mental picture. "What's wrong with that?"

"It's messy. My mother hated messy. You hate messy."

He shrugged. He supposed it was true. At least it was now. But he'd been a kid once.

"Tell me a messy story," he encouraged her.

"I had a cocker spaniel named Ralph."

"That's a start."

"He loved the beach," she continued. "We'd spend hours down there, getting wet, sandy, the wind tangling our hair. It drove my mother crazy."

"Kids tend to get dirty."

His words seemed to surprise her. "Did you get dirty as a kid?"

"I told you I mostly lived in hotels, right?"

She nodded.

"We stayed in the city locations more than the beach resorts, so there wasn't much dirt around. I spent a lot of time with tutors and my nannies. There weren't many opportunities to make friends when I was young."

"I didn't realize." There was sympathy in her voice.

"I mean, I hadn't thought about how all the other kids in the hotels would come and go every few weeks."

"That was the reality."

"Did it bother you?"

"It took me a long time to realize it wasn't normal."

Her eyes took on a faraway expression. "When I was about eight," she told him, "I realized living in a castle wasn't exactly normal. Before that, I just assumed anyone who wanted a castle would buy themselves one. I thought my friends' parents preferred smaller houses in town."

Colton found himself smiling. "It wasn't until my mom died, and my dad left, that I realized my life was very different from most kids'."

"Have you heard from him?" Tessa asked.

Tessa was well aware that his dad was a reclusive writer living in Paris. What he'd never shared with her was the pain he'd felt when his only living parent turned his back on both the family and the family business.

"He doesn't bother with Christmas cards," Colton stated flatly, intending to change the subject.

"You should go see him."

"Why would I go see him?"

Charles Herrington had descended into inconsolable grief when Colton's mother had been killed in a car accident. Apparently deciding he was incapable of providing emotional or any other kind of support to his grieving thirteen-year-old son, he left Colton in the care of his grandfather. Charles had absolutely no interest in the family business. He'd come home only rarely, and the company had eventually passed directly from Colton's grandfather to Colton.

At twenty-three, when his grandfather died, Colton had become CEO of the multinational corporation. It would have been invaluable to have had some guidance from his father, but Charles had remained too self-absorbed to notice or to care.

"He's your father," said Tessa.

"And?" Colton demanded.

"And, you'll regret it if you don't make peace. Every day, I think of things I should have said to Sophie, done with Sophie. I wished she'd told me more stories about her life, her paintings, my relatives—anything."

Colton dropped the coats over the back of one of the armchairs. "What would he tell me? The man lives almost entirely inside his own head. He's been cloistered in some crappy little Paris apartment for years, pounding out those dense, inaccessible stories that only the most pretentious academics can stomach."

Tessa stared up at him in silence for a long time. "Have you ever told him you're this angry?"

"I'm not angry." Colton regretted his emotional outburst. He'd long since come to terms with a life without his parents. It wasn't like him to care about his father's circumstances, never mind talk about them.

"Then what are you?"

"Resigned."

She paused again. "It's okay to have feelings, Colton."

He had feelings. He had plenty of feelings. He simply wasn't in the habit of letting them out for the world to see.

"You ever do something just because you felt like it?" Tessa asked.

"I do most things because I feel like it." Why did she think he was trying to buy her land?

"I mean, not because it's smart, not because it's right, just because it makes you feel good in the moment?"

He gazed down at her soft, flowing hair, blue eyes,

flushed cheeks, red lips. He could think of something that would make him feel very good in this particular moment. But it was a colossally bad idea. He'd kissed her twice since arriving yesterday. Each time, he'd walked away with his heart hollow, his longing for her even more acute. If he was going to get over her, to forget about her and get on with the rest of his life, not kissing her would be a good place to start.

"No," he answered huskily.

"Why not?"

"Because it would be foolish." Feelings were all well and good, but the world didn't run on feelings, especially the business world. It ran on cold, hard facts and logical decisions.

"You should think about trying it," she tossed off loftily.

"I think about trying it all the time."

"You do?"

"I do."

She cocked her head sideways. "So, give. What is it you feel like doing?"

Staring down at her, desire rippling through him, wanting so damn badly to throw caution to the wind, he realized how dangerous the conversation had become. He was about to do exactly as she suggested, do something very stupid based on emotion alone. He couldn't let that happen.

He girded himself, shaking his head. No way, no how was he telling her that what he wanted was to kiss her, ravish her, make hot, hard love to her until they both cried for mercy.

He scooped up the fur coats, relieved her of the hangers and turned for the door.

"Playing hooky from work," she guessed from behind him.

"I'm the boss," he called back, pushing down hard on the emotion in his chest and his gut.

"Eating a giant hot fudge sundae."

"We really have to do something about your sweet tooth."

"Skipping a day at the gym."

He paused at the door, without turning. "I like the gym."

"Dressing up in lacy ladies' underwear."

"No. What is the *matter* with you?"

She gave a little pout. "I like dressing up in lacy ladies' underwear."

That was it. He was done. No man could be expected to fight the image that bloomed inside his mind.

He turned and marched down the hallway, rounded the staircase and made his way back to the safety of the great room. Bring on the financial sales pitch. It was better than dueling with Tessa.

TESSA DIDN'T KNOW what it would take to actually pierce Colton's logical shell. Maybe it couldn't be pierced. She knew he didn't operate on emotions. But maybe he didn't even have emotions. Maybe she was fighting to find something that didn't exist.

As she entered the great room, she forced herself to face the truth. The Colton she needed didn't exist. And she couldn't be the Tessa he deserved. Impasse. There was nowhere for them to go.

Sherry's voice chirped from the big sofa, regaling Colton with tales of the exclusive clubs they belonged to, the fabulous vacations they took, all the work and money that had gone into their new house and her husband's plans to work his way up to VP in the company. It was a tag-team conversation, with Sherry lobbing Jack an opening, and him taking over, presumably so she could catch her breath.

Tagged in, Jack went on about his international business trips, his wealthy clients, their success and the stellar service available through Faust and Michaels. It was a fairly shameless commercial.

Emilee moved up beside her, mumbling in her ear. "Are we having fun yet?"

Tessa's attention was stuck fast to Colton. "He looks so lifelike."

"Huh?"

"He's so sexy and handsome, and his deep voice just strums across your nervous system like it was custom-designed."

"Uh-oh."

"But there's no way to break through that iron-hard, emotional control. If he can't let himself be imperfect, how's he ever going to forgive it in someone else?"

"What the heck happened up there?"

"We hung up some coats."

"Tessa." There was a warning tone in Emilee's voice.

"And Colton was Colton. As usual, just like always. In his wildest fantasies, he'd never consider dressing up in ladies' underwear."

"Excuse me?" Emilee squeaked.

"I guess skipping the gym was a more realistic expectation," Tessa admitted.

"Are you supposed to be making sense?"

"Not really."

Sherry laughed very loudly, her hands fluttering in the air as she made some kind of a point. "You're so right, Jack. And the third-floor balcony is to die for. We had Aberdeen and Questin on retainer. You know, the New York City firm that—"

"I have to admit," Emilee growled. "The more I listen to them, the less I like their house."

Tessa forced her gaze away from Colton, looking out the dining room window, hoping against hope for a little light at the end of the tunnel. But the storm was still going full force.

"Any good news on the weather front?" she asked Emilee.

"Government offices and businesses staying closed. The governor is asking people to stay off the roads. They're forecasting fifteen inches of snow by nightfall."

"What about the power situation?"

"Crews can't even start work until the wind lets up. They're saying lines are down, trees are falling, but a full assessment will have to wait."

Tessa puffed out a hard breath. "So, I guess the Biddles are ours for the night."

"Maybe not," Emilee ventured. "Take a look at Rand's expression. If that annoying woman doesn't stop talking, this whole thing could turn into a murder mystery."

Tessa couldn't help a dark chuckle as she moved her attention to Rand. "So, enough about me. How are things going between you and Rand?"

"So far, so good." There was a smile in Emilee's voice. "He asked for my number."

"Which you gave him."

"I most certainly did."

"Any stolen kisses in dark corners?"

"No, but I'm working on it. I'm also worried about you. Please tell me your head's on straight where it comes to Colton."

"My head's on perfectly straight."

Emilee linked an arm with Tessa's. "Stay strong, sister."

"Staying strong."

"It's certainly not to my taste," Sherry was stating, a hand raised delicately to her chest as she gaped at the suit of armor. "I'm partial to Zander Corbel, or anything from the Shenzille Circle. Subtle is always better than ostentatious. In fact, last Christmas, Jack bought me the most amazing set of glass shelves, custom-made for that corner near the pool deck." She gave a self-deprecating giggle. "But you obviously don't know what I'm talking about, Colton, since you've never seen our house. You *must* come visit someday. But, what do you think? Subtle or ostentatious?"

Colton appeared to give the armor a moment's thought. "It takes a big room to pull something like that off."

For some reason, Tessa felt let down. She didn't know what she'd expected—for Colton to put Sherry in her place? Had she expected him to declare his staunch respect and regard for medieval armor as a decorating choice? It was silly. She was the last person who should care about his opinion. Let the simpering Sherry worry about impressing him.

"Let's go find something to feed these people," she suggested tightly.

"I'll happily whip something up for Sherry Biddle. You got any arsenic lying around the basement?"

"I was thinking more along the lines of pasta."

Sherry let out a rather shrill, false-sounding laugh as she reached out to pat Colton's knee.

"Then again, I'm flexible," Tessa finished.

A sudden boom thundered through the house.

Colton jumped to his feet, while the high pitch of shattering glass and rending whine of metal on metal reverberated through the air. Tessa felt the noise right into her chest.

"Car accident," Colton declared, rushing for the front door.

Rand and Barry appeared at a run, turning out from the hallway.

"Did you hear?" Rand called to Colton.

"Let's go," Colton returned.

CHAPTER FIVE

TESSA RUSHED ACROSS the room, intent on following the men. Emilee was with her. Only Jack and Sherry sat dumbfounded.

"I have to get my bag," said Barry, turning back to the staircase.

Fuelled by adrenaline, Tessa grabbed her coat, stuffing her arms in the sleeves as she rushed out the door and up the driveway. Colton was out front, running toward the sound of engines. Rand followed him closely while Tessa jogged next to Emilee, praying they wouldn't find anyone seriously injured.

Around the bend in the driveway, she saw lights through the blowing snow. Headlights, taillights, yellow flashers, all seemed to be pointing at different angles.

"There're at least three cars," Emilee gasped.

"Check the sedan," Colton shouted to them. He moved toward a passenger van that had rammed an oak tree. Smoke was billowing from under its hood.

Tessa and Emilee rushed to the upside-down car. Tessa dropped to her knees, peering into the gloom of the shattered driver's-side window. She cursed herself for not bringing a flashlight.

"Go get flashlights," she said to Emilee. "As many as you can find. They're in the cupboard beside the fridge. And bring blankets. Get Sherry and Jack to help."

"Can you hear me?" she called to a woman who was hanging by her shoulder harness.

Emilee ran off into the darkness.

"My daughter," the woman rasped.

Tessa couldn't tell for sure, but she thought the woman had blood running down her cheek.

"I'll check her," Tessa assured the woman. "But are you okay?"

"She's in the backseat. I'm fine."

The woman was obviously very far from fine. But Tessa crawled to the backseat window.

"Sweetheart?" she called to the little girl.

She looked to be about five and, like her mother, was suspended by the seatbelt.

The girl blinked her eyes open.

"Hi," said Tessa, lying down on her belly and crawling partway into the car. "My name's Tessa. Can you tell me your name?"

"Christie," the girl responded in a shaky voice laced with tears.

Tessa inched closer, maneuvering her arms inside the small passageway, ignoring the shards of glass and the snow melting into her clothes. People shouted behind them, men's voices, women's voices, crying and screaming. She was vaguely aware of Colton working on the van behind her, helping people out of it.

"Can you tell me what hurts, Christie?"

"I want my mommy," Christie cried.

"I'm here, baby," came the woman's breathless voice from the front seat.

"Your arms or your legs?" Tessa asked Christie.

"My arm," she cried. "Ouch. My arm."

"Okay," Tessa crooned, as she moved to half sitting to be closer to the little girl. "My brother's here with us.

He's a doctor. Doctor Ambroise is his name. He's going to be here in just a few minutes to help you."

"Is she okay?" asked the woman, tears obviously choking her voice.

"Does your tummy hurt?" asked Tessa, putting a soothing hand on Christie's shoulder.

"Yes. No. A little bit."

"How about your head?"

"My arm hurts."

"Tess?" came Barry's voice.

A wash of relief rushed through her. "She says her arm hurts."

"Anything else?" asked Barry.

"I don't think so."

"She's talking? Seems coherent?"

"Yes."

"Okay. I'm going to check mom first."

"My baby," cried the woman.

"I'm Doctor Ambroise," came Barry's soothing, professional voice as he made his way through the window opening.

"Christie. Please help Christie," said the woman.

"We're helping her," said Barry. "What's your name?"

"I'm Summer," the woman gasped, obviously in pain. "Summer Torill."

"Does that hurt?" asked Barry.

"Yes," hissed Summer.

"This?"

"Yes."

"Less or more."

"More." She groaned out loud.

"Mommy?" cried Christie.

"It's okay," Tessa cooed. "Doctor Ambroise is helping your mommy."

"I'm cold," the girl whimpered.

Feeling a powerful urge to hold Christie in her arms, Tessa called out to her brother. "Can I undo her belt?"

"Do her ribs hurt? Touch them very gently."

Tess carefully placed her hands on Christie's chest. "Does this hurt you, honey?"

"No," the girl whispered.

"No," Tessa called.

"Her neck? Her back? Get her to move her hands and feet."

Tessa carefully checked the girl's neck and back, having her move and watching carefully for signs of pain.

"She can't move her left arm," she called back to Barry.

"I've got blankets," Emilee's voice came from outside the cars.

"I'm going to need a back board to move Summer," Barry told Emilee in a low voice.

"Can we improvise?" she asked him.

Tessa mentally catalogued the contents of the castle, picturing all the stuff she'd found in the basement.

"The boathouse," she called to Emilee. "There are surfboards in the boathouse."

"I'll get Rand," Emilee responded.

"Do it quickly," Barry instructed.

"Can I wrap Christie in a blanket?" Tessa asked her brother.

"Can you get her out without bumping her arm?"

"I think so."

"Okay. Move her very carefully. I need to stay here with Summer."

Tessa found herself giving a rapid nod. She felt a hand on her back and twisted her head to see Colton there to help.

"Mommy?" Christie whimpered.

"Okay, Christie." Tessa turned back, forcing herself to sound calm and confident. "Let's get you out of here and wrapped up in a nice warm blanket."

The girl met Tessa's eyes. "I'm scared."

"I know you're scared, sweetheart, but I'm going to help you. I'm going to get you out of here so you can see your mommy, okay?"

After a moment, Christie nodded.

"Good girl. Okay, can you put your good arm around my neck?"

Christie nodded again, raising her little arm.

"Fire's out," Colton said to Barry. "Rand's getting the surfboard. What else do you need?"

"How are the people in the van?" asked Barry.

"They're walking and talking, mostly teenagers. Battered and bruised, but we've sent them down to the castle, and they're getting warm. Sherry and Jack are there."

"And the semi driver?"

"He seems fine. He's on the radio with emergency crews seeing if he can get some kind of transport vehicle."

Tessa was encouraged by Christie's strength as she wrapped her arm around Tessa's neck.

"I know your arm hurts," said Tessa, maneuvering herself so that she could lie on her back and slide out feet first with Christie resting on her stomach. "And I'm going to try really hard not to touch it, okay?"

"Okay," Christie whispered in her ear.

"I'm right here," said Colton.

She felt his touch again.

"Tell me if I hurt anything," she told Christie, easing the little girl toward her until she was lying down on Tessa's stomach.

"Owie," whimpered Christie.

"I know, sweetie. Colton, can you pull us out?"

"There's a lot of glass," he warned.

"I know," Tessa acknowledged, bracing herself for scrapes and cuts.

"Lift your butt," he instructed.

"What?"

His deft hands were under her, slipping his coat beneath her, covering the worse of the shattered glass.

"Here we go," he murmured, and then she was moving smoothly out of the car.

"Watch her left arm," she warned Colton.

He gently put a blanket over Christie, supporting her arm as he lifted her into his arms.

A rumble grew louder, a big diesel engine shaking the ground around them. Flashing lights came into view, and Tessa recognized it was a loader. Her thoughts immediately went to Barry's former schoolmate, Henry "Red" Redmond. She knew he was a member of the volunteer emergency crew.

Christie was cringing against her chest, and Tessa covered the little girl's ears.

The loader came to a halt, and a man jogged into view. She recognized Red immediately.

"Hey, Barry," he said as he stopped in front of them, taking in the accident.

"Hey, Red."

"How's everybody doing?"

"Two with injuries," Barry reported.

"Everyone's okay in the other vehicles," Colton put in.

"I'll send in a report on the accident." Red nodded to Tessa. "It'll likely be tomorrow before they can tow away the vehicles. But we can set up some warning lights on the road. And I've cleared a path with Betsy, so the paramedics will be here in a few minutes."

"That's good to hear," said Barry.

For the first time, Tessa heard the stress in her brother's voice. She reached out to him, putting a hand on his arm.

"Everything going to be okay?"

"We're all good here," said Barry, his voice back to being completely calm and professional. "But I want to get everybody out of the cold. Red, is your cab heated?"

"It is," Red confirmed. "I can take the little girl, leave the ambulance for her mom." He crouched down in front of Tessa.

"Watch her arm," Tessa warned.

"Hey, there," Red said gently. "You want to come for a ride in my loader?"

"Mommy?" Christie whispered, her voice shaking.

"Your mommy's going to ride in the paramedics' truck," Tessa explained. "But it's a little small, and both of you won't fit. Red here is our friend. He's got a big, big digger that can make it through really deep snow. I've been in one before. It's fun. It's like being on a carnival ride. Do you think you can go with him?"

Again, Christie hesitated. But then she bravely nodded her head.

As Red carefully lifted her into his arms, the sirens and flashing red lights of an emergency vehicle penetrated the gloom. "Can you direct them?" he asked Colton.

Colton moved toward the emergency vehicle, waving his arms, directing them to the sedan.

The paramedics descended on the scene, talking with Red about the logistics of getting Summer and Christie to the hospital. Tessa quickly moved out of the way. Rand arrived with the surfboard, but it wasn't needed.

With Red on his way to the hospital, it took Barry and the paramedics about twenty minutes of painstaking maneuvering to get Summer out of the driver's seat. By then, she was unconscious, and Tessa could tell Barry was worried.

"There's nothing more we can do here," said Colton, putting a comforting arm around Tessa's waist.

Tessa bit down on her bottom lip. "She *has* to be all right."

"She's in good hands."

"I know."

"You were amazing," he told her in a low voice.

Tessa was confused. "What do you mean?"

"The way you comforted that little girl. She was hurt and frightened, and you knew exactly what to say."

The compliment took Tessa by surprise.

"You've got that human touch that I can never get right," Colton continued.

Tessa had a hard time sorting out what she was hearing. Colton wasn't good at something? Colton was good at everything.

"It was nothing," she found herself answering. She couldn't even remember what she'd said.

His arm tightened around her, and his tone was husky. "It was everything. I'm incredibly proud of you."

Tessa's chest swelled. He was proud of her? She'd followed her instincts, yet she'd gotten it right?

"You must be cold." He started to gently steer her toward the driveway.

She quickly glanced around. "Do they need anything else?"

"Not up here," said Colton. "But there are a dozen fifteen-year-old boys milling around your castle."

"From the van?" she asked.

"Yes, from the van. I'm thinking we might want to get down there and supervise."

Tessa regrouped and refocused.

"The van was carrying a wrestling team on their way back to Augusta," Colton continued. "It sounds like their GPS messed up and sent them down the wrong road."

"Are any of them hurt?"

"They seem fine," he answered as they started down the driveway. "I'm more worried about your great room."

COLTON COULD SEE the boys were restless. And fuelling them up with pasta just made it worse. He'd heard from the paramedics that there was a shelter set up in a local school, but there was no way to transport the boys and their coach to the center of town. And it seemed unnecessarily cruel to both the active fifteen-year-olds and the families already staying at the shelter to force the two groups together.

The coach was doing his best to keep them corralled. Jack and Sherry Biddle were next to useless and had retreated into a far corner, watching the goings-on with round eyes. Rand was too busy lusting after Emilee to be of much use and Tessa was trying valiantly to clear dishes up after the ravenous group had devoured a huge spaghetti dinner.

Colton decided to get things rolling in a better direction.

He clapped his hands loudly to get their attention, wishing he had a whistle. A whistle would work great.

"Ned, Allan, Bobby and Sam." He'd made sure he memorized their names over dinner. "You are table-clearing detail."

"Awww," the boys groaned in unison.

"No complaints," Colton snapped in his best board-room, I'm-the-CEO-don't-mess-with-me voice. "Rick, Kevin, other Rick and Jason, you're washing up."

Another round of groaning complaints filled the air.

"Peter, John, Chris and Piper, you'll be drying."

"This is lame," said Kevin, one of the larger boys and obviously a leader of the pack.

"Use the dishwasher," said Sam, more of a flyweight, with glasses and shock of dark hair that continually fell into his eyes.

"There's no dishwasher in the world big enough to clean this mess up," the coach noted.

"This is your fault, Coach Redding," Ned accused darkly. "We should have stayed on the interstate."

Of all the boys, Ned seemed most likely to end up in a juvenile detention center.

"Not another word," Colton warned them all sternly. "Miss Ambroise over there," he nodded to Tessa, "cooked and served the dinner. She's not going to do the cleanup, too."

"Are *you* going to help?" Kevin asked Colton.

"I absolutely am. And I'll be watching all of you every step of the way. So, no messing around."

"Who died and left you king?" asked Ned.

"My grandfather," Colton responded, looking Ned straight in the eyes.

Ned stared back, obviously not sure how to respond.

"He's Colton Herrington," Jack Biddle spoke up. "He can buy and sell each and every one of you—"

"Jack," Colton interjected.

"And he can kick your asses," Jack finished.

"Jack," Colton barked. He looked to the boys. "That wasn't the point I was making."

"Are you rich?" asked Sam.

"The point is, we're all stranded together, and we're all going to share the work."

"Like, *really* rich?" asked Kevin.

"For tonight, you probably need to care more about the part where he can kick your ass," the coach intoned.

Colton struggled to suppress a grin. "So, we're all agreed? We share the workload?"

There was more grumbling from the boys, but they made their way toward the dining room and the kitchen. Colton started with the clearing.

Tessa sidled past him. "Tough guy?" she mumbled under her breath.

"Don't you mean thank you?"

"You're a regular knight in shining armor."

"Go sit down."

"I can help."

"You've done enough. Relax. Read a book or something."

Her glance went to the messy table, but he could see she was tempted.

"Now," he ordered. "I've got this."

Her shoulders dropped ever so slightly. "You do seem to have a way of keeping order."

He couldn't help but grin, but then he warned himself not to care about her opinion. "I'll take that as a compliment."

"And I'll go find a good book."

"You do that."

The coach had gotten up to help, as well, and the Biddles had made themselves even scarcer. So the great room was suddenly quiet and empty. Colton couldn't help but be glad about that. Tessa deserved a little peace.

It took about an hour of bickering, reluctance and petty complaints to get through all the dishes. When they finally finished, Colton felt as if he'd put in a full day's work.

Barry had called to tell them Christie was in good shape with a cast on her arm. Her mother, Summer, had required surgery, but she was now recovering nicely. Barry was staying over at the hospital since they could use his help. There were a number of storm-related injuries coming in, and emergency crews were stretched since many of them were still out looking for the missing April.

Now the boys were clustered in the castle kitchen, and Tessa appeared in the doorway. She had showered and changed, wearing a pair of skinny jeans, heeled shoes and a black-and-purple sweater. Her brown hair glistened under the lights and, even without makeup, her blue eyes were deep and intense.

"As a reward," she said to the boys.

A dozen heads swiveled her way and gaped at her. They might only be fifteen, but they recognized a pretty woman when they saw one, and she had their complete attention.

"I'm going to take you all on a tour of the basement."

"The basement?" asked Kevin.

"Do we have to clean it up?" asked Ned. "Basements are lame."

"Any more of that battle armor down there?" asked Sam.

"Plenty more stuff like that," said Tessa. "Shields and swords, all kinds of interesting things." She handed around a few flashlights, keeping one for herself.

"Let's do it," one of the other boys called out.

"Can't be worse than dishes," Kevin capitulated.

Ned scowled, but the tide was against him.

"This way," Tessa called out.

Colton fell into the back of the pack, intending to keep order through the tour.

It turned out he needn't have worried. The boys were absolutely fascinated with the collections amassed in the Ambroise basement. Tessa's grandfather had been a skilled metal worker, with a passion for the medieval period. The boys were impressed with the weight of the swords and shields, clearly imagining what it must have been like to live in a different era. In the 1600s, they'd have been old enough to fight.

They also seemed to like Sophie's paintings. It didn't hurt that there were a few nudes, causing jokes, guffaws and a few catcalls. They were fascinated by the size of the wine cellar, and intrigued by the passageways and hidden rooms, though they were disappointed to learn the castle didn't have a dungeon.

Colton had to admit, offering the tour had been a stroke of genius on Tessa's part. By the time they finished and emerged from the dusty caverns, it was time for the boys to roll out their sleeping bags. Luckily, their van had been full of their overnight gear from the trip.

It became very obvious, very quickly, that it would be all but impossible to settle twelve excited and rambunctious boys down for the night. But Tessa surprised Colton again. She produced a book to read to them.

Predictably, they groaned and complained that they were far, far too old to be read a bedtime story. Tessa made them a deal. If they'd lie there quietly and listen for fifteen minutes, she'd let them decide whether or not to have her finish the book. They grumbled but agreed.

She began reading the tale of Prince Colby of Bersa-
dia, a fifteen-year-old boy who'd lived in a kingdom,
long, long ago. At first, the boy's name startled Colton,
because Colby had been his father's nickname for him
when he was little. But he soon forgot about the name as
Tessa's sultry voice drew them all into a tale of swash-
buckling betrayal and danger. It was a coming-of-age
story, perfect for the audience, and completely appropriate to the castle tour they'd just completed.

At the fifteen-minute mark, nobody uttered a peep.
Soon, Rand and Emilee were listening, and even Jack
and Sherry crept into the room, hovering near a doorway. Tessa read on while the young Colby lost his parents and then his grandparents, having to take charge
of the kingdom at a young age. The land was plagued
by drought and marauding bandits, and the young king
was betrayed by those he trusted, nearly killed as others schemed for power.

By the time the story ended, the boys had completely
settled. It was coming up on midnight, and it was obvious they'd be able to go to sleep.

The coach thanked Tessa for making his life so much
easier. He was going to sleep on the couch with the
team, while the Biddles had been given a room in the
empty south tower. Colton and Rand had spent last night
in the north tower, where Tessa, Emilee and Barry had
rooms.

Now, Colton watched Tessa cross the great room toward him, unable to pull his gaze away from her long,
shapely legs, the sway of her hips, the curve of her
breasts and especially the brilliance of her smile. She
was so smart, so creative, yet so incredibly down-to-
earth. She was unique. There wasn't another woman
like her anywhere.

"You coming up?" she shocked him by asking as she sashayed past.

He immediately rose to his feet. "Absolutely."

"There's something I want to show you."

She didn't mean it the way he'd heard it. His hormones were in overdrive because he was being so starkly reminded of why he'd fallen in love with her. It made him hear a lilt in her voice that simply wasn't there. She probably had another painting, or maybe a pink ceramic cat sculpture created by some long-lost relative that she thought he needed to see. Whatever it was, he'd go. The hard truth was, he'd go wherever she led him.

CHAPTER SIX

TESSA WAS RELIEVED and glad that the boys had settled down easily. She was happier still that the Prince Colby story had gone over well. She'd never read it. It had caught her eye today in Sophie's library—an extraordinary find.

Now, she wanted privacy to share her discovery with Colton.

"What's going on?" he asked as she led the way into her bedroom.

She was slightly nervous, slightly excited. She couldn't wait another minute to share.

"Take a look," she told him, handing over the slim hardback book.

The cover was a picture of a pensive boy. He wore period costume, with a leather tunic. A falcon soared in the background, high above a crumbling stone castle.

"It was a good story," said Colton. "Reading them to sleep was a really good idea."

"Look at it," Tessa prompted.

His gaze moved down. "What?"

"The author, Colton. Look at the name of the author."

He read aloud. "Charles Herrington." Then he instantly went still. "Is this a joke?"

"No. It's him. Read the dedication."

Colton didn't open the book. "Where did you get this?"

"I found it in Sophie's library."

"When?"

"Today. What does it matter? Read what he wrote."

Colton's jaw went tight. For a moment, she thought he was going to refuse. But then he pulled open the front cover. Tessa had memorized the words.

For my darling son. When I am not there, I am there, because you are there, and you are me through the clutter of imagination and noise.

Colton was silent for a very long time. "I never know what the hell he means."

"He means he loves you and he's proud of you."

Colton's tone hardened. "No, he doesn't."

"Colton."

"He doesn't have any right to love me and be proud of me. He left me."

Tessa shared what she had realized in the reading. "Your father couldn't run a resort company any more than Roble in the story could have been king."

"You're staying the story is a parable."

"The story is atonement."

"It's not that simple."

"Maybe not," Tessa allowed. "But you always said he was oblivious to everything around him, especially you. He's not. He knows when he fails. He realizes he failed as a father. And I bet it hurts him."

Colton tossed the book unceremoniously onto her dresser.

She put a hand on his arm. It was hot through his dress shirt, muscles tense as steel. "Charles couldn't bring himself to stay in Boston, and he knew Paris wouldn't work for you."

"There's food and shelter in Boston. He could have written there."

"Oh, Colton." She sighed heavily, wondering how he could be so smart yet so oblivious to emotional drivers.

"What now?" he demanded.

"We're not all as tough as you. We can't turn off our emotions. The rest of us *want,* the rest of us *feel.*"

His eyes went hard and dark. "You don't think I want? You don't think I feel?"

"No," she admitted, taking a plunge to where she'd never gone with Colton. "I don't think you do."

"Well, I do," he admitted. "But we can't always operate on emotion and want."

"We can sometimes," she countered, refusing to back down.

His eyes drilled into hers. "How about now?" he rasped, leaning in. "Is now a good time to operate on emotion and want?"

Cascades of longing washed through her. "What do you want?"

It was transparent in his expression, of course. And she wanted it, too. It might be wrong. It might be foolish. But she wanted Colton more than she'd ever wanted anything in her life.

"You." His arms went around her, jerking her against him, his mouth coming down hard, fast and determined, robbing her of breath.

She gave into it, gave into Colton, dove into her first glimpse of his unvarnished desire.

The giddy sensation lasted all of thirty seconds. She could feel the exact moment he brought himself back under control. He carried on with the kiss, but it was choreographed instead of raw with emotion.

Each kiss was perfect, as were his words, as was each and every caress. His fingertips skimmed her stomach as he removed her sweater. He effortlessly released the clasp of her bra. His tongue teased hers in a way that made her knees weak and brought moans of desire to her lips.

He tossed her bra, gathering her against him, his shirt abrading her tender skin. When his hands cradled her face, raking into her hair as he covered her in tender kisses, she felt as though her soul was melting.

He scooped her into his arms, carrying her to the bed. There he lay her down, stretched out beside her, brushed his knuckles across the tips of her breasts, making her gasp in reaction as shards of exquisite desire darted to her stomach and below.

He knew just how to touch her, exactly what to say. She couldn't remember when he'd learned it all, and she certainly hadn't given him any pointers. He seemed to have an innate aptitude for perfect lovemaking.

She, on the other hand, fumbled with his shirt buttons until he took over. She caressed his bare chest, working her way down his washboard stomach, thinking she'd change things up a bit. But he stopped her with a gentle hand.

"Let me," he whispered.

Then his hands roamed free, bringing her deftly to heights of arousal, stripping off their clothes, checking to see if she was ready before kissing her deeply, moving their bodies to perfect symmetry and starting a rhythm that led her both gently and passionately, inexorably to completion.

She didn't complain. There was nothing to complain about. It was all so perfect, as it always was. She shimmered at the edge of ecstasy, longer, and longer still, hovering in slow motion before catapulting over the edge to absolute, blinding, oblivious pleasure.

As her breathing stabilized, he moved to one side,

pulling a quilt overtop of them, brushing her messy hair
back from her face, kissing her swollen lips with just
enough pressure to be meaningful without hurting. He
settled on his side, cradling her, making her feel warm
and cared for in the aftermath.

"How do you do that?" she found herself asking.

"Do what?" He straightened the quilt so it was even
around them.

"Make it so perfect."

She could hear the smile in his voice. "It's you."

"It's not me. I just lay here."

"No, you don't."

"Colton."

"What?"

"I'm serious."

"I'm serious, too." His tone went low. "I've missed
you, Tessa."

She didn't know what to say. She'd missed him, too.
There were so many things about him to admire and
respect. And he was the best lover she would ever have.

He reached off the bed, fumbling for a few moments.

"What are you doing?"

He came up on his elbow, gazing down at her, ad-
miration clear in his eyes. "You know, you are the most
amazing woman in the world."

"You don't need to flatter me just because we made
love."

"It's not flattery." He drew a deep breath. "I made
mistakes, Tessa. I don't know what they all were, but I
know it was my fault. And I want, no I *need* to make it
better, to fix it between us."

Trepidation came to life in the pit of her stomach.
"Colton, don't."

"You deserve everything good in the world, Tessa. I promise you—"

"Let's not talk now."

Nothing had changed. They'd made love, and it was perfect. But perfect wasn't what she needed, perfect wasn't the thing she could do.

He moved his hand in front of her, opening his palm, revealing a tiny, blue velvet pouch. "I've been carrying it around with me." He loosened the delicate drawstring. "For months now, it's been next to my heart."

Before Tessa could even breathe, her engagement ring popped out of the little bag, landing on his broad palm.

She could have cried. It was a perfect reproposal. He was such an amazing man. What woman wouldn't die to hear words like that from her lover, to experience such a romantic gesture?

"Marry me, Tessa. I'll get it right this time. I promise."

Tessa felt tears sting at the back of her eyes. "You didn't get it wrong last time."

He smiled. "That's good."

"You got it perfect, Colton." She forced herself to look into his eyes, chest aching so badly she thought her ribs would burst. "That's why I had to leave. That's why I can't come back."

His expression faltered. Then his eyes narrowed, and his lips pursed. "You want better than perfect?"

"You don't understand."

"I'm trying to understand, but you're not making sense."

Tessa swallowed. She gripped the quilt on top of her, balling it in her hands, trying desperately to regroup.

"You're too perfect, Colton," she whispered hollowly. "And I can't keep up."

His hand fisted around the ring, and his expression turned remote. "Who's asking you to keep up?"

"You are."

"That's ridiculous."

"It's as honest as I can be."

He rolled from the bed, rising beside her. "What do you want from me?"

She sat up, clutching the quilt to her chest. "I can't describe it. It's impossible to describe. It's not something to be fixed. Either you have it or you don't."

He stepped into his pants, maintaining an admirable level of control considering what had just happened. "So, you won't marry me because I'm too perfect. Yet I have flaws you can't describe, that I apparently can't fix, even if you could describe them?"

Tessa didn't have an answer.

"Are you truly crazy?" he asked, shrugging into his shirt.

"I might be," she allowed, realizing this was a complete and final breakup. Colton wasn't going to come anywhere near her ever again. And who could blame him.

COLTON SLEPT FITFULLY all night, then stewed in isolation for most of the next day. Jack and Sherry managed to track him down a few times and keep him captive for a while. He pretended to listen to their endless stories, each time excusing himself as soon as he could.

Alone, Colton alternately berated himself for staying in love with Tessa all this time, and for being such a fool about it. Giving her the ring so quickly— What had he been thinking? They'd been apart for months.

He should have waited, let her get used to the idea of them being together again.

But she'd been so sweet in his arms, so great all day long, so beautiful, so incredible, reminding him of all the reasons he loved her. He'd known what he wanted. He'd known it made sense. And he'd been impatient to seal the deal.

The door to the second-floor library groaned open and Colton braced himself, guessing it was Jack and Sherry again. It was ridiculously cold up here, but at least it had been quiet.

"There you are." It was Rand's voice.

"Hey." Relieved but still irritable, Colton responded with a short greeting from his seat in a big, emerald-green armchair.

Two of the chairs were angled in front of a window. The boys were outside running off steam in the front yard, the occasional shout coming through as their blurry shapes put together a snow fort.

"Everything okay?" Rand entered the room, swinging the door shut behind him.

"I thought you were hanging out with Emilee."

"She's helping Tessa put something together for dinner. I think they're down to potatoes and spam."

"Whatever." Colton would have plenty of time for five-star dining once he got out of Tucker's Point.

"Why're you hiding?" asked Rand, plunking down in the opposite chair. "It's frickin' cold up here."

"It's also quiet."

"The boys are outside." Rand nodded toward the window.

"It's not the boys I'm worried about."

"You have a fight with Tessa? I mean, she seems

upset, too. She was quite viciously attacking a turnip down there."

"I'm not attacking anything up here."

"That doesn't surprise me." Rand paused.

The shouts below grew louder. It looked like the fort-building had turned into a snowball fight.

"So what's up?" Rand prompted, stretching one arm across the back of the chair. "Or are you just stir-crazy? I know if it wasn't for Emilee being here to flirt with, I'd have gone about nuts by now. My phone is out of batteries, and I'm dying to read the Friday status reports. Man, never thought I'd miss those. But there was a glitch in Hawaii's profitability last week, and I want to see if the trend is holding."

"I asked her to marry me," said Colton.

"What? Who? Tessa? Again?"

"To marry me. Tessa. Yes, again."

"Why would you do that?"

"Because we made love. And I had the ring with me."

"You had the ring with you?"

Colton didn't bother to answer this time.

Rand thwacked his head against the chair. "Oh, buddy, you've got it bad."

"She said no."

"No kidding. I doubt she'd be attacking a turnip if you'd patched things up."

"It was a stupid thing to do," Colton admitted. "But, she was… She's… It's just so…" His voice died away.

"She give you a reason?" There was genuine sympathy in Rand's voice.

Colton searched for the right words. He'd been mulling it over all day long. "She has this thing. She keeps telling me I'm too perfect. She can't tell me how or why, and she can't tell me what to do about it. And she seems to want the world to operate on emotion instead of logic."

Rand was quiet for long enough that Colton looked at him.

"You're a bit of hard act to keep up with," Rand admitted in what was obviously a cautious voice.

"No, I'm not."

"Yeah." Rand nodded. "You are. You do what's right, always. And you do it in such an icy, linear fashion, that nobody can ever argue with you."

Colton felt as if the whole world was losing its mind. "What's wrong with doing the right thing?"

"Not everybody can do that."

"They can try." It was a laudable goal.

"They can try, but they'll rarely succeed, not like you do."

"So what?"

"So, you make the people around you feel inadequate. I don't think I'd want that twenty-four seven."

"So you're on Tessa's side?"

"I'm just saying, maybe if you made a mistake once in a while."

"I make plenty of mistakes."

"Name one."

"I proposed to Tessa."

Rand chuckled. "That wasn't a mistake. Since you're crazy in love with her, it was a perfectly reasonable course of action."

Colton was starting to get annoyed. "It was illogical and emotional. It was stupid."

"You might be onto something there," said Rand.

"You're *agreeing* that I'm stupid?"

"I'm agreeing that you may be onto something. Maybe you should do something really illogical, something really selfish and emotional, something that shows Tessa and the rest of us that you're human."

"Is that what she wants? Is that what *you* want? Is that what the world wants from me?"

Rand's expression turned thoughtful. "I can guess a bit of what it must have been like for you. Your father was flaky and unreliable, and then he left you. And you seem to have vowed never to be like him. Understandable, completely. You've had to be an adult for a very long time now."

Colton almost stepped in to defend his father. Despite his knee-jerk reaction last night, the details of Prince Colby had impacted his opinion of his dad. He was actually thinking about going to see him.

"See those kids down there," said Rand. "They're nothing *but* selfish emotion and primitive energy. They're probably going to do each other an injury before the afternoon is over, but it's perfectly natural."

"Your point?"

"My point is they're even older than you were when your father left, and you had to rein everything in. Maybe, just maybe, you're allowed to be selfish and emotionally motivated once in a while. It might help you become a more rounded human being."

Colton tried to wrap his head around Rand's opinion. He didn't agree. But Rand was smart, and Colton respected him. Should he try to let go? *Could* he actually let go? What would it look like if he did? The image actually frightened him.

"You wouldn't like it if I was selfish," he finally told Rand. "Nobody would like it if I was selfish. Things would go wrong. They'd come off the rails. I'm the CEO of a multimillion-dollar company, I can't operate on emotion."

"Try it."

Colton shook his head. "It's too dangerous. I have too much power, and I affect too many lives."

"Wow. What a narcissist you turned out to be."

Colton shot his vice-president a sharp glare.

But Rand didn't back down. "Just for kicks, what exactly would you do?"

"You sound like Tessa."

"Then it's two against one. What would you do?"

"If I was completely emotional and selfish?" Colton mentally ticked through the possibilities.

"You're applying logic to this, aren't you?"

"I'm simply mulling the possibilities."

"And?"

"And…" Colton made up his mind. They wanted to see his selfish side? He'd give them his selfish side. "Here's what I'd do. Tessa and Barry's backs are financially against the wall, giving me all the power."

Rand smiled. "What are you going to do with that power?"

He would be an absolute bastard. "Give her a choice. I buy Land's End and destroy the castle. Or she marries me, and I save it."

"Blackmail?"

"Yeah."

"You'd actually blackmail a woman into marrying you?"

"See why I can't behave like this? I'd turn into one selfish son-of-a-bitch."

"You slept with him?" Emilee confirmed as she tossed some more chunks of potato into the soup pot.

"Looking back, it seems inevitable," Tessa admitted, forcing herself to keep her feelings at bay, as she'd been doing for the past fourteen hours.

Their lovemaking had ended in disaster, of course. But they'd been flirting around their physical attraction to each other from the moment he'd arrived at Land's End.

"Tessa." Emilee glanced around the room, obviously making certain they were completely alone. "Are you still in love with him?"

"I still want him."

That was as much as she'd dared allow herself to face. But there was a prickling feeling growing in the base of her belly. And, deep down inside, she feared heartache was only a whisper away.

Emilee made her way along the counter to where Tessa was chopping carrots, her tone gentle. "I mean all-out love."

"He took his dad's book," Tessa said instead. "When I showed him it was his dad's, he pretended he didn't care. But he took it with him when he left my room."

"That's a good thing, right?" Emilee accepted the change of topic, even as she watched Tessa carefully. "I mean on a human level, it's nice if you can help heal a rift."

"Truth is, it made me feel greedy," Tessa admitted, pausing to take in the kitchen, her mother's pottery vases, Sophie's pictures above the table, the old cast-iron pans hanging from cupboards. "All this stuff I have at Land's End, years and years of it. I have all this, and all Colton has is a book."

"Well, that and a multinational corporation," Emilee noted.

"It's not the same thing," said Tessa.

"I suppose not."

"He owns public buildings, decorated by strangers. He owns a business, not a home. You know, he grew up in hotel suites. How sad is that?"

"Maybe sad," Emilee allowed. "But also profitable. Your inheritance here is a money sink."

Tessa set down her knife.

She'd reluctantly admitted to herself that Barry was right. The castle was crumbling beneath them, and she was incredibly selfish to insist they keep it. It cost far too much money to maintain. Tessa could never manage it herself, and her brother's life and dreams were hundreds of miles away.

She realized she'd been operating on emotion since Sophie's death. But she needed to apply a little logic to the situation. Setting aside her selfish desire to have it all, what did she truly want to keep? Could some things be donated to museums? The castle itself might be made of stone, but even stone eventually wore out.

"I'm going to have to give it up," she said out loud.

"Would you sell it to Colton?" Emilee asked gently.

"Might as well be him." Tessa would honestly rather Colton tore it down than a stranger.

She started to work on another carrot, the sound of her chopping echoing through the huge kitchen.

"You love him," Emilee stated.

"It doesn't matter," said Tessa, fighting back a wave of emotion. "He'll never change, and I'll never measure up."

Emilee's tone went soft, and she leaned in. "Maybe you should let him decide that."

"You know I'm right," Tessa responded in a pained whisper, resting the side of her head against Emilee's. "You've been telling me I'm right for months now."

Emilee gave a self-deprecating click of her teeth. "I may have been wrong about some things."

"You wanted emotion," Colton's voice boomed suddenly and shockingly though the kitchen doorway. His footsteps echoed as he paced into the room.

Tessa jumped at the sound, her knife clattering to the countertop.

"I'll give you emotion," he continued with barely a breath in between.

Both Tessa and Emilee whirled around to gape at him.

"You want selfishness?" he asked, coming to a halt directly in front of her, eyes gun-metal gray.

She shrank back, pressing the small of her back against the lip of the counter.

"I'll give you selfishness."

"Colton—" she began.

"My turn to talk," he interrupted.

"Rand?" Emilee questioned, her attention going to the doorway where Rand had stopped.

"Here are my terms," said Colton.

"Your terms for what?" Tessa interjected, confused, alarmed, but somehow excited at the same time. There was a fire in his eyes she'd never seen before.

"When Barry gets home from the hospital, I'm going to make an offer for Land's End. It'll be an offer that the two of you can't possibly refuse. It'll be so far over market price that your heads will literally spin."

Tessa was about to tell him she'd already decided to sell, but he leaned in, not letting her get in a single word.

"And then I'll level it. I'll flatten the whole thing and pave it over."

Tessa was stunned by the bitterness in his tone. It

might be the logical thing to do, but he made it sound so horrible.

"Or—" he drew out the word "—or, you can agree to marry me. You marry me, and I'll save your castle. I'll spend whatever it takes to rebuild or do anything else you want with it."

Tessa felt the floor sway beneath her. As she clutched the counter, trying to get her bearings, Rand crossed the kitchen. He grasped Emilee firmly by the elbow and led her away.

When they were alone, Colton drew himself up, lifting his chin, crossing his muscular arms over his chest. "What do you think of *that?*"

Tessa swallowed, finding her voice around a dry throat. "Damn the torpedoes, it's all about Colton?"

"Yes."

"That has got to be the most illogical, self-centered, emotional decision I have ever heard."

He gave a sharp nod. "I'm not perfect, Tessa. And nobody, *nobody* needs to be perfect for me."

She struggled to wrap her mind around what he seemed to be saying. She thought she understood, and her heart wanted to sing with joy.

Still, even as she spoke, she barely dared to hope. "Finally, after all this time, the thing you want—selfishly, emotionally, deep down inside…" She found she had to draw a shaky breath. "Turns out to be me?"

His expression softened, and his eyes lightened to smoke. "It turns out to be you."

She was giddily, deliriously happy. Colton was human, after all.

A smile twitched at the corners of her mouth, and she reached up to smooth her palm across his face. "I'm so proud of you, Colton."

"I'm so in love with you, Tessa. And I've got your castle as leverage. You're not escaping from me this time."

"You think I love the castle more than I love you?"

"I think we're a package deal, and you're going to take us both."

"Well, I'm not."

His eyes went wide, jaw lax.

"I'm taking you, Colton. The castle we can talk about later."

"But—"

"I love you more than any old castle."

His shoulders relaxed. "I love you, Tessa. I love you exactly the way you are, and I'm sorry if I ever made you feel otherwise."

"You made me use spearmint toothpaste," she reminded him, vowing to put everything out in the open from here on in.

He gave his head a little shake of confusion. "You said it was your favorite. I bought it for both of us so that we wouldn't clash."

"You made me shower before sex."

A grin grew across his face. "I made *me* shower before sex. I didn't think you'd want me sweaty. I don't care if *you* take a shower."

"You won't let me make mistakes."

Now he really looked confused. "During sex?"

"You take over and make it perfect."

He laughed at that. "I want it to be good for you."

"Well," she admitted. "It was."

"But make as many mistakes as you want. Seriously, Tessa, if that's what it takes, you go ahead and mess it up. I'll just lie there and smile."

It was her turn to grin. "Well, okay. But that might be overkill. I'm sure we can work out something."

"With absolute pleasure." He drew her into his arms and kissed her softly.

She all but melted into his arms.

"The ring's still in my pocket," he whispered in her ear. "Still sitting next to my heart."

She drew a shuddering breath, holding back tears of joy. "Will you quit being so darn perfect?"

"I'll do my best, Tessa. I'll do my best."

* * * * *

REQUEST YOUR
FREE BOOKS!

2 FREE NOVELS
FROM THE ROMANCE COLLECTION
PLUS 2 FREE GIFTS!

YES! Please send me 2 FREE novels from the Romance Collection and my 2 FREE gifts (gifts are worth about $10). After receiving them, if I don't wish to receive any more books, I can return the shipping statement marked "cancel." If I don't cancel, I will receive 4 brand-new novels every month and be billed just $6.24 per book in the U.S. or $6.74 per book in Canada. That's a savings of at least 22% off the cover price. It's quite a bargain! Shipping and handling is just 50¢ per book in the U.S. and 75¢ per book in Canada.* I understand that accepting the 2 free books and gifts places me under no obligation to buy anything. I can always return a shipment and cancel at any time. Even if I never buy another book, the two free books and gifts are mine to keep forever.

194/394 MDN F4XY

Name	(PLEASE PRINT)
Address	Apt. #
City	State/Prov.	Zip/Postal Code

Signature (if under 18, a parent or guardian must sign)

Mail to the **Harlequin®** Reader Service:
IN U.S.A.: P.O. Box 1867, Buffalo, NY 14240-1867
IN CANADA: P.O. Box 609, Fort Erie, Ontario L2A 5X3

Want to try two free books from another line?
Call 1-800-873-8635 or visit www.ReaderService.com.

* Terms and prices subject to change without notice. Prices do not include applicable taxes. Sales tax applicable in N.Y. Canadian residents will be charged applicable taxes. Offer not valid in Quebec. This offer is limited to one order per household. Not valid for current subscribers to the Romance Collection or the Romance/Suspense Collection. All orders subject to credit approval. Credit or debit balances in a customer's account(s) may be offset by any other outstanding balance owed by or to the customer. Please allow 4 to 6 weeks for delivery. Offer available while quantities last.

Your Privacy—The Harlequin® Reader Service is committed to protecting your privacy. Our Privacy Policy is available online at www.ReaderService.com or upon request from the Harlequin Reader Service.

We make a portion of our mailing list available to reputable third parties that offer products we believe may interest you. If you prefer that we not exchange your name with third parties, or if you wish to clarify or modify your communication preferences, please visit us at www.ReaderService.com/consumerschoice or write to us at Harlequin Reader Service Preference Service, P.O. Box 9062, Buffalo, NY 14269. Include your complete name and address.

ROM13F

New from
The Mysteries of
Angel Butte series!

Everywhere She Goes
by Janice Kay Johnson

Standing between her...and danger

Returning to her hometown is Cait McAllister's chance to stand on her own. That means taking a break from men and relationships. Then she meets her new boss, the intriguing Noah Chandler. As the mayor, he's got bold plans for Angel Butte.

The most persuasive part of him, however, could be the way he looks out for Cait. Because when a threat from her past puts her in danger, Noah is there to protect her. And there's no way she can resist a man who has so much invested in keeping her safe.

AVAILABLE JANUARY 2014 WHEREVER BOOKS AND EBOOKS ARE SOLD.

HARLEQUIN®

American Romance®

Friends, to roommates…to lovers?

Living with the Cupid of Blue Falls, Texas—her aunt
Verona—Elissa Mason should be married and pregnant
by now. Or so her friends tease. But Elissa's baby is the
family nursery. Following a devastating tornado, she has
to rebuild, and nothing's going to distract her. Not even
her strange, new feelings for neighbor-turned-roommate
Pete Kayne.

Deputy Sheriff Pete Kayne understands having a dream
and doesn't want to get in Elissa's way—especially after
the tornado has taken everything but his horse and his
friends. All he's got left to share is his heart. He has his
own ambition: a chance to join the ultimate in law
enforcement—the Texas Rangers. Elissa is his friend.
That will have to be enough…for now.

Marrying The Cowboy
by TRISH MILBURN

**Available January 2014,
from Harlequin® American Romance®.**

HARLEQUIN®
Romance

The Man Behind the Mask
Barbara Wallace

A weekend to change everything...

Delilah St. Germaine fell for New York's most in-demand bachelor, Simon Cartwright, the moment she began working for him. Four years later, her heart still flutters every time he saunters into the office—much to her frustration.

Thrown together for a working weekend, Delilah glimpses the cracks in Simon's glittering facade. And now that she's tasted the sweetness of his kisses, she's determined to learn who the *real* Simon Cartwright is. But will Delilah's life ever be the same once the truth is revealed?

Available next month from
Harlequin Romance,
wherever books and ebooks are sold.

HR7427